my tuscan star

WITH LOVE FROM ITALY

TESS RINI

ISBN: 978-1-7376372-5-7 (e-book)

ISBN: 978-1-7376372-6-4 (paperback)

Tessrini.com

Publisher: One Punch Productions, LLC

Cover design and interior formatting by *Hannah Linder Designs*

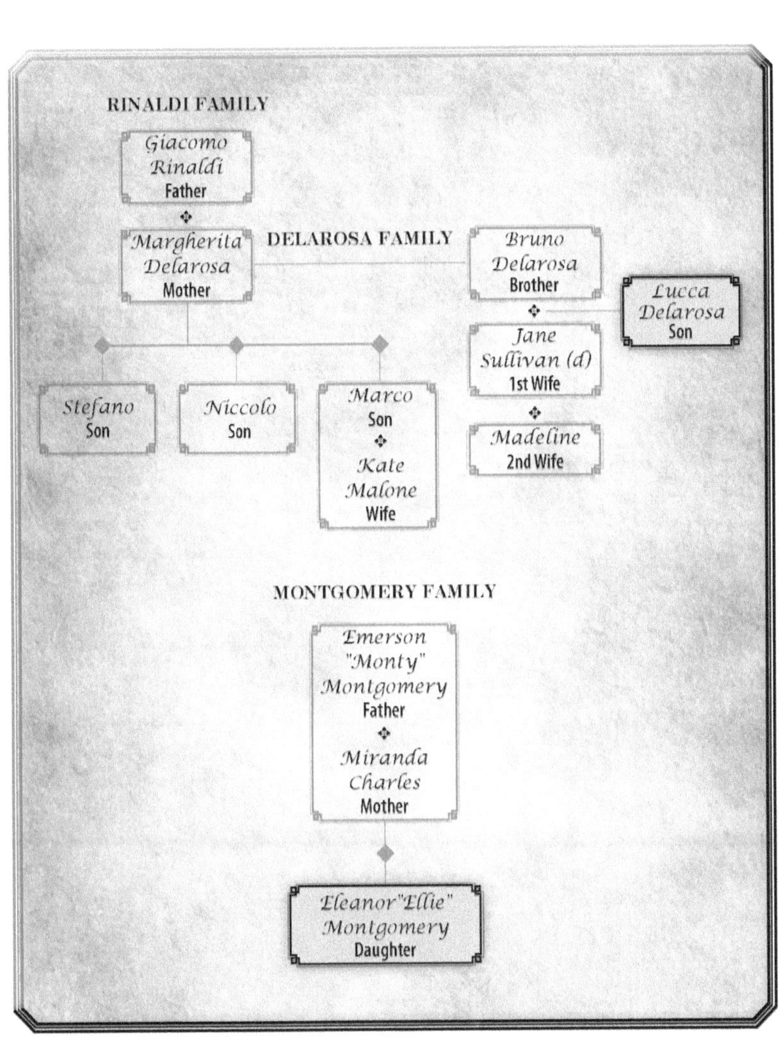

RINALDI FAMILY
Giacomo Rinaldi
Father
Margherita Delarosa
Mother
DELAROSA FAMILY
Bruno Delarosa
Brother
Lucca Delarosa
Son
Jane Sullivan (d)
1st Wife
Madeline
2nd Wife
Stefano
Son
Niccolo
Son
Marco
Son
Kate Malone
Wife
MONTGOMERY FAMILY
Emerson "Monty" Montgomery
Father
Miranda Charles
Mother
Eleanor "Ellie" Montgomery
Daughter

Where we travel in *My Tuscan Star*

For Mary M—
Thank you for your wisdom, creativity and for believing in
me. Most of all, thank you for your patience and hours you
spent unsticking me when I faced those annoying writer's
blocks. Our porch time means everything to me.

one

Ellie James peered out the van's dirty windows, anxiously looking for a house number. Would it kill them to display addresses in Beverly Hills? She rolled her eyes. Ellie knew the wealthy homeowners wanted their privacy, but still, this was ridiculous. Pulling over, she checked her phone again. According to her navigation app, she was at the location. She glanced around, still confused, but resignedly put the van in park. Undoubtedly, she would have to go the rest of the way on foot and figure this out.

She glanced in the mirror and laughed with sick humor. Her long, straight, light-brown hair was tied up in a messy bun on her head and had partially come loose. She wore no make-up, and her face was shiny from the hot day. To top it off, she sported white frosting in her hair. Wetting her finger and rubbing it for a second seemed to only spread it. Oh well, once she got this delivery over with, she could go home and take a long, much-needed shower.

Ellie climbed out and went to the van's side door to retrieve the last cake she had to deliver. Lifting the cake box out of the built-in cooler and juggling it gingerly, she glanced around nervously, hoping she had the right place. The last thing she wanted to do on this hot day was deliver a lemon cream cake. It was probably melting as she stood there. She glanced down at her light blue Brigid Bakes T-shirt, black yoga pants and tennis shoes. Oh well, no one of importance would see her.

Ellie walked up to the house she thought was the delivery location. Its massive, wrought-iron gate greeted her. She noticed a keypad and punched the button, juggling the cake. If she dropped it now, she might as well just call it—it had been a long day.

She could hear the ringing and knew the buzzer worked. After twenty or so rings, it went dead. What a joke! She stubbornly pushed the button again. *Ring, ring, ring.* Sighing, she adjusted her weight from one foot to the other. After ten hours in the bakery, her feet were killing her. She stumbled a little into the gate and quickly grabbed the cake. In doing so, the gate swung open a few inches. Okay, well, that is weird. Why have a security gate if it's not secure?

That wasn't her problem, though. Ellie shrugged and stepped through the gate, pausing and glancing around. Still no one. She started walking up the long drive toward the colonial white mansion, with its black shutters and black door. Its white columns created a picturesque porch. It helped to concentrate on the charming scenery rather than her aching feet. She thought about turning around and driving her van up to the house now that she knew the gate was open, but with her luck, it would swing close and lock. It made more sense to just hurry up on foot and drop the cake off with a housekeeper or whoever answered the door.

Finally reaching the front door, Ellie rubbed her shoulder against her forehead to wipe the sweat off. Shifting the cake to her one hand, she rang the doorbell. Glancing around, she took in the perfectly manicured extensive lawn and hedges, the colorful flower beds perfectly enhancing the landscape. Off to the side, a groundskeeper's truck was parked. She could hear motorized buzzing from the back—it was clear someone was there tending to the yard. If only they could take delivery of this cake!

Ellie knocked, desperate to finish the delivery. The door creaked open, moving several inches. Now things were getting even weirder. She quickly decided she wasn't going inside. After-all, she had listened to enough crime podcasts to know that's how the delivery girl always got it. The cake would just have to be left on the doorstep. If the sender complained, the bakery would refund their money. Stepping back, she hit something solid. She opened her mouth to shriek when she felt something cool pressing against her neck.

She heard a deep voice in her ear—so close she could feel his breath. "Freeze right there, or I will be forced to hurt you."

Ellie swallowed hard. She glanced down to see tennis shoes and bronze legs standing behind her. He was so close. Without even thinking, her instinct kicked in, and she stomped her foot as hard as she possibly could on his, swung her elbow into his chest, turned, and when he staggered back, she hit him square in the chest with a round kick. He fell backward onto the ground, the knife clattering near him. Unfortunately, the cake had also hit the ground—Ellie glanced over to see the precious box flat-tened, and now a gooey mess all over the brick area in front of the door.

Grabbing the knife by instinct, she decided to take it and run. Her assailant was lying on the ground, flat on his back, wearing cargo shorts and a faded T-shirt. His crystal blue eyes stared up at her, a stunned expression on his face. She gasped.

She had just flattened Lucca Delarosa—Hollywood's hottest actor.

Two men appeared from around the corner suddenly—they began running toward her at a frantic pace.

Lucca was slowly sitting up, running a hand through his

wavy black hair that was only slightly disheveled. He rubbed his lightly bearded chin. Glancing toward the men—he put up a hand to stall them. They stopped running but continued advancing at a slower pace.

"Who are you, and what are you doing here?" His rich baritone voice, even though it was curt, was so familiar to her, it made her eyes widen.

"I'm delivering a cake," Ellie answered, her voice high-pitched and wobbly, not sounding like her normal self-assured self. They both glanced over at the doorstep.

"You *were* delivering a cake," he noted dryly.

Ellie nodded, grimacing. "Yeah, sorry about that. We'll get you a new one. But you scared me! You had a knife. I didn't know it was you. It was a natural reaction." She knew she was babbling, but this whole situation was out of control.

Lucca looked at her speculatively. "Try to stab me with it."

Ellie stared at him dumbfounded. Had he lost his mind? Did he hit his head?

"Um, no thank you. Just the same, I don't think so." She dropped the knife to the ground without looking at it.

Lucca leaned over and picked it up, a slight smile on his face. "I'll stab myself then." He grabbed the knife, plunging it into his chest, his hand resting near it. He made dramatic faces before falling back toward the ground, more gently this time. His body shook before it went still.

He sat up then, giving a slight bow with his torso. Ellie looked closely at the knife, which had fallen on the ground.

"Oh, duh, prop knife." She could feel her face flushing with embarrassment. "Listen, thanks for the free show. Sorry I forgot to clap. We'll send you another cake. Try not to attack the delivery person next time," she said, her voice dripping with sarcasm.

Ellie turned and was about to walk away when he jumped to his feet with ease.

"Hey, listen, I'm sorry. I usually don't sneak up on delivery people with a weapon—even a fake one."

She turned her head to look at him and opened her mouth for one last retort when she saw a flash from the right. Before she could react, she was blindsided and knocked to the ground. As she lay there, she gazed into the anxious face of a Golden Retriever looking at her longingly before one big pink tongue came out to lick the frosting in her hair.

two

"Sophia! Stop! Get off of her!" A blast of Italian commenced, as Lucca struggled to push the dog off Ellie and help her sit up.

"Well, geez, I guess we're even," Ellie said, looking down and seeing blood on her T-shirt. Looking at herself quizzically, she saw her elbow and hand had sustained most of the blow to the ground, and both were slightly bloody. Then she saw the jagged cut that was bleeding profusely from her upper arm.

"*Dio*, you're bleeding. Come on, let's go into the house. I'll call a doctor."

Ellie felt his hands on her waist, helping her to stand.

"Are you okay? Can you walk?" He looked at her, his eyes concerned.

"I'm fine. Really." She glanced around and saw a rectangle copper planter. "I think I must have cut my arm on the edge of your planter. The rest are just scrapes. I'm just going to go. I probably have a bandage in the car."

"No, you can't leave while you're bleeding all over. We'll go inside. At least let me find you a bandage."

Ellie looked at him and sighed. He was right. She knew she

didn't have any bandages in the car. Blood was running down her arm now. What a mess.

"Okay, fine. I'll come in, but just to grab a paper towel or something. I don't want to bleed all over the bakery van. It's new and it's not mine."

Lucca glanced around. "Where is it? In fact, how did you even get in here?" he asked, his eyes narrowing suspiciously.

"I walked. Your gate was open," Ellie snapped.

He shouted that information to the two men, who took off running toward the gate.

"Your front door is open, too," she added.

"WHAT?!"

She shrugged, indicating the running men. "Thing One and Thing Two aren't too good at their jobs."

He stared at her hard before muttering under his breath. He started walking toward the door, holding it open for her. She followed him into the massive entryway, its black-and-white checkerboard tiles glinting with polish. A round, mahogany table with a large and colorful floral arrangement in an expensive crystal vase greeted them. A spectacular chandelier hung over it.

"Let's go into the kitchen," he said. She followed him uneasily, glancing around. The coolness felt great against her hot skin, but she felt grubby and tired. She didn't want to bleed all over his house.

They walked into the large modern kitchen. Lucca grabbed paper towels, swinging them off the roll in one pile and handing them to her. "Here, hold this on your arm and let me go find a first-aid kit."

He disappeared, leaving Ellie standing alone, applying pressure to her wound. She glanced around curiously. The white kitchen featured gleaming stainless-steel appliances, dozens of white cabinets, and expansive white marble countertops with a stone backsplash. Black lantern fixtures hung over the island. The kitchen was gorgeous, but the whole place looked untouched. She sniffed and was certain no one ever cooked there. She rolled her eyes—celebrity homes.

Lucca came back, looking triumphant. "I found this in my housekeeper's closet. She's off today. He opened the case, displaying neatly organized bandages, creams, various scissors, and tweezers.

"Uh, we're not operating. Just a bandage will be fine," Ellie said.

He laughed, raising an eyebrow wickedly. "Well, I have played a doctor before."

Ellie gave him a small glare. "Let's just get this done." She took the paper towels off, but her arm was still bleeding profusely.

He winced. "I think you should let me call a real doctor. You might need stitches."

"No, no, it's fine. I don't know why, but whenever I cut myself, I just bleed a lot. Let me just hold this for a few minutes, and then we can bandage it up and I'll be on my way."

"Aren't you supposed to hold the wound above your heart to stop the bleeding?"

Ellie looked at him with narrowed eyes. "Movie experience again?"

He grinned. "No, Boy Scouts. Here, sit down. I'll grab some ice. That's supposed to help, too."

Ellie let him ease her onto a stool at the massive island, and watched him grab a kitchen towel and load ice into it. He came around to the side of the island and gently held it next to her hand that was holding the paper towel. She opened her mouth to ask him about Boy Scouts, only to stop herself. It didn't matter— she didn't need to know anything more about him. She was completely aware of him now, though—she could feel his breath. Her heart was skipping suddenly, and it unnerved her.

As if reading her thoughts, he asked softly, "Not to be cliche here, but you obviously know who I am."

She made a small face. "I didn't before I knocked you down. I had no idea who the cake was for—it only had the address."

He was looking at her suspiciously. "Let me guess. You're an actress. You haven't gotten your first break yet, but it's right around the corner," he said sarcastically.

Ellie's eyes grew big. She would round kick him again. No, this time it would be a full frontal one right where it would hurt the most!

"Wrong, Hollywood. I hate actors. Especially arrogant ones," she said pointedly. "In fact, I'm done with L.A. I don't know why I thought I could ever stand living here again. Everyone is so fake."

His eyes widened. "Wow, that's quite a huge pronouncement on an entire industry," he said dryly. "You don't even know me. I'm as nice as you are stubborn."

She looked at him coldly.

He smiled, the well-known movie star grin he was known for. Deep dimples lined his cheeks, his white teeth gleamed. "Look, let's start over." He held out his hand. "Lucca Delarosa, Arrogant Actor. But not fake at all, I can assure you."

She smiled a little grudgingly, grasping his hand. "Ellie James, Injured Cake Deliverer."

She looked down at their hands, feeling electricity shooting up her arm. She dropped his hand quickly.

He frowned at her. "Are you afraid? Geez, I'm not going to hurt you. I'm sorry about the prop knife. I thought you might be here to hurt *me*. It was the first thing handy."

Her eyes widened. "Hurt you with a lemon cream cake?"

He smiled gently. "I didn't know the cake was legit until it was spread all over my doorstep. My dog probably likes it. I think she's out there eating it now."

As if she heard herself being discussed, Sophia now burst through the open door, running straight to Ellie and trying to jump on her.

"No, missy, down. Down."

The dog stopped jumping for a moment.

"Do you have any treats?" Ellie asked, glancing around at the spotless kitchen.

Lucca looked confused. "I'm not sure…"

"Give me something—a piece of cheese if you have it."

Lucca opened a door to the sub zero refrigerator. "Brie?"

Ellie rolled her eyes. "Not unless you want her to get sick all over. Do you have a piece of cheddar or sliced cheese?"

Lucca's head was deep in the refrigerator now. He pulled out a package and handed her a piece, looking smug. "It's provolone."

Ellie nodded impatiently. She grabbed the slice, ripping off a piece.

"Down. Good girl. Stay." She gave her another piece before asking, "Sophia, right?"

He smiled. "Sophia Loren."

She grimaced. "I should have known. How old is she? You need to train her."

"She's six months or so. I know nothing about dogs. But yes, I was going to hire a trainer. Are you one as well as a cake deliverer?"

"Not really, but I have watched them and helped," she admitted, thinking back to the professional pet trainers her family hired over the years. "She's still a puppy. There's a lot you can do."

He bent to pet Sophia's head. "I hadn't planned on this. It just kind of happened—long story. But I got her for protection."

"You got a Golden Retriever for protection?" she asked incredulously.

"What's wrong with that? She tackled you, didn't she?"

Sophia was licking Ellie's hand now. Ellie laughed, "Well yeah, but afterward, she just licked me to death. Hardly a trained killer."

Sophia stood then and looked at them calmly. She walked over toward the other end of the kitchen, which featured a long table and a dozen chairs. Sitting for a second, she continued assessing them, her tongue hanging out of mouth, her face resembling a smile. She then stood, her tail went up, and she did her business right on the carpet.

"*Mamma Mia*, Sophia!" Lucca yelled at the dog, bursting into Italian. The frightened dog now retreated, giving one last longing look at Ellie before she scurried away.

Lucca walked over, surveying the expensive Persian carpet that anchored the table and chairs. "Every time. She can't go two feet over to the wood floor. She has to do it on the carpet. He sighed, grabbing paper towels and a spray bottle that was on the counter.

Ellie put a hand over her mouth, trying not to laugh. To see this world-famous movie star on his knees cleaning up after a dog was almost too much. She had seen all his movies, of course. He was a versatile actor who could play both the tough guy action hero and the gentle love interest with ease. She had seen him win countless awards. He truly was good at his craft; she'd give him that.

Lucca stood and looked at her suspiciously, almost daring her to laugh. "If you took a photo of that, I *will* hurt you this time."

"Not with a prop knife!"

He smiled then and went to the sink, washing his hands. "Sorry about that interruption—let me get the ice back on your arm."

Ellie gently took the paper towels away. The cut was jagged, but it didn't go deep. Blood was still oozing, but not as quickly.

"I think it's good. Let me just take care of this, and I'll be out of here."

Lucca dug out some cotton squares from the first-aid kit. Getting them damp with the antiseptic spray, he handed them to her. She dabbed at it and cleaned the cut up as much as she could.

"You better put this cream on, too," he said. "I really wish you would see a doctor."

"I'm not going to sue you," Ellie remarked dryly.

He stopped and looked at her seriously before shrugging. "I don't know you. You could. But that's not my reason for wanting you to see one. I just don't want it to get infected or something."

Ellie nodded and looked away. She believed him. She knew he was a great actor, but his eyes were sincere. And she had a lot of experience with actors. Her radar instantly knew when they were lying.

He handed her some more cotton squares to put over the cut. His head was bent over the bandage now as he quickly wound it around her arm, concentrating intensely. Suddenly, he cursed in Italian, unwrapping and trying again. She breathed in; he smelled of soap and something else. Whatever it was, he smelled darn good.

She straightened up, feeling uncomfortable. "It doesn't have to be perfect," she teased. "It just has to go around my arm."

"Look, remember I am the doctor," he said, looking up briefly, giving her a smile. Their eyes held for a moment. Ellie felt her heart beat a little faster and was glad when he broke the spell. "By the way, who sent me the cake?"

Ellie felt her face flush. "Oh, yeah, sorry. I have the note here in my pocket. She dug it out with her other hand, placing it on the island.

Lucca had finished applying the bandage and now impatiently cut the medical paper tape with his teeth, before sticking several on for good measure. He put the tools back in the suitcase again and picked up the note. Opening it, he smiled. "It's from my cousin, Marco. Why would he send me a cake?"

Ellie shrugged. "We just take the orders. Like I said, I'll get you a new one."

Lucca shook his head. "It's fine. I don't need it. How's your arm feeling?"

Ellie rubbed the bandage gently. "Fine, I think. I just have a headache now, but that's probably just the result of this entire day." She grabbed her used cotton squares. "Where's your garbage?"

He indicated under the sink. "I'm sorry. I should have asked if you wanted something for pain. Let me get you something. I'll be right back."

Before she could answer, Lucca quickly exited, and she heard his phone ring and him answer it and then switch to Italian. His footsteps were heavy as he ran up the staircase toward where she assumed the bedrooms were.

Looking around, Ellie made a sudden decision. She slid down the stool and went quickly toward the entry hall. Sophia was lying on the cold tile but got up when she saw Ellie.

"Shhh, there's a good girl. You just need a little attention, don't you? Sorry, I have to go. Stay. Stay." Ellie gave her a pat, and the dog laid back down.

Opening the massive black door, Ellie exited, quietly closing it behind her. She hurried down the driveway, almost breaking into a jog. She pushed a button, and the gate opened. She ran through and jumped in her van. She felt her heart racing. For some reason, she just wanted to get out of there. Starting the van, she sped down the street. It was then she started to breathe.

"I'LL GET YOU SOME WATER," Lucca said to the empty kitchen. He glanced around. Ellie was gone. He went to the front door where Sophia was sleeping, opening her eyes to peek at him.

"You let her leave?" he asked gently.

He slid her out of the way and opened the front door. He

looked down toward the gate and saw nothing. He closed the door and went over and pushed a button—a panel opened and he reviewed his security cameras. At least the one near the street was working. He saw Ellie looking around nervously before jumping into a van and roaring down the street.

Closing the panel, he looked at Sophia intently, thinking back to the phone call he had just had with his cousin. He would see Ellie again at the bakery. He smiled.

"She didn't even want my autograph," he told Sophia and then gave a small chuckle. Sophia just closed her eyes, now uninterested.

three

Ellie towel-dried her hair, as she sank into a comfy chair in her bedroom. She had put on a tank top and some shorts and now unwound the wet bandage. She had stopped at the store and bought some medical supplies on her way home. She re-did it now, applying an antibiotic cream, she put a sterile strip on it to keep the cut together and put a large bandage over that. She dabbed some cream on a few of her scrapes for good measure.

With the traffic, it had taken her forever to return the van to the bakery and then drive home in her own car. It had given her plenty of time to think. She was still feeling unnerved about meeting Lucca. She had told the truth when she said she was not a fan of actors. Ellie had grown up in the industry, her parents a giant looming presence. They both starred in dozens of movies—movies now deemed classics by Hollywood standards. Their love story was a highly publicized legendary tale—so much so that they were called Hollywood Royalty. The fact they were still married was often marveled at, with gossip columnists trying frequently to find any fissure in their relationship. To Ellie's relief, none had been found.

She loved her parents, but she hated their lifestyle and many of the people they worked with. The security, the scrutiny, and the ugly side of fame had always weighed heavily on her. Every awkward move of her adolescence had been photographed and detailed to an ever-greedy audience. She grimaced, thinking about her braces, her awkward teen years. Then there was her first boyfriend—who she later found out was only using her because his dad wanted to sell his screenplay. She shuddered. Hollywood was not for her.

Ellie walked into the spare bedroom of her cottage in Malibu—well, that's what the Realtor had called it; to Ellie, it was simply a small, extremely expensive house. On the floor sat canvases scattered awkwardly. She sighed. She hadn't been able to paint for more than a year. Oh, she had tried. She had spent hours in front of blank canvases. She had finally forced herself to paint, knowing that it was a muscle memory she had to keep up—like an athlete. So far, she had cast her attempts aside. She nudged a few of them on the ground—kicking them gently. Would she ever be able to paint something she was proud of again?

Ellie had made a name for herself early in her career as a rising young artist. Her paintings became highly sought after. She had dropped her last name long ago to ensure people weren't just buying her artwork because of her famous parents. She had desperately gotten out of the spotlight when she had studied art in Italy. Her mentor there had encouraged her and had called in favors to host her first few art shows. The reviews had been extremely positive and Ellie had moved to New York to achieve even more success.

It was only when the limelight was turned on her and not her paintings that she felt uncomfortable. She didn't realize people wanted to know the artist personally. She remembered her last show in New York—the fancy hors d'oeuvres, the expensive champagne flowing freely. The night had been shattered when the waiting photographers pounced, chasing her when she had left, taking photos as fast as they could before she jumped into her waiting town car. Her driver sped away, but Ellie had been shaken. She impulsively moved to Los Angeles the next day, leaving her penthouse apartment in New York. Suddenly, the anonymity she had felt in New York was compromised.

Ellie had stayed with her parents briefly before renting the beach house. She thought living alone near the ocean in Malibu would be inspiring, and she could try her hand at beachscapes. She had spent hours dragging her easel all over the sand. She was wrong. Nothing came to her.

It was only after running into her old friend Brigid that she felt a sense of calm. She and Brigid had gone to an ultra-private high school together and had lost touch for a while. Brigid's father was an award-winning producer and her own upbringing had been like Ellie's, only Brigid's parents hadn't remained married. In fact, Brigid had often laughed at the array of starlets lined up, trying to get her father's attention. She had come to terms with it long ago and simply rolled her eyes now, counting her "wicked stepmothers" on her fingers.

Brigid had opened a bakery catering to affluent celebrities, creating spectacular wedding cakes, unique birthday cakes, and more. Her hard work was paying off, and she was gaining in popularity. She had invited Ellie to come see the bakery and then over lunch, confided to her that she was pregnant. Brigid and her husband, Matthew, had been trying to have a baby for a long time. After a devastating miscarriage, Brigid was thrilled to be in her second trimester, but she was also feeling stressed, she told Ellie. Her dream was finally coming true, but her beloved bakery was also in need of her attention. That's when Ellie, feeling compassion for her friend, had offered to help out a little where she could. She soon dove in, tackling any small chore for Brigid so the only thing Brigid had to do was concentrate on the intricate cakes she had become known for. Brigid had other staff as well, but she told Ellie it felt wonderful to have a person she trusted right there.

She even began to show Ellie how to do some of the cake decorating. Ellie found her creativity coming out and enjoyed some of the work, spending hours perfecting her piping techniques under Brigid's watchful eye. Brigid, who was a perfectionist, had proclaimed Ellie's artistry excellent. Ellie knew deep in her heart she was spending so much time at the bakery to procrastinate and ignore her real artistry. She couldn't help it, though.

Ellie's phone rang, and she saw it was the object of her thoughts. "Hey, Brig, sorry I didn't call you when I got back. The van is parked behind the bakery."

"That's okay, Ellie. I can't believe you were nice enough to even make those deliveries. I fired George."

George was the ultimate surfer dude, always running off to catch the waves. Brigid fired him once a week at least. George knew how to play Brigid's soft heart, and he would undoubtedly get re-hired. He had disappeared shortly after lunch, and that was why Ellie had been charged with making the last few deliveries in Beverly Hills.

"Well, let's see if this firing sticks." Ellie couldn't resist teasing her friend.

"Listen, I have to tell you something," Ellie said, quickly getting serious. She explained the cake's demise at the last delivery.

"Oh, Ellie, you kicked him?"

"Well, he had a fake knife to my throat!" Ellie defended herself. "What was I supposed to do? But, yeah, sorry about the cake, Brigid."

"It's fine. I'll refund the order. No worries. What was he like? I'm dying to know!"

Ellie exited the bedroom now, walking out to the French doors that led to a deck overlooking the ocean. She sat down on an Adirondack chair, contemplating the question.

"Ellie?"

"Oh, sorry, I was just thinking. I didn't think you'd be interested. I mean, you and I have met so many actors."

Brigid sighed deeply. "Ellie, I'm a normal red-blooded female. Lucca Delarosa is hot. Capital H. And he's reported to actually be nice."

Ellie frowned. "I guess he was. I mean, looking back at it, he was kind when Sophia tackled me."

Brigid gave a small shriek. "Who's Sophia? His girlfriend?"

Ellie laughed and proceeded to fill her friend in on the rest of her afternoon.

"Wow. He bandaged you up. That is pretty sweet."

Ellie smiled at the memory of him trying to get the bandage perfectly rolled around her arm as if someone was going to take measurements. "Yeah, I mean he tried. He said he was a Boy Scout, but that doesn't make sense. Didn't he grow up in Italy?" Ellie questioned, suddenly remembering that she had wanted to ask him about that.

"Could you read a magazine or go online once in a while? I know you hate the industry, but you need to know basic facts," Brigid teasingly implored.

Before Ellie could answer, Brigid continued patiently. "He grew up in Italy, but then when he was still a kid, his parents had this messy divorce. His mother brought him to the states—somewhere near Manhattan. He eventually ended up in Hollywood and got his big break, and the rest is history. Come to think of it, I haven't read that much about him personally. Just the usual stories about the string of ladies he has on his arm."

"I bet," muttered Ellie.

"Well, for goodness' sake, you can't begrudge the guy. Why would he waste those eyes staying at home? Share them with the world! You know of all the celebrities right now, he is one I would like to meet. I should get my dad to produce him in something."

Ellie smiled and then said: "Or next time, *you* deliver the cake."

Brigid laughed. "Yeah, that's what I need to do. Waddle up to his house almost six months pregnant and deliver a cake."

"You're one of those beautiful pregnant women, and you know it," Ellie told her.

"Okay, if you say so, but man, it's getting more uncomfortable by the minute. See you tomorrow?"

"I'll be there," Ellie promised.

four

The next few days passed quickly for Ellie. She had spent some time contemplating her future, running on the beach, staring out into the ocean before climbing the enormous number of stairs back to her house.

She had finally come to terms with the fact that she needed to leave California. It had been in the back of her head that travel might stir up her creative juices. She didn't want to let her friend down, but she couldn't keep procrastinating. She had to find a way to make herself excited to paint again.

The idea had come to fruition when the mother of her former roommate had emailed her, asking if she was interested in a commission. Ellie and her roommate, Gemma, had attended art school and lived together the entire time. Gemma's mother, Madeleine, visited often. She had been very sweet to Ellie, always including her in their plans. Madeleine told her she was newly married and moving into her husband's villa in Tuscany. She wanted something of her own to bring to the villa. She had asked if Ellie was interested in painting something that she could hang prominently—something that would make her feel like it was also her home, too.

Ellie had responded, but she was honest about her art struggles. Madeleine was sympathetic and offered the guesthouse on the villa's property for Ellie to live in and try to paint. It would make a perfect studio, she told her. Ellie could come and see if she was inspired. If not, she would completely understand. If nothing else, it would be fun for Ellie to come back to Italy and she would love to see her. She missed her daughter, who was trying to make a living as a sculptor, and lived in Amsterdam. Madeleine explained she and her new husband would be on an extended honeymoon, and Ellie could live at the guesthouse for a few weeks before they would return. Ellie was excited to hear it was outside of Siena, a city she loved. It seemed like fate, since she had been toying with the idea of going back to Italy where she had truly felt inspired.

Ellie took a deep breath. Tuscany. She had felt at home there. Now she had to break it to Brigid that she had plans to leave. She stared at her pregnant friend, who was sitting on a stool, a pastry bag in her hand.

"Brig, I need to talk to you," Ellie started cautiously.

Brigid looked at her excitedly. "I have something to ask you about as well. You go first!"

At her friend's raised eyebrows, Ellie blurted out the whole story. Instead of the expected tears—Brigid was so hormonal these days—she was nodding enthusiastically.

"It's as if it was meant to be," she said, putting down the pastry bag and grabbing her water bottle. She took a swig and smiled broadly at Ellie. "I'm so excited."

"That I'm leaving?" asked Ellie, clearly confused.

"No, of course not. That part sucks. No, I have a super huge favor to ask, but this makes it so much easier. Listen, do you remember my cousin Kate Malone?"

Ellie shook her head, and Brigid continued quickly. "Well, it doesn't really matter. I think you met her when we were kids.

Anyway, Katie traveled to Italy, and now she has this hot new book out and has started a podcast. I have to show you all her social media stuff. It's amazing. She's built this whole business about Positano and the Amalfi Coast."

Ellie smiled. "I love it there! I went there with my parents when I graduated from art school."

Brigid looked thoughtful. "Good, good. Even better. So Katie met this gorgeous man in Italy. They are getting married in a little over a week, and as a surprise, her groom wants me to make their wedding cake! Katie told him how much she loves my cakes, but she couldn't think of a way to get it from here to there. She forgot she's marrying a billionaire!"

"Wow, I guess that's handy," Ellies joked. "But I still don't understand."

"He called me a few times, and we finally decided that he would ask his cousin to fly it on his private jet to ensure it makes it there successfully. There's no way I can go. I double-checked with my doctor, but he wants me to be over-cautious with this baby. International travel just isn't in the cards." She smiled weakly, putting a hand on her stomach. "The problem is, you know what a perfectionist I am. I can't trust someone there to assemble it and decorate it. But I trust you..." Brigid trailed off, looking at her pensively. "Would you even consider it, Ellie? You could spend some time down on the Amalfi Coast and then head up north to Tuscany. We did that on our honeymoon. It's a beautiful drive or you can take the fast train."

Ellie thought about it. Picking up the pastry bag, she slid the frosting down toward the tip, frowning in thought. "Are you sure you trust me? I mean, I've never done a wedding cake—only birthday cakes and stuff."

Brigid laughed. "They may have only been birthday cakes, but some were for my dad's fancy Hollywood friends. Fancy— which is a code word for extremely picky, as you know. I wouldn't have let you do those if I didn't know you were talented at it."

Ellie frowned. "Who's going to help you here? I already feel bad about leaving."

Brigid smiled. "My surprisingly thoughtful husband and I had a long talk last night. He knows how important the bakery is to me. Matthew looked at the books, and he says we can hire more staff. He is also going to take a leave of absence and help a little more here. You know what a pushover I am. My husband will be a better businessperson than me," she said with a chuckle, nodding her head as George sauntered through the door in his boardshorts and tie-dyed shirt.

George stared at them innocently. "Got any deliveries today?"

Ellie burst out laughing and hugged her friend. "Okay, I'll do it. I guess we can talk more about it later. But I hope you know what you're doing."

Brigid's smile grew. "Most definitely."

LUCCA WALKED through the front door of the bakery. His new Chief of Security, Mike Donnelly, held the door open for him, quickly glancing around.

"I think you could have waited in the car," Lucca said.

Mike shook his head. "Sorry, boss. I'm sticking with you for now."

"Can I help you?"

Lucca watched Ellie come through the double swinging doors. She stopped short, as she spotted him. Lucca smiled widely at her, flashing his deep dimples. "Well, if it isn't Ellie James, Injured Cake Delivery Driver."

She looked at him with narrowed eyes. "Hey, Hollywood. Nice to see you again. Did you come for your cake?" she asked sweetly.

He let his gaze travel over her, from her top knot down to her apron, which was stained with various colors of frosting.

"Well, you do owe me one, unless you'd rather practice your judo—or whatever that was—on me again."

Ellie smiled smugly. "No need to practice. Obviously, I'm already really good at it."

She glanced away from him, her eyes widening. "Mike!" she yelled as she ran around the counter, hurling herself into Mike's arms.

"Hey, kiddo. Great to see you." The buttoned up, steely-eyed, burly security officer who Lucca had hired on the sheer fierceness of his demeanor was now looking like a proud father, dabbing away tears from the corner of his eyes. Mike, in his fifties, was a former police officer who now ran a powerful security agency. Lucca already trusted him implicitly.

"Hello, Lucca. I'd know those dimples anywhere!" Lucca turned to see a small woman behind the counter. Her blonde hair was also pulled into a bun, but she was much shorter and curvier than Ellie. She laid a hand across her visibly pregnant stomach. "I'm Brigid. We talked on the phone. Come on back. We have a lot to discuss."

Lucca glanced back to where Ellie was busy whispering in Mike's ear. He walked behind the counter and saw Mike nod in his direction. He went into Brigid's cramped office.

He glanced back toward the lobby. "Any idea how they know each other?"

Brigid looked evasive and shrugged. "Hard to say. Ellie knows a lot of people."

Lucca was trying to focus on what Brigid was saying, but his mind kept going back to the woman out front. He had thought about her several times over the last week, and he wasn't sure why. Certainly, she was very pretty, but she was too normal—if he was going by L.A. standards. There were beautiful women everywhere. He wasn't sure what it was that made her stand out to him.

Tall and thin, Ellie didn't appear to wear any make-up, but maybe she didn't need to. She had a heart-shaped face, a small nose, and full pink lips. Everything on her face was natural and untouched—no fillers or plastic work. He could see that from a mile away. Her light brown hair was up in that thing on her head, though some of it had fallen out the other day and he could see it went halfway down her back. She did have nice eyes —he had thought about them after she had left. They were a pretty soft brown that went well with her hair. They seemed to look right through him. There was something about her—maybe it was her sheer displeasure at meeting him or her disdain for the industry. What had soured her so badly? He was intrigued. Was she a failed actress? It didn't seem likely. There was something about the way she carried herself, even when she was injured, that had stood out—as if she was royalty or something. Yet, she had a fresh, girl-next-door quality about her. He found her perplexing.

"When did you want to leave for Italy?" Brigid was asking, breaking into his thoughts.

"Is three days before the wedding enough time for you?" Lucca asked.

Brigid nodded. "I'm so happy you're willing to fly the cake over. When Marco first called me and insisted he wanted to do this for Katie, I was thrilled. She always loved my lemon cream cake—even when I was just practicing on her. She's been such a cheerleader for me—when I went to pastry school up north, she let me stay in her apartment. But I had no idea how to get the cake to the wedding unscathed and then get it decorated. I would do anything to be at the wedding," she said, patting her stomach. "Timing is everything."

"Yes, *mio cugino* had no problem asking me to do him this favor," Lucca said dryly. "Though I guess the cake he sent to my house was supposed to be the explanation as to why this was so important. He said according to Kate, your cake is the best she's ever had." Brigid was beaming at the praise and he continued, "But what about the wedding cake once we get there? Does the staff know how to assemble it? The last thing I want to do is ruin the cake for this wedding. I am really happy for Marco and Kate."

Brigid smiled. "She's simply the best. I can't wait to meet Marco. He sounds so dreamy. Sorry," she flushed, and looked uncomfortable. "I mean, you're nice, too."

Lucca laughed. "That's perfectly fine. There's actually more of us. I have a lot of cousins!"

Brigid giggled. "I'm definitely not single, but Ellie is."

"What does Ellie have to do with it?" Lucca asked, turning around and watching her greet customers from behind the counter.

"So that's what I wanted to talk to you about, actually. If you agree, Ellie would go to babysit the cake in transit. Then she would assemble it there and do all the finish work. She was talking about going to Tuscany, anyway. So then she can just take off from there. But I mean, if it's an imposition..."

Lucca grinned. For some reason, this new plan was extremely agreeable to him. He would get a chance to get to know Ellie and see what was behind her disdain of actors. He assured Brigid now that the idea was perfectly acceptable, and they began making logistical plans. Suddenly, this wedding was going to be a lot more interesting!

"MIKE, please don't tell Lucca how you know me," Ellie whispered to the older man. As her head of security, he had been her lifeline as a teenager, her confidant and, at times, a substitute father. He had gotten her out of more jams, covered for her, and was there for her at her lowest and highest points of adolescence.

Mike was looking at her now quizzically, his dark eyes narrowed. "He doesn't know who you are?"

Ellie looked down uneasily. "He knows me as Ellie James. I mean, that's what I go by, mostly. And he just thinks I work here—it's not like my being an artist came up. I didn't want to go into the whole thing. You know how it is. People change when they find out who I am. Or rather, who my parents are."

"Lucca is just as big as your parents. He may not have the longevity, but he's got a lot of movies under his belt and he's not hurting for money or fame, kid. I'm sure he won't be fazed," Mike pointed out.

"I know—but just say you're a friend of my dad's or something for now. I mean, I'm not about to ever see the guy again, so it doesn't really matter. I just like to stay private."

He shook his head sadly. "You know, Ellie, if I could have changed things, I would have. I'm sorry your childhood was so chaotic. It wasn't fair to you. You didn't choose that life. I tried to mitigate it as much as I could, but the press was relentless when it came to you."

Ellie put a hand out and clasped Mike's over the counter. "You did the best you could. I honestly don't know what I would have done without you. Sorry I fell off the radar. I've been kind of going through a weird time."

He nodded. "You know I'm always here for you. By the way, where *are* your parents?"

Ellie furrowed her brow. "The South Pacific? I'm not really sure. They're sailing all over on their yacht. They asked me to go, but they wanted to be gone for a couple months. No, thank you. That's a lot of my parents, if you know what I mean." She laughed.

Mike laughed, too, before straightening and saying abruptly, "Hey boss, all squared away?"

Ellie looked over her shoulder to see Lucca standing behind her, eyeing the cupcakes in the case. She felt a twinge of guilt about his ruined cake. "Do you want something? We could substitute cupcakes for the smashed cake."

He gave her a quick smile. "I didn't think I did, but man, they look amazing. Sure, if you want to put some in a box, I'm certain my staff wouldn't object if I bring them home. I might even have one."

Ellie quickly got one of Brigid's signature light blue boxes and began to fill it with various flavors. She was conscious of him behind her, watching intently.

"How's the arm?" his deep voice rang out so close to her, she almost jumped.

"Uh, fine. I made sure it's clean. The cut is starting to close. I actually asked a friend who is a nurse to look at it and she didn't think it needed stitches but she had me go get a tetanus shot."

Lucca nodded. "That's good. You know you didn't need to run off. I'm harmless without my prop knife, I assure you."

Ellie looked over at Mike, who had now moved over by the door, his face impassive. He was always good about pretending he wasn't listening. She turned to meet Lucca's eyes, his dimples were on display as he gave her a mocking glance.

She made a quick face at him. "It had nothing to do with you. I just needed to leave. It had a been a long day," she said casually.

"Well, that's good. I'm glad it wasn't me. I mean you made it pretty clear how you feel about those in my industry, so I was thinking you might want to limit time around me. But now that I know it didn't have to do with me personally, we can plan on having some fun on our trip."

Ellie almost lost her grip on the box. Unsteadily, she placed it on the glass counter and turned to him.

"What trip?" She felt a dread coming on.

He smiled smugly. "We're going to Italy together, Ellie James, Injured Cake Deliverer. And I can't wait."

"I'M NOT GOING WITH HIM," Ellie said defiantly to Brigid. After Lucca's announcement, he had told her to ask Brigid about it. She had simply thrust the box at him and stomped off to do just that. She heard the tinkle of the bell on the door and knew he and Mike had left the shop. She turned to face Brigid who was putting a cake on a turntable ready to frost.

"Ellie, it's the easiest way to get the cake there. I can't send you commercial with a five-tier wedding cake! It's simple. You get on the plane and Lucca's staff will do the rest. You won't have to do much until you get to the wedding venue."

Ellie shook her head. "Send the cake with him and I'll just take my own flight and meet him there."

Brigid rolled her eyes. "That sounds horrendous and so complicated. Um, you're also being weird. Most women wouldn't balk at having to be on a private plane with Lucca Delarosa for nine hours or so."

Ellie frowned. "I'm not most women and you know it. I don't want to have anything to do with the guy."

Brigid's eyes narrowed, as she looked up from frosting the cake. "Has he been a jerk to you? Cause if so, I'll cancel this whole thing and tell Marco to just have a cake made there."

Ellie sighed. "No, he actually hasn't," she admitted. "He's just...I don't know. He's nice one minute and then the next minute I want to take off my shoe and throw it at him!"

Brigid laughed. "Okay, well let's all try to keep our shoes on at least until the cake is cut. Then I don't care what happens."

Brigid sat down on the stool near the decorating station. Ellie could see the fatigue on her face and felt instantly contrite. "Little one active today?"

Brigid smiled weakly. "Yeah, like prizefighter active. I think she loved Lucca's voice or something. Every time he spoke, she punched me. Probably wants a peek at that gorgeous hunk of man."

Ellie laughed and slumped down into a chair opposite Brigid. "Look, I don't mean to be difficult. I'll do it. But I'm going to just get there, do the job, and then take off."

Brigid smiled widely. "That's all I can ask."

five

The next few days flew by. Ellie packed, throwing random clothes in a suitcase, not sure when she'd be back next. She got her hair done—getting a few blond highlights put in and freshened it up with a cut. She wasn't sure why—she certainly wasn't doing it for Lucca. Just thinking about it made her frown.

Brigid gave her detailed instructions and even drawings about what the finished wedding cake should look like. When Ellie had spare time, she practiced her piping. Brigid had reassured her that her technique was perfection, and she trusted her completely.

Ellie still didn't know how this all had unfolded, but Brigid reassured her that it was kismet. Ellie had wanted to go back to Italy, and it had come together. Plus, Ellie was doing Brigid this favor, which partially eased Ellie's guilt over leaving.

Their departure date arrived early. Brigid had given Lucca Ellie's number, and he texted that he had moved up their flight time to the night before in order not to waste daylight hours. Ellie gave Brigid a long hug goodbye and looked back, a little teary to see her friend waving cheerfully. Matthew had arrived and came to put an arm around his wife. Ellie knew Brigid was in good hands and smiled back. She hopped into the bakery van with George driving. The cake was in the back, carefully packaged into separate coolers.

Traffic was light since it was the late evening hours, and they arrived at the airport on time. Two men in Lucca's security detail met them at the gate for private planes and charters. They were ushered quickly through, and before she knew it, Ellie was entering the plane, glancing around quickly. No Lucca. She sat down tentatively. The security team had helped George carry the coolers. They had all been set in the back, belted down with special straps so they would not bounce around in the event of turbulence.

She heard a commotion and straightened up in her chair. Sure enough, she heard Lucca's voice. He sounded frustrated, and she couldn't quite make out his words. She smiled when a sudden face appeared at the door: Sophia.

Sophia yanked on the leash, and Lucca came flying in as the dog bounded toward Ellie.

"No, Sophia. Down. Down." Ellie tried to calm her.

"You really ought to train this dog," Ellie said.

He frowned. "I'm trying. But do you know how hard it is to get a dog trainer in L.A.? Seems like every single person has a new puppy. My assistant tried for hours. Nothing. So she's coming to Italy, and we'll try to find one there."

"Do you at least have a crate for her? It will be more comfortable for her if she gets scared or if there's turbulence."

Lucca nodded. "That I have. She's crate trained at least. I did follow that advice."

One of the crew was carrying the crate in a few seconds later, putting it in a bulkhead space and securing it. He opened the door, and Sophia happily entered, settling down with her toys.

Lucca sat across from Ellie in the comfortable leather seats and suddenly smiled widely. "*Buonasera,* Ellie."

Ellie's eyes narrowed. Oh, so that was how this was going to go. He had decided to bring on the charm. Well, he was going to find it wasn't going to work on her!

"*Buonasera*," she answered firmly, deciding to stick to business. "The cake is on board."

Lucca's smile didn't waver. He was busy now assessing her, his eyes traveling over her white blouse and black jeans, ending with her black sandals. Ellie used what willpower she had to not reach up and fix her hair at his close scrutiny. She had worn it in a ponytail. She wasn't sure why, but she had rebelliously worn no make-up either. She didn't want Lucca to think she got all glammed up for him.

He stared at her intently, but only said, "Good. We're all set then. Thank you for agreeing to move up the flight. I like flying at night, and we'll have to make a pit stop in New York for Sophia. We should arrive in the evening—I'd love to be able to have dinner with my family."

"It's fine. I'll probably just sleep a lot," she said, wanting him to know she didn't care if he was there or not.

"Do you need anything at all before we take off?"

At the shake of the head, he murmured to the flight attendant, and the pilot soon came over the loudspeaker to tell them to prepare for take-off and what their flying time would be. Ellie glanced around—the plane was much larger than she had imagined, much to her relief. She never did well in small spaces.

Turning her head, she saw Mike's full head of black hair that now had hints of silver in it. He must have gotten on with the other security detail. She had been distracted with Sophia. She waved at him, and he gave her a big smile, his eyes crinkling in the corners. He then turned back to his laptop.

She turned back to Lucca. "Do you usually travel with so much security?"

He gazed at her seriously. "Yes," he answered. He looked like he wanted to say more, but chose instead to open his leather bag and get out a script.

He glanced down at her hands, which were gripping the seat handles. "Ellie," he said gently. "Are you scared to fly?"

She returned his gaze, trying not to show him her fear. She lifted her chin with pride. "No," she said curtly. "Of course not."

Ellie didn't want to tell him her heart was galloping like a runaway horse. Her throat was starting to close. Oh, dear God, why now? She hadn't had a panic attack on a plane for years. She thought she'd gotten over this phobia.

Lucca stared at her for a moment. Suddenly, he clicked his seatbelt off and was moving to the chair next to her.

"What are you doing?" she asked a little more loudly than she intended.

He grabbed her hand, holding it. She felt the tingle from his fingers shoot up her arm and didn't want to analyze it. She must be more nervous than she thought.

"I just came over so we could breathe together. Let's do a simple box breathing technique."

Ellie looked at him suspiciously but listened to his instructions. She inhaled while he counted to four, held her breath for the count of four, and then exhaled for another count of four.

"No, no, no. It's got to be deep down—not shallow. That will just get you hyperventilating. It's got to come from here." She felt Lucca's other hand on her stomach. She instinctively flung his hand away with her arm. "Don't touch me!"

"Okay, I'm sorry. I'm just trying to help. Let's try it again. Deep breaths."

Ellie looked at his face. Lucca's eyes were closed, and he was dutifully going through the exercise. She found herself holding her breath for longer than four counts. God, he was fantastic looking. She may not like actors, but there was no denying how simply beautiful this man was, his long black eyelashes covering those signature eyes of his. His olive skin looked so smooth. He had shaved, and there was only a small shadow of a beard now. His short wavy black hair was styled, but not overly so. Many men had tried to copy it and hadn't achieved his casual cut. Suddenly, he opened his eyes, and Ellie jumped.

"No, no. You have to keep breathing. You only hold your breath for four counts."

Ellie smiled weakly and continued with the exercise. Eventually, she began to feel her heart rate slowing down, her throat opening.

"Wow, that worked!" she exclaimed, forgetting to be cool.

He smiled. "Always does. I do it all the time before a scene."

"Why?"

He looked at her, his blue eyes serious. "Stage fright. Not just any stage fright. It's crippling. It took a long time for me to get to the point where I can de-stress myself. It was actually my father who ended up teaching me to breathe. I didn't think he had it in him, but I found out later he suffers from panic attacks."

Ellie looked down at their clasped hands. She withdrew hers now. "I feel better, thank you. It hasn't come on like that for a long time."

He nodded. "When you least expect it, right? I'm glad you're feeling better."

"Um, you can go back to your seat now. I'm okay."

"I was hoping to stay here in case you need distracting," he said with a wicked grin, raising his eyebrows.

"And just how do you think you'd distract me?" she asked coolly.

"I figured you could punch me or something. That would make you feel better."

Ellie laughed. She couldn't help it. She had to admit he *was* funny.

Lucca smiled. "See that's better. Okay, Slugger, I'll move back to my seat." He slid back across from her, settling into his chair. "You know what else works besides breathing?"

Ellie shook her head.

He looked at her steadily as if he was weighing telling her. "Crying," he finally admitted.

She opened her eyes wide. "Are you joking?"

He shrugged. "Why not? I mean, it's just like taking the valve off of a pressure cooker. Crying releases all that energy—good and bad. It's fantastic."

Ellie stared at him for a second and then decided to busy herself. She desperately didn't want the conversation to turn personal. She opened her backpack and gently moved her canvas roll of brushes out of the way so she could safely remove her sketch pad. She glanced through it, evaluating some of the work she had done over the last few months. It was awful.

Lucca seemed to be absorbed in his script. She eyed him for a minute. It was too much to resist. She folded the tablet to a blank page, and her pencil began to fly across the page. She tried to only take small looks, absorb as much as she could, and then draw. She tilted the pad upright—trying to ensure he couldn't see.

"What are you working on?"

Ellie jumped slightly and felt herself flush. "I was just kind of drawing the cake. You know, making sure I understand all the last detail work. I don't want to get this wrong."

He nodded absentmindedly. Then he threw the script down next to him and stretched his legs out a bit. The flight attendant brought him an orange juice without him even asking. She seemed poised to drop everything to run to Lucca's every whim. Ellie almost rolled her eyes. She asked the flight attendant for a water, and the woman looked like she didn't want to leave Lucca's side to get it. Grudgingly, Ellie was given a water bottle, and the flight attendant finally seemed to admit defeat and went to check if the security detail wanted anything.

"Did Brigid tell you much about the happy couple?" Lucca asked.

Ellie carefully closed her sketch pad. "No, not really. Just that Kate Malone was her cousin and they were super close growing up and when Brigid was in pastry school."

"Kate is wonderful. Very kind and funny. My cousin is a lucky man," Lucca said wryly.

"You sound in love with her yourself," Ellie commented dryly.

He smiled, as if he was thinking about another time. "We shared a special dinner together one evening. It was fantastic tormenting my cousin. But no, Kate is decidedly his bride. And they make a better couple than we would. And there's also the fact that I will never marry."

"Why not?" Ellie asked curiously.

He shrugged. "I don't believe in it. My parents had a nasty divorce. It tore our family up. My father recently remarried, but time will tell how that turns out. Marriage isn't normal. I don't know any happy marriages."

"That's because you live in the Land of Divorce," she said. "A lot of people have good marriages."

"Really? That seems a rather optimistic and sunny outlook for you," Lucca said mockingly.

Her eyes narrowed. "I'm a very pleasant person. I am also optimistic. You don't know me at all."

He smiled, a more genuine one this time. "I'm sorry, Ellie. It's so easy to give you a hard time. You're right, I don't know you. I'd like to, though. Especially since we're on this adventure together. Forgive me?"

Before she could answer, he continued. "My cousin Marco is the one who should be soured, but now he's met the love of his life and is getting married."

"Why would he be soured?" Ellie asked, relieved to have a safer topic.

"Marco didn't have it easy growing up. We are the same age and very close." At her look, he added, "Thirty-three. Anyway, he struggled at school, and it was very hard on him. It turned out he had some kind of learning disability. He overcame it, and when his uncle died, he became CEO of Oro Industries."

"I've heard of them," said Ellie nervously. "Only it wasn't good. I think I saw something about fraud or that people were going to prison."

Lucca nodded. "Yes, it was unfortunate. When Marco took over, he found out his uncle's trusted friend, who was his Chief Financial Officer, had been doing all kinds of shady stuff. It was Kate who uncovered it," he told her. "Marco didn't believe her at first, and they had a big fight. Then she saw some photos of Marco with his ex-fiancé, and Kate ended up back in the states."

"How did it all work out? This sounds like a movie!"

He laughed. "Almost. Maybe I should hire a scriptwriter. Well, Marco's ex-fiancé had literally left him at the altar. The thing was—he never had any real feelings for her. He was just doing what he thought he should be doing. Fortunately, she ran off and married someone else. But that left him kind of broken. When he happened to be in Rome, he met up with her because her husband needed a job. It was all innocent, but Kate didn't know that. No matter what, she still wanted to help him. She sent her sister, Meara, to help Marco unravel what was happening at our corporation. I met Meara just once and let me tell you she's a force of nature."

Ellie stared at him for a minute. "Wait, Meara Malone? I've read articles about her. She's like the top female CEO in the Silicon Valley. She has broken all kinds of glass ceilings. *That's* Kate's sister?"

"Yep. And she got Marco to come back to San Francisco with her to convince Kate to marry him. Meanwhile, Kate had built up her business, but she's going to run it from Italy."

Ellie smiled a little. "I actually was introduced to Meara one time."

Lucca gazed at her thoughtfully. "Brigid was right. You do know a lot of people."

She waved her hand dismissively. "Oh, it was some party or something."

"While you were working?"

Ellie nodded before she had a chance to think. She still wanted to maintain her privacy, and for some reason, it was important that Lucca didn't know anything about her. Once they got this cake to Italy, they would go their separate ways and would never see each other again. She told herself she preferred it that way. He unsettled her in a way that she didn't want to think about.

It had been a long time since Ellie's last relationship. Not that she hadn't had a lot of offers to go out, but she knew it was her own paranoia. She didn't trust easily—for good reasons.

Lucca was staring at her now, as if he were trying to figure her out.

"I'll let you get back to your script," she said abruptly.

He continued to study her, grinning a little. "Dismissed!"

Ellie chose not to respond, closing her eyes instead. She would pretend to sleep a little. She heard the pages rustle, which gave her comfort. Hopefully, he had stopped staring at her. She nestled into the seat. So far, their flight was very smooth.

A couple of hours later, Ellie started to wake up. She couldn't believe she had fallen asleep. Now her head was nestled into something soft. She rubbed her cheek against it and gave a little sigh of contentment. It felt really nice. Something smelled good, too. Suddenly, she bolted straight up. She turned to the owner of that soft piece of material. Lucca opened his eyes. He had obviously been dozing. He stared at her innocently. She took in his gray T-shirt and faded jeans. He looked more like a rock star today than a movie star.

She stared at him now indignantly. "When I went to sleep, you were over there." She pointed to his seat across from her.

He gave her a smug smile. "You're a head bobber."

"I'm what?" she snapped.

"A head bobber." To illustrate, he dramatically shook his head up and down and back and forth. "I felt bad for you. I wanted you to be able to sleep without killing your neck, so I just gave you my shoulder for a pillow for a little while. I got some sleep, too."

Ellie felt herself frowning, but a small piece of her wanted to crack. Was he being thoughtful or just annoying her? She didn't want to like him. "Thanks, but you could have just given me a pillow."

He shrugged. "Seemed like the best option."

Lucca moved now across from her and closed his eyes. "If I start to bob, will you help me?" he asked, his eyes closed, his mouth twitching.

"Highly doubtful."

She waited for his retort, but there was none. He was already asleep. How could he fall asleep that fast? She studied him. His face was completely relaxed. He had shadows under his eyes, as if he hadn't been sleeping well. In fact, the other day he had looked exhausted. She wondered if he was working on a new movie or something.

Ellie took out her sketch pad again and sent her pencil flying. She was able to study him as much as she wanted and quickly made several sketches of him. She could add more detail to them later. The shapes and shadows of his face intrigued her. She looked at him to make sure he was asleep and heard a small snore and smiled. Ellie kept working for quite a while, but when he stirred, she snapped her pad shut. Getting out her phone, she pretended to look at it and not focus on him.

He was staring at her, before stretching. "Do you want something to eat? I know it's weird to eat in the middle of the night, but I got us some food for whenever we want. It's better than the stuff they always have on board."

Ellie's stomach rumbled just at the mention of food. She nodded. She hadn't had much dinner and might as well eat. He got up quickly, returning with an assortment of sandwiches, salads and homemade potato chips.

Ellie's eyes widened in excitement. This is from "Rocco's!" she said, knowing the distinct paper wrapping anywhere. Rocco's was one of the most popular delis in town and was the popular go-to for many celebrities. In fact, Ellie hadn't been there for a long time because paparazzi often hung out around there. She wasn't sure if anyone would recognize her anymore, but she wasn't taking any chances. She tried to dress down most of the time, and she didn't often wear make-up. Still, even the presence of a lot of cameramen gave her PTSD. She almost shuddered now just thinking about it.

"Yeah, I had someone pick it up. It sounded good for the flight."

"Oh, well, thanks. It's always delicious." She chose a sandwich and some chips.

He raised his eyebrows. "You've been there?"

Ellie nodded, taking a bite of her sandwich so she couldn't be expected to answered.

Right then, she felt a knuckle rub her head. She looked up and swallowed. "Mike, if you give me a noogie, I'll take you down."

Mike was standing in the aisle, looming over them. "Try it, kiddo. That would be interesting. Hey, boss, we have a few things to go over regarding security at the lemon grove. When you get a moment, come on over to our side of the plane—we'll show you some of the plans we've drawn up."

Lucca nodded. "Mike, make sure you and the guys eat at some point. I ordered a lot of food."

He smiled. "Thanks—we'll do that." As he walked away, he gave Ellie a wink.

Lucca stared at her. "So I don't remember. How do you know Mike?"

"I never told you. That's why you don't remember."

He looked a little sheepish. "Mike said he knows your father. What does your dad do? Is he in security?"

"Sort of," Ellie mumbled. "He knows a lot about it." She thought back to the half dozen movies her dad had made in a series about an arrogant CIA agent.

Lucca seemed satisfied and continued eating. He changed the subject now, telling her about his cousins and aunt. He seemed very close to them. "My aunt—Zia Margherita—is my dad's sister. She's the kindest human I know. And Marco has two younger brothers, Stefano and Nico."

Lucca talked about visiting the lemon grove where they lived as kids, running through the fields and creating havoc. "Zia Margherita and Zio Angelo were so good to me even when I was a hellion." He laughed. "I loved visiting. Zio Angelo wasn't even my uncle, but he treated me like I was his nephew."

"I don't understand."

"Angelo's brother was the boys' father. Their father left them high and dry—it's a long story. But Angelo took over, almost like a father to the boys."

"Wow, that's really nice," said Ellie. Lucca seemed in the mood to talk. She wasn't really sure what to say.

"Definitely very nice. I often wished he were my father, too."

She shifted in her seat. Lucca confiding anything in her was making her uncomfortable. She'd much rather be sparring with him. Done eating now, she pushed her food gently away on the retractable table that Lucca had pulled out from the window area.

"Do you think it's okay if I get up and walk around?"

He stared for a minute but nodded. He looked away, taking a bite of his sandwich.

Ellie got up and walked to the back, where Sophia was in her crate. She knelt down next to her. "Hi, sweet thing. I'm sorry you have to be in here. But we have to keep you safe. I promise to play with you when you get out."

Sophia paused, chewing on a toy. She put her paw up on the crate, and Ellie smiled. Dogs meant unconditional love. She had only had that from her parents and wondered what it would be like to have that from a man—Lucca may be right about marriage. She frowned. She really hoped his opinion was wrong.

LUCCA WRAPPED the rest of the food and put it in the bag. The flight attendant scurried right over.

"Oh, Mr. Delarosa, I'll do that. That's part of my job." She continued talking, but Lucca was nodding, not listening. He was watching Ellie sitting on the floor by Sophia's crate, whispering to her earnestly. Ellie seemed much happier doing that than sitting talking with him. He ran his hands through his hair and was only partly aware that the flight attendant had finally walked away.

Ellie's long ponytail swung down her back. He could see her side profile. She wasn't wearing any make-up, but he had noticed her eyes as soon as he had gotten on the plane, clearly assessing him. Everything about her was uniquely natural—especially since she came from the Land of Make Believe. He found himself watching her expressive face. She seemed to try to keep her feelings to herself, but the emotions that crossed her face were very telling.

Lucca wondered why she disliked him so much. He tried to be kind and polite to her. Maybe he had needled her a bit. For some reason, he had found himself naturally wanting to tell her about his family in Italy. Lucca was proud of them and loved being included in their lives. She had listened, but then abruptly got up as if she couldn't wait to escape.

He watched her, now laughing at Sophia's antics. Had he even made her laugh? She may have smiled at a few of his comments, but nothing like the animated face she was showing his dog. Lucca wasn't even sure why it mattered, but suddenly he felt like he was competing with Sophia. He frowned. This meant he would have to pick up his game.

six

When the wheels touched down with a giant thud and the plane screeched to a stop, Ellie sighed with relief. Thank God the long flight was over. She had come back to her seat and found Lucca reading his script. They had briefly stopped in New York, and she was relieved when they had taken off that she didn't have any more panic episodes. Still, she had caught herself trying to do Lucca's box breathing. He had looked over at her, a smug smile on his face.

She had closed her eyes again, worried he would resume a conversation. She had drifted off for a couple of hours. When she woke up, he had been absorbed in his reading, and she didn't know why that annoyed her. She knew it was irrational but couldn't help feeling just a little peeved. She took out her sketch pad and resumed for a few minutes. It was only after he glanced up, his eyebrows raised, that she tried to unobtrusively turn the page.

He had stared at her steadily for a minute, but didn't ask any questions. Instead, the pilot had come on to tell them they were descending. Ellie looked at Lucca suspiciously when he changed seats and came to sit by her again. "What are you doing?"

"Just thought I'd come over in case we need to breathe," he said.

"I'm fine. I was fine when we landed in New York. I'm not scared of landing."

"I was asleep. I didn't notice. But maybe I'm not so fond of landing." He gave her a charming smile.

Ellie frowned but said nothing. As they descended, she felt him grab her hand. She looked up at his handsome face and noticed he did look a little pale.

"Four breaths in," she said softly.

He nodded.

THE SMALL PARTY quickly checked in with customs, took care of Sophia's needs, and the luxury vans were loaded. Ellie watched the coolers being placed into the second van. Lucca told her it wasn't necessary for her to supervise, and that his people were on it. Stubbornly, Ellie had remained rooted to the spot, counting the coolers and checking that they were well wedged into the van and no heavy suitcases were piled on top. She was not doing this for nothing. The cake had to arrive in perfect condition.

Lucca waved to her, holding the door open to a roomy SUV. She looked behind her, watching his staff and security personnel getting into the vans. She walked slowly to the SUV and got in. Mike got into the front seat next to the driver. One van headed off, and the other was behind them.

She knew the drive from Naples Airport was scenic, and she felt herself relaxing. She was tired and felt sticky, even though the plane had been comfortable. The air in the car felt good. Lucca pointed out some sites in Naples as they sped through and then, since it was a clear afternoon, they could see a little of Mt. Vesuvius in the distance.

Finally, they left the busy thoroughfare and settled down to the windier roads near Sorrento. Brigid had told her the wedding was to be held at the family's estate on the lemon grove and there was a house for her to stay in. Ellie assumed there was some kind of staff housing. It sounded like a massive property.

They soon arrived at a wrought-iron gate, and Lucca got out to use a key card. Ellie thought it was strange he hadn't asked Mike to do it. She had noticed that about him, though. He had gotten their food on the plane himself and not asked anyone to do it. He didn't seem demanding or expecting everyone to wait on him.

The small motorcade continued up the gravel road, which eventually turned into a paved one. They pulled up to a circular drive, where a picturesque fountain stood in the middle, ringed by flower beds. The nearby expansive cream-colored house with its arched windows and covered wraparound terrace was breathtaking in its simplicity. Despite its size, it radiated warmth and family. Ellie began to see why Lucca loved coming here as a kid.

"Mike, I'll give you a call in the morning. We can talk further about the issues we discussed on the plane," Lucca said. Getting out, he ran over to Ellie's side of the car and opened her door. "This is our stop," he said proudly. "My family's home."

She got out automatically but narrowed her eyes. "Do you want me to meet them or something before I go to my room?"

"You're staying here with the family," he said, smiling.

She shook her head. "I can't."

"Why not?"

"Lucca, I'm the cake decorator. I'm here to do a job. That's it. Period."

Mike had already gotten their luggage out of the trunk and had carried it to the porch. Sophia's crate had been unloaded, and she was now free, bounding all over the nearby grass.

"Mike, stop. You traitor! I'm going with you guys," called Ellie nervously.

He set her bags down on the porch and came back down toward her. "Don't worry about the cakes, Ellie. I have strict instructions. I'll make sure they are unloaded without a scratch and placed in the walk-in at the venue."

She glanced around nervously, hoping for an escape. "Lucca, this is ridiculous. I'm not comfortable staying here with your family. I'd rather just go with the security team."

"Lucca!" shouted a male voice. Suddenly, people were pouring out onto the porch. A tall, gorgeous man bounded down the stairs and was hugging Lucca enthusiastically.

"You know you can trust me with the cake," Mike said quietly behind her.

"I'm not worried about the cake. I'm worried about this," whispered Ellie, gesturing to the family and the house.

"You're going to be fine, kiddo. Trust me on that, too."

Ellie turned and gave him a long look. "I hope you're right."

He disappeared into the SUV and they drove off, with Ellie looking longingly after him. He gave her a small salute and an encouraging smile. His eyes were hidden behind his sunglasses.

She turned around to watch Lucca's family embracing him. All three brothers were either hugging him, playfully punching him, or slapping him on the back. An older woman stood on the stairs, looking clearly amused. Ellie guessed who was who by Lucca's descriptions of them on the plane. Marco must be the one who hugged him first. Clad in a polo shirt and shorts, he had broad shoulders, but was lean. He had wavy black hair that looked like he tried to tame it into submission. He was the more commanding of the three brothers. Ellie guessed even if he hadn't been head of the family's dynasty, he simply would be in charge of everything.

Stefano must be the tallest of the three. He was dressed up a little more in gray pants and a long-sleeved shirt, with the sleeves rolled up. He was lean as well, and though he resembled Marco, his hair was closely clipped, his features more chiseled and serious. The youngest brother, Nico, was in faded jeans and a T-shirt. He also had the trademark hair, only his was ruffled and on the longer side. He had a big smile on his face and seemed to be teasing everyone in classic little brother fashion.

Ellie stood there awkwardly, waiting for Lucca's introduction. She didn't have to wait long. He came over and threw an arm around her shoulders, a big grin on his face.

"Everyone, I'd like you to meet my girlfriend, Ellie."

<h1 style="text-align:center">seven</h1>

Ellie turned to Lucca in astonishment. He put both arms around her now, hugging her frantically, whispering in her ear. "Remember, the cake is a surprise! No one knows but Marco. It's the only explanation of what you are doing here."

He let her go, but kept an arm around her. She put her arm around his waist and dug her nails into his back with all her might. He arched his back, but apparently was using every acting skill he had not to show pain.

She was greeted warmly by all three brothers, with Marco being the first. He came forward, kissing her on both cheeks. "*Buonasera*, Ellie. Thank you for doing this," he whispered. He pulled back and stared at her hard, his black eyes warm.

She nodded, swallowing the protest in her throat. After the brothers were done greeting her, Margherita came down the stairs to embrace Lucca and then Ellie. She was a tall woman, elegantly dressed in white pants and a blue silk blouse. She wore simple gold hoop earrings and a heart locket. Her black hair with just a hint of gray was pulled back in a gold clip.

"Ellie, we are so happy to meet you. When Lucca told me he

was bringing a date, I was thrilled. I knew it had to be someone special for him to bring a date to Marco's wedding."

Ellie smiled weakly. "Thank you for having me," she said, digging her nails into Lucca's hand that she was now holding. He smiled rather than wincing.

"Let's go in, everyone," Margherita urged. She turned to Ellie. "Kate—the bride—went to Positano with her sister and one of her bridesmaids. Her dad is resting upstairs, as he recently had some health issues. She said not to wait for them, so Stefano has made dinner a little early for the family. We figured you would want to eat when you got here. We'll show you to your rooms first and if you want to shower and change, please feel welcome."

Everyone was filing up the stairs toward the front door, laughing and talking at once. They entered the house, and Ellie used the opportunity to swing Lucca around by the wrist.

"Stop manhandling me," he said, rubbing his wrist and hand.

"You stop. Are you kidding me? Girlfriend? When were you going to tell me that bit of news?" she whispered urgently.

He looked chagrined. "Look, it was kind of underhanded and I probably should have involved you, but I knew you'd say no. This surprise means a lot to my cousin. He has never once asked me for anything, and I just want to make it happen. I can't trust his brothers to keep a secret. It means that much."

He looked at her now, his crystal blue eyes pleading with her.

She frowned at him. "God, you're good."

"I know, right?" he said smugly.

"You're totally acting right now!"

He shook his head, laughing. He crossed his heart with his finger. "Honestly, Ellie, I'm not. I am 100 percent serious."

"You're going to owe me so much, Hollywood."

"I know, I know. I promise I'll make it worth your while," he said, a different look crossing his face.

Ellie felt her heart do a little somersault at the look on his face. They stared at each other for a minute.

He elbowed her. "C'mon, Ellie James, Injured Cake Deliverer. Let's go spend some time with the family."

LUCCA SMILED, sitting back from the big table on his family's back terrace, his arm loosely behind Ellie's shoulders. She subtly shifted away from him but had a pasted smile on her face. It made him smile even more to see it.

For the first time in months, he felt relaxed. It was good to be home—what felt like home for him, anyway. He had many homes around the world as well as his dad's villa in Tuscany, where he had spent some of his teen years. His summers as a child on the lemon grove had the most impression on his heart. He deeply trusted his aunt and cousins, and these days, he didn't trust many people.

Lucca studied Ellie as she joined in the conversation. In a way he trusted her already, too. Of course, he knew very little about her except that she didn't make a big deal about his fame, and that definitely scored points with him.

He admired her from the side. She had changed before dinner and now looked pretty in her casual gold-colored sundress. Her straight hair hung behind her back, and her face was bare of make-up. She was quietly talking with Nico, the youngest of his cousins who could talk to a fencepost. He was already teasing Ellie, it appeared, and she was laughing. She had a nice smile that lit up her face. He found himself reaching up and gently touching her hair. For a moment, it almost appeared as if she didn't notice, but then she turned to him slightly, giving him a quick glance that probably stopped most people in their tracks. Not him, though. He stroked her hair again. It was so silky soft and he realized appreciatively there were no hair extensions. It spread across his hand, and he combed his fingers through it, looking at the way the evening colors bounced off of it. She turned to him now, putting her hand on his thigh. He squirmed a minute, misreading her intention until she dug her nails into his leg. He had changed into shorts before dinner, and she was making the most of attacking his bare leg.

He covered his hand innocently over hers. Instead of trying to pry her hand off, he finally was able to turn it over and stroke her palm gently. He saw with a glance it was having his desired effect. She squirmed a little in her seat, still talking to Nico. She couldn't take her hand away without being obvious. He now raised it to his lips. This time, she did pull it away—gently, but enough that he saw his aunt raise her eyebrows slightly. He decided to deflect her attention.

"Zia Rita, I heard you are bringing a date to the wedding!" he teased.

She laughed, flushing a little. "No one can keep a secret in this household! Yes, I am bringing Sergio to the wedding. We've...well, we've been enjoying each other's company," she added softly.

Lucca had known Sergio for years. He had been the manager of the property for as long as he could remember. He had always liked the friendly man, who seemed so capable at his job.

"I think that's wonderful," he said softly, putting his hand over hers on the table.

Marco nodded. "I'm happy for you, Mamma. I know that I was a little shocked at first, but not anymore. Sergio is a good man. And at least you and Lucca have dates. My two brothers here are as single as they come."

"Hey." Nico smiled. "Don't you know weddings are the best place to find someone? I'm being smart. Don't lump me in with Stefano."

Stefano frowned. "It's no one's business who I date, and I certainly would not bring a woman to anything involving you all." He looked over at Ellie, giving her a rare smile. "No offense, Ellie."

She smiled. "None taken. I'm sure it's like any family. There's certain steps in this process: interrogation, embarrassment of involved family members, and then acceptance."

They laughed. "You forgot the hazing part," said Lucca. "Usually we throw that in!"

Margherita protested. "That is not true, Lucca! Not under my roof. Kate was definitely not hazed, and now you're scaring Ellie!"

Lucca put his arm around Ellie's shoulders again. "Ellie doesn't scare easily. She can handle herself."

"Are you an actress?" Margherita asked innocently.

"Oh God, never! I mean, no, I'm just not part of that world. I work in a bakery," she said.

"How did you two meet?" Margherita persisted.

"Well, let's see. She stomped on my foot, elbowed me, and then round kicked me," answered Lucca.

"Only after he attacked me with a knife," Ellie pointed out calmly.

The family began talking at once, and Lucca put up a hand with a smile. "Listen, we'll save that story for later. Maybe when Kate comes home. She will find it entertaining," he said. "Meanwhile, how about you and I clear the plates, Ellie?"

Margherita protested, "Lucca, she just got here. We don't make our guests work—that's for you and my sons to do."

Ellie was already standing. "Margherita, I don't mind. It feels good to move around anyway after the long flight and drive."

"Leave everything, and instead, you should take a walk with Lucca in the lemon grove. You two need to stay awake so you can get over the jet lag."

"That's a great idea," said Lucca, standing. "By the way, where's the little monster?"

"Don't call her that!" Ellie protested. She turned. "Sophia? Come!"

Sophia had been down on the grass, romping with Max, who belonged to the foreman, but treated the house as his second home. Sophia came running now at Ellie's voice, jumping on her.

Ellie grabbed something from her pocket. "Sophia, down. Down. Sit." Sophia sat, and Ellie handed her a treat.

"Where did you get that?" Lucca asked.

"I borrowed some of Max's. Your aunt showed me where they were. We need to start training her." She held out a bag with some dog treats in them.

"Come, Sophia," she said, giving the dog a treat after Sophia got up to follow them. Ellie turned back to the group. "Thank you so much for dinner. Stefano, that ravioli was amazing, and the caprese salad was so fantastic. I love fresh mozzarella. I don't know if I've ever had a better meal."

Stefano nodded his thanks, and Lucca grabbed Ellie's hand to lead her back into the house. Silently they wove through the massive kitchen before getting to a formal entryway. He held the large mahogany door open for her, and she and Sophia quickly exited. They had just descended the front stairs when Ellie turned on him.

"What the hell, Lucca! This is nuts. I can't keep up this charade. Are you out of your mind?"

Lucca was standing staring at her with those glittering blue eyes, and for some reason, it was making her even angrier. How dare he look so flipping cute after a long plane ride, car ride and now while she berated him? He put his hands in his shorts' pockets, his untucked shirt hanging loosely. He was silent, his head to the side, as if he were just waiting for her to lose steam.

"You put me in a horrible position. I don't even know these people. And I certainly don't know you like that. And now I am your girlfriend? They are nice people in there, and now I have to lie to them!"

"*Mi scusi?*"

They both turned toward a voice. Marco was running down the stairs now, looking behind him anxiously.

"Ellie, I wanted to apologize to you. I feel like Lucca was forced to put you in this awkward position because I insisted he keep this a secret. It's not fair to you, and I wanted to tell you that after the wedding, I'll make sure and tell everyone this was all done at my insistence. Please, don't blame Lucca."

He swung a friendly arm around Lucca's shoulders now. "He's a big lug and as ridiculous as they come, but he's my cousin and I love him. He's just trying to do me this favor—and Katie—though she doesn't know it yet! I can't thank you enough for all you're doing. I know it's a lot to ask."

Ellie was charmed despite her predicament. She smiled weakly. "I hope it's okay I said I worked at a bakery. I just blurted it out without thinking."

Marco nodded. "No one will think twice. You probably think this is all a little weird. Katie has given me so much already and I want to give her the world. I figured out early on, though, that she's not wanting the stuff I normally think of. She isn't impressed by things, if you know what I mean." He laughed for a second, as if he was remembering another time. "That's why I had to get creative. When I thought of this idea, it was to not only get Katie her favorite cake but also to reunite her with Brigid. I had no idea Brigid wouldn't be able to make the trip and that I would have to ask so much of a stranger. I can't thank you enough for helping me."

He was looking at her now with warm black eyes, and Ellie found herself melting by his obvious love for his fiancé. She opened her mouth to acknowledge his kind speech when suddenly a white SUV swung up the path. A woman about her age jumped out, her brown hair tousled. She wore a simple red sundress and carried shopping bags.

Marco dropped his arm from Lucca and went to throw them around the woman. Kissing her soundly, he grabbed the bags and led her back toward them. Lucca walked forward and whispered to the woman, kissing her on each cheek. She hugged him in return, laughing.

"Stop teasing me, Lucca. I'm the bride. None of your mischief." She noticed Ellie and smiled at her. Lucca walked back to Ellie and put his arm around her, kissing her cheek. "Katie, I want you to meet my girlfriend, Ellie. I've decided she can handle the lot of you for a few days. It's risky, I know."

Ellie was still painfully aware of Lucca's kiss, even if it had been for show. She pulled herself together and accepted Kate's warm hug. Ellie instantly took a liking to her. "I hope you don't mind, Kate. I guess I'm crashing your wedding," she said, giving Lucca a meaningful glance.

"Of course not. Oh my God, I'm thrilled! It's lovely to meet you." She turned then and gestured toward a short woman with black curly hair who was helping the driver get more bags from the back of the car. "That's my best friend, Teresa, from home." She looked at them seriously now, but with a twinkle in her eye. "I apologize in advance for anything she might do or say."

Teresa walked forward slowly, and Kate made the introductions. Lucca also kissed Teresa on both cheeks, and she stood there silently, her eyes wide. She looked utterly starstruck. Kate stood next to her, smirking.

The driver approached as well, and Lucca gave him a big hug, introducing him as Sergio. His brown eyes were warm, and his smile was genuine. He looked perfect for Margherita.

Ellie recognized the tall redhead who was standing near the car, looking at her phone. Kate yelled: "Meara, look up." Meara glanced up and waved. Ellie saw Meara's earbuds were in and realized she was on the phone. Ellie wondered uneasily if Meara would remember meeting her. It was almost a year ago, and she probably met a lot of people.

"She's making last-minute arrangements for a bachelorette party for me tomorrow night." Kate rolled her eyes. "I told her it was not necessary, but trying to budge Meara from an idea is like rolling a boulder up a hill."

Kate looked at her. "Ellie, now that you're here, you'll have to come! Please! It's just me, my bridesmaids, and some new friends from Positano. We'll have a great time."

"Well, I..." Ellie stammered.

"I'm not going to take a no. I can't leave you alone with all these men. You have to come out with us." She laughed, grabbing Marco's hand. She gazed up at him now, and he was staring down, completely besotted.

Ellie sighed despite herself. She looked at Lucca, who was watching her with narrowed eyes. She turned back to Kate. "I'd love to come. Thank you for the invitation."

Kate smiled widely at her. "We'll tell you more about it tomorrow. I have a fitting during the day and some last-minute errands, but I'll see you at some point. You're staying at the house, right?"

She didn't wait for an answer but looked at them both. "Looks like you guys were about to go for a walk. I highly recommend it," she said, smiling dreamily at Marco again. "It's very romantic in the grove." She let go of Marco and elbowed Teresa now. "Teresa? Hello? Are you still with us? I have never, ever seen you at a loss for words!" Teresa smiled weakly at Kate's teasing.

"Wait till she sees the real Lucca." Kate rolled her eyes before looking at Ellie, as if sizing her up. "You don't look like the type to be swayed by him," she commented.

Ellie smiled. "Correct."

"Good." Kate said and then laughed. "Keep it that way."

Lucca grabbed Ellie's hand, and they began to walk down a

path, looking very much like a couple. Sophia, who had been roaming the fields, came at Ellie's first call. Ellie handed her some treats absentmindedly. Glancing back, she saw the party loading bags into the house, laughing and talking. She felt a sudden sense of warmth. Now that they were away from his family's sight, she tugged her hand away. He gave her a smile. She frowned, but couldn't resist admitting, "Your family is wonderful."

Lucca nodded, his grin deeper, his dimples out in full force. "I'm very fortunate. They are who I hold most sacred. I'm glad you will have the opportunity to get to know them."

"Why?"

"I'm not sure." He shrugged. "Look, Ellie, I know we put you in a weird position, but to be honest, I'm not too sorry. I think you'll have fun, and I know I'm going to. Let's just relax and enjoy a few days together. After that, I promise I'll get you up to Tuscany."

"How did you know I was planning to go to Tuscany?"

"Brigid told me. I'm actually headed up there as well. I told her as a thank you I'd make sure you got there okay."

She shook her head. "No, she didn't say anything. But that's fine. I need to rent a car anyway."

"Why would you do that when I'm also going that direction? We'll get to spend more quality time together," he teased.

She frowned. "Lucca, despite what you may think, I'm immune to your charms. I told you before, flat out, no Hollywood for me. No actors, producers, writers—no one. So don't start something." She paused for a second and took a deep breath. "I don't want to start something I can't stop."

He wiggled his eyebrows at her. "That makes it sound even more fun." He stopped walking and his face became serious. "You've made it very clear. What is it, though? Who wronged you? What makes you so hostile about people in my industry?"

She looked away, afraid to meet his eyes. "It's just a lot of fake people. People who use others for their own gain. I just don't trust anyone in the business. I'm sorry."

Lucca was watching her intently, and it made her uncomfortable. She struggled to fill the silence. "I'm not going to be hostile while I'm here. I won't embarrass you or anything. Just don't have any expectations. And honestly, I'm sure I'm not even your type, so I'm probably embarrassing myself just assuming that you're even into me."

Lucca's voice was dangerously soft. "Oh, Ellie, you won't have to assume. You'll know when I'm into you." Her heart started hammering at the thought.

He held out his hand. "Shall we call a truce, then? Can we just appear to get along even if you've sworn off actors? I will be a gentleman and won't cross any lines. I'd like to be your friend," he said softly.

She felt a small sense of irrational disappointment. He didn't have to give in so quickly. She eyed his hand now before sliding hers into it. She immediately felt the jolt of electricity shoot up her arm—the same one that traveled down her spine every time he touched her.

"Truce," she finally said, eyeing him warily. She wasn't sure what she saw in his face—relief, smugness, charm or all three.

She looked over and saw Sophia running around the lemon trees at full speed. She laughed. "She has the zoomies," she said, pointing to the dashing puppy.

Lucca lifted an eyebrow. "I know the feeling," he said dryly.

eight

Ellie stared at herself in the mirror, deciding if she needed to do anything to her hair. It had felt good to take a long shower last night. After her and Lucca's truce, they had walked through a small part of the lemon grove. She hadn't realized how vast the property was. He was very knowledgeable about the family empire, though he admitted he was not involved in the slightest. He told her he had enjoyed picking lemons and doing chores around the farm growing up. He adored his cousin's uncle, and apparently, Zio Angelo had adored him back, giving Lucca substantial shares in the business. Lucca spoke lovingly about the man who had died shortly before Marco had taken over his title of CEO. Lucca told her more about Marco's rocky start, given that his CFO had done everything to thwart his efforts and now faced fraud charges. While the brothers were all involved in the business, Stefano and Nico were probably going to slowly remove themselves to pursue their interests.

Ellie had stayed silent, letting Lucca talk. He seemed content to keep things light, proudly telling her about his family. When they had returned to the house, he had taken her straight upstairs to the room he had shown her when they first arrived.

With a quiet goodnight, he had left her, and she had felt strangely alone.

She had gone to bed and slept well in the big comfortable bed with its soft, cream comforter. She woke up and looked around the room. The walls were painted in a soothing shade of green and when she knelt on the upholstered window seat, she was able to look at the gorgeous view of the vista beyond the lemon grove. The bathroom was everything she could ask for, with a luxurious stone shower and expansive vanity. There were even toiletries and hair tools well-supplied on nearby shelves. A welcome basket from Margherita had greeted her with even more expensive Italian toiletries. Ellie took off the top of a cream now, smelling it. Lovely. She applied a little on her face now, feeling its light silkiness.

Ellie dressed in white jeans and a simple pale yellow top. She wasn't sure what the day was going to bring and wished she had remembered to tell Lucca that she wanted to go to the venue to double check the cake. Tomorrow she would begin decorating it, as she wanted to give herself a little extra time in case of any catastrophes. She was trying not to think about it—it made her nervous to be given so much responsibility. A video call to Brigid was always a possibility if needed.

Walking down a few hallways, Ellie was relieved to see the stairs. She had been so tired yesterday, she hadn't even remembered all the twists and turns they had taken. She walked into the quiet kitchen and realized she should have asked what time she should come down or what time Lucca was going to get up. He was probably still in bed.

Margherita was sitting at the big table near the French doors to the terrace. She looked up and smiled. "*Buongiorno*, Ellie! I hope you slept well!" Rising now, she came toward her. "Everyone has had an early start. The boys went up to the wedding venue. Marco is insisting on double checking my work." She rolled her eyes. "I did ask them to do a few chores while they were there. They might as well help our staff. This is a big lift for them. And Kate took her family and Teresa to go to her last fitting. She was hoping if everyone saw her ahead of time, there would be less crying at the wedding," Margherita said with a laugh. "It's a slim chance. And not everyone is here—her other two bridesmaids couldn't get here until tomorrow."

"Oh, I'm sorry to have missed everyone. I usually don't sleep this late. I was more tired than I realized," Ellie said.

"It's completely fine! I am sure you were exhausted. Would you like a cappuccino and some breakfast? Stefano usually cooks breakfast, but everyone was up so early we just grabbed what was easiest." She pointed toward a big tray of pastries. "Or we can make some eggs, or we have meat and cheese."

"Oh no, I might just have some cappuccino, if you don't mind. My stomach is all mixed up. I'm not sure what time zone I'm in!"

The older woman quickly made her a cappuccino, handling the big red machine with practiced ease. "Thank you, Margherita," said Ellie, taking the Italian ceramic mug from her.

"Please, call me Rita," the older woman said kindly, as she made herself a cup. Looking at her for a minute, she seemed to make a decision. "Let's take our coffee into the living room," she offered, leading the way.

Ellie followed her, glancing around. Although the house was massive and perfectly furnished, it seemed lived in and warm. The big furniture was comfortable and inviting, the wooden antique tables were glistening with polish.

Margherita indicated a couple of comfortable upholstered chairs in the corner near French doors. Ellie sat down and took a big sip of her cappuccino. She choked as she looked at the wall opposite her, behind Margherita's head. She coughed, and Margherita expressed concern.

"Wrong pipe," Ellie managed to stammer, taking a deep breath. Ellie glanced again at the wall. Yep, it was there—she hadn't imagined it. One of her paintings was hanging on the wall.

MARGHERITA WAS WATCHING Ellie closely as she took another sip. The older woman turned and looked at the painting. It was one of Ellie's first works she had sold—a Tuscan village scene captured on a linen panel.

"Stunning, isn't it? My brother gave it to me—he bought it in Florence. It reminds me of home."

Ellie swallowed hard, staring into her cup. She felt her face flushing. She finally looked up at Margherita, whose eyes were twinkling at her.

"And now, Ellie, do you want to tell me why you are here pretending to be my nephew's girlfriend who works in a bakery?"

"How did you know?" Ellie stammered.

"Know which, dear? That you are a well-known artist, don't work in a bakery, or are not dating my nephew?"

Looking at her intently, Margherita seemed to take pity on her. "Let's start with the artist part. I actually saw you years ago at one of your shows. I don't think you would remember. The place was packed, and you probably met a lot of people. I was so impressed with your work, my brother bought me a piece. I've treasured it ever since."

Ellie nodded, finding that she still couldn't talk.

"And as for Lucca, well, let's just say I'm really good at reading body language."

"I imagine most women he brings home practically sit in his lap," Ellie said dryly.

"Well, no, dear. He's never brought a woman home."

"Never?" Ellie was astounded.

Margherita shook his head. "This is his private world. One he fiercely protects. He never wants reporters sniffing around or bothering us in any way. That's why we were all a little surprised."

It was suddenly important for Ellie that Margherita understand the situation.

"Rita, I am very sorry to lie to you. It wasn't my intention. But you have one thing wrong, I do work in a bakery. I'm here to decorate the wedding cake." Ellie went on to explain the whole story. When she was finished, she felt relief.

"You promise not to say a word? I don't want to let Marco down. He wants so desperately to give this surprise to Kate."

Margherita smiled. "I have never seen my son like this—he's so happy and so in love. And Kate is already a daughter to me. I cannot be happier for him. Of course, I won't say anything. And I won't say anything to Nico or Stefano either. I'm sure they can be trusted, but since Marco went to such extremes, I don't want to risk it." She laughed then. "Kate's father, Finn, is a talker. We definitely won't tell him!"

Ellie smiled. Taking the last sip of her cappuccino, she almost choked again at Margherita's next question.

"Now tell me, do you see your parents often? They were very proud of your art."

Ellie looked at her steadily now. "You know who my parents are?"

"Yes, I'm sorry. Is that a secret, too? Doesn't Lucca know anything about you?"

Ellie put the cup down now on the nearby table. She stared down at her hands before finally looking up guiltily. "No, he doesn't. I hope you won't say anything. It's just...people act differently when they find out. I don't talk about my parents—ever. You are like clairvoyant or something. How do you know about them?"

Margherita smiled a little. "I actually met them at your show." At Ellie's surprised look, she continued. "No, they weren't inside the gallery. They were standing nearby outside. When I was leaving, I saw them. They were taking turns, casually peeking through the window. I asked them if they wanted to go inside, but they told me no. Maybe it's because I'm a mother, but I instantly could tell what was going on. They were being very careful to not overshadow your big night, but they desperately wanted to be there. I almost didn't recognize them. Your mom was wearing a wig, and your dad had this crazy hat on.

"Oh, God, that hat. It's an old-style Irish walking hat he got in Dublin. He loves to wear that thing. I think it causes more attention!" Ellie rolled her eyes. But then she softened. "I never knew they were there. I didn't see them."

Margherita nodded. "I'm sure you didn't. I introduced myself and took them across the street, where we could have a glass of wine and something to eat outside at a café. They just loved watching how crowded it was, and once in a while, we got a glimpse of you. They had arranged to go inside the gallery once it closed for the night. You were long gone by then. We said our goodbyes after dinner, but I remember it well. It's not every day one gets to dine with such legends."

Ellie smiled. "They actually are very sweet. They are traveling now. I only hear from them sporadically. Of course, they want me to go back to painting, but they are trying to understand. You see, I'm kind of going through a dry spell. Nothing is coming. After I get finished decorating the cake here, I'm heading up to Tuscany to see if it inspires me like it did when I was in art school." She shrugged. "Maybe that's why I didn't tell Lucca. I don't even think of myself as an artist right now. Unless you count wedding cakes!"

Margherita laughed. "The wedding cake will be an Ellie James original. How fabulous."

～

AFTER FINISHING THEIR TALK, Margherita assured Ellie her secrets were safe with her. "It is your business," she said firmly. Changing the subject, she asked Ellie if she'd like to go see the wedding venue.

"I'd love to!" exclaimed Ellie. "I was thinking I'd have to sneak up there with Lucca and make sure the cake is okay. I know they put it in the walk-in cooler, but I just want to make sure nothing was damaged."

Margherita agreed that would be prudent and ushered her outside. Instead of getting into the sedan that was right there, she hopped into a large golf cart. "I hope you don't mind. I prefer using this."

As they traveled up the hill, Margherita talked about moving there as a young bride and living in an old farmhouse. "My brother-in-law, Angelo, remodeled it for the staff. He built the house we live in now where the boys grew up. My husband had left by then. Lucca might have told you about that." She glanced at Ellie inquisitively.

"Yes, I'm so sorry. That must have been really difficult."

Margherita smiled sadly. "It was. It was such a waste, too. He would have made a wonderful father. But it's water under the bridge."

She swung the golf cart up to the expansive stone building with little balconies and arched windows.

Ellie's eyes widened. "It looks like something out of a fairytale."

Margherita smiled. "We're very proud of it. And for Kate, there was no other choice but to have the reception here. The boys will be out in the back—it's quite a set up out there. We'll sneak in and go check on the cake."

Ellie followed her inside the cool building, its intricate stone highlighted by Italian pottery. "Oh Rita, I love it. It's so enchanting."

"Yes, we'll have cocktails in here and then go outside for the wedding banquet," she said. "You should see the to-do list I have. I'm so happy I have so much help!"

They went into the venue's massive kitchen. She introduced Ellie to Luciano, their chef, explaining Ellie's role with the cake. Pointing to the walk-in, Margherita told Ellie to go help herself while she talked with Luciano.

Ellie entered the walk-in and immediately spotted the carefully marked cake coolers over to the side, out of the way. She opened each, inspecting the rounds. All seemed well. One had a small dent toward the bottom, but she'd be able to easily cover that with the flowers she had made before she had left. The flowers were in the final cooler. She double-checked everything, breathing a huge sigh of relief.

"Zia told me you were in here."

Ellie jumped. She was kneeling before the last cooler. Putting its lid gently down, she turned to see Lucca. Dressed in faded jeans and an old T-shirt, he wore a baseball cap. He looked like a teenager, hands in his pockets, smiling at her. "Everything okay?"

Ellie stood. "Yes, thank God."

"They looked okay when I checked them this morning, too."

"You did?"

"Of course. Don't worry. I was very, very careful. I didn't even breathe on them. I told you I'm just a part of this whole charade as well. I want everything to be perfect for Kate and Marco. When do you need to start decorating?"

"I guess tomorrow I should assemble them and start. On the morning of the wedding, I'll do the final bead work and flowers. There's just a balance of making sure it all gets done, but nothing droops or falls off. I'm a little worried about the heat."

"Didn't Marco tell you?"

"Tell me what?" She raised her eyebrows.

"He had a cooling table installed just in case. I have never seen him this nervous to have everything perfect. He also doesn't want the cake brought out until right before it's to be served."

Ellie smiled. "That makes me feel better. I imagined it melting if it's too warm."

Lucca returned her smile, and Ellie found herself not able to look away. Staring at him now, she could almost forget his image on the big screen.

"Um, so Rita kind of figured things out. She knows I'm not your girlfriend."

His grin got larger. "That doesn't surprise me. That woman should be a spy or something. She used to know when any one of us did anything. And I mean *anything*. She's cool, though. I'm sure we can trust her."

"She promised not to say a word," Ellie said, and then felt a sense of guilt, knowing Margherita had promised to keep all her secrets.

"Want to see outside?" he asked suddenly.

Ellie nodded. "I can't wait!"

nine

Lucca watched Ellie's reaction to the outdoor space. Margherita had a fleet of staff and landscapers working on the area for the last few weeks. While the venue regularly hosted weddings and outdoor dinners, Margherita had pulled out every single stop. The lemon trees that were intricately woven into a pergola were now draped in lights. Italian ceramic pots were everywhere. A new gleaming dance floor was nearby, and the tables had all been assembled.

"It's beautiful!" Ellie exclaimed, looking at everything.

"Wait until you see the table set and all the lights. This morning we strung more down in those trees," he said, pointing down to the lemon grove. "You're going to be able to see this place from space!"

She laughed. "I can't wait to see it. I'll peek out once the cake is wheeled out. I want to see Kate's reaction."

He gave her a surprised look. "Ellie, you're coming to the wedding!"

"But I can't. After the cake is out, Marco will tell everyone the truth. I don't need to be here. It will be so awkward."

"You are my guest. You have to be here! The family will think it's odd and ask where you are. You don't want to spoil the surprise. And Marco said after the wedding. He's not going to run around outing us during the wedding. Believe me, he'll be plenty busy." Lucca smirked.

"But I hadn't counted on it. I mean, I don't even have a dress."

He waved his hand dismissively. "You can find a dress anywhere."

"Spoken just like a man," came a voice from behind them.

They swung around. How long had Meara been standing there?

Meara was tall like Ellie, made even more impressive by the high heeled Italian leather sandals she wore. She was wearing a simple white sheath dress that looked amazing on her. She narrowed her large green eyes at them. "I take it you didn't plan on coming to the wedding, Ellie?"

Lucca laughed, putting his arm around her shoulders. "I didn't think she would come if I told her it was a big family wedding."

Meara's eyes widened. "So was she supposed to wear some random dress from her suitcase? Honestly, I don't even know what to say to that, Lucca."

"Say to what?" Kate came up so quickly, Lucca saw Ellie almost jump.

"This lunatic brought his girlfriend here without telling her they were attending your wedding," Meara explained dryly to her sister.

Kate laughed. "Oh my God, is it genetic? I am so sorry, Ellie. Tonight, I'll tell you the story of what I was wearing when Marco brought me home to meet his mother." She made a face. "I swear I wanted to wring his neck." She looked at Ellie thoughtfully. "But in the meantime, we need to find you a dress, and I know just the place—Meara's closet!"

Meara laughed. "It's true. I brought tons of clothes down

here over the last couple of weeks. Every time I go up to Rome, where I'm living right now, I end up bringing more. I think I have two or three dresses you can choose from, and if you don't like any of those, we can figure something out. We can go shopping tomorrow if we have to."

Lucca looked at Ellie's face and saw the nerves run across it. She was probably thinking about all the work she had to do on the cake. They hadn't talked about how that was going to all happen with no one noticing.

"I had planned on showing Ellie some sights tomorrow," he said smoothly. "One of those dresses better work out!"

Meara rolled her eyes. "If they don't, you'll be shopping tomorrow, and that's the way it is. Come on, Ellie, let's go and sightsee in my closet."

He watched Ellie being ushered off by both women. She glanced back apprehensively, and he nodded reassuringly. There was actually a part of him that would love to take her shopping. He wondered if she ever had the opportunity to wear a really nice gown—like Rodeo Drive nice. He laughed, thinking of how she didn't even wear make-up. That last thing she'd ever do was wear a designer gown. He found more and more he liked the naturalness about her—no fussing with her hair, no weird smells. In fact, Ellie usually smelled like frosting. Today he had smelled a hint of lemon. She was fresh and authentic. He went in search of his cousins, who had wandered down to Nico's greenhouses. He reminded himself of his words to Ellie. Friends only.

ELLIE LOOKED around the table happily. Kate's bachelorette party was being held on the waterfront in Positano. Lights were traveling up the hills with the pastel houses glowing in the sunset. The crowds were thick with couples and families enjoying the pleasant evening. The ferries were still shuttling visitors from Sorento and Capri. Ellie sat back, taking it all in. She had loved Positano when she had visited a few years ago.

She could relax now after her ad hoc fashion show at the house. Things had gotten a little tense when Meara had asked her speculatively if they had ever met. Ellie had bit her lip and shook her head. Meara had stared at her for a second, but then continued getting dresses out of her closet.

After obediently trying on dresses for almost an hour with Meara and Kate lounging on the bed, they had finally chosen one for her. It was an emerald green slip dress with spaghetti straps. Its silkiness fell over her body, with the bodice dipping lower in the front than she was used to. There was also a rather high slit, showing off a good deal of leg. Ellie had been anxious, but even she had to admit after looking in the mirror, it was very flattering on her. Meara didn't have much of a chest either, she thought glumly, looking down, but it was cut in a way to make the most of what she did have. The dress had been a little long, but that problem was solved when Kate produced some amazing heels. She admired the sisters. They had so much fun together, bantering back and forth. She instantly felt like their new project. Teresa had joined them toward the end, declaring she had the perfect clutch for her, bringing it to her for inspection.

Ellie was warmed by their new friendship. After they felt Ellie was set, they had all gone to get dressed and one of the men who worked for Sergio had driven them into Positano, where they were driven in hired golf carts down the pedestrian street toward the sea. The restaurant Meara had chosen was nestled near the walkway, parallel to the sea, and they had a whole cornered off area to themselves. Two other friends of Kate's, Francesca and Allegra, soon joined them. Both were Italian and worked nearby, they told her. They were lively and funny, and the group was soon shrieking with laughter.

"I wish Rita would have said yes and joined us," Kate

commented. It was obvious she already adored her future mother-in-law.

"Something tells me she was looking forward to having the house to herself with Sergio," Meara said with a laugh. "Think about it. She's had all these built-in chaperones and nothing could be worse than her sons!"

They all laughed, with Francesca and Allegra sharing stories about the brothers. They had all known each other since they were young, Francesca explained.

Francesca turned to Ellie, raising her eyebrows. "So are you and Lucca serious?"

"Uh, no, not right now," Ellie stammered, taking a sip of her wine to stall. "I mean, we haven't known each other that long."

"Yet he brings you to a family wedding." Francesca nodded. "That has to say something."

"He's super hunky. Even better than he is on screen," said Teresa matter-of-factly. "Oh, sorry, Ellie. I don't mean that in a bad way. I'm not going to try to make a play for him or anything. But man, can I just stare at him for a few minutes when you're sick of him?"

"Teresa, I swear you're like a stalker," said Meara, rolling her eyes.

Kate frowned. "That's not funny, Meara," she said quietly. "Sometimes fame brings out a dark side."

Ellie leaned in and waited, but Kate seemed determined to not say anymore. Ellie rushed to change the subject, seeing the uncomfortable look on Kate's face. "We're just taking it slow. Like friends."

Francesca narrowed her eyes. "Men like Lucca Delarosa seldom come along."

Kate burst out laughing. "Frannie, you told me the same thing about Marco!"

Francesca smiled smugly. "I was right, wasn't I?"

"You sure were!" Kate responded and then smiled, her whole face lighting up.

"So, what are the guys doing tonight?" asked Allegra, changing the subject.

Ellie had wondered the same thing. They had left before she had come down, and she didn't even get a chance to say goodbye to Lucca. She had found herself oddly disappointed.

"They all went on Marco's yacht," Kate said. "They're sailing around and probably smoking cigars," she pulled a face. "They only do that when they are miles away from Rita, or she'll box their ears. They better not give our father one—that's the last thing he needs."

Meara clinked her glass with her knife. "Before the food comes out, I just want to make a toast to our beautiful bride. Katie, I am so excited for you, and I'm so happy we are all here for you. Even if I did try to break you guys up once!"

The group all laughed, except Ellie who was confused. "Long story!" Meara told her. "But once in a while, I guess I make a mistake." She laughed. "To old friends and new. Let's get you married, Katie."

They all drank a toast with the prosecco the waiter had just brought. Suddenly, a trio of waiters were putting down platters of food. Pastas, seafood, bruschetta, salads, were filling up the table. Kate was laughing. "Meara, how much did you order?"

"Gotta go big or go home! One of each, sister. Pretty much everything! Dig in!"

ten

Ellie crept down the stairs in her stocking feet. She didn't dare put her tennis shoes on. She was wearing her yoga pants and a T-shirt, her hair pulled back in a ponytail. Last night, Lucca had texted her late, telling her to meet him in the kitchen at the crack of dawn. It was important they get up the hill before anyone got up. She walked into the kitchen now.

"*Buongiorno!*"

Ellie jumped. "Lucca, keep your voice down! What if someone hears you?"

"In this house? Are you kidding me? Their bedrooms are like a mile away."

"Still! Shhh. We need to leave."

"What about breakfast?"

"I'm too nervous to eat," she said. She went over to the table now to sit down in one of the chairs and put on her shoes. "Okay, I'm ready."

He was watching her. He was wearing his faded jeans and T-shirt again. "Cappuccino?"

"Are you out of your mind? I can't have caffeine. I'll be all jittery, and my hands will shake. My piping has to be perfect!"

He held up his hands in a surrender. "No breakfast. No cappuccino. Okay, let's go!" He picked up his backpack then.

"What's in the bag?" she asked.

"Just some scripts my agent sent me. I thought I'd read while you decorate."

She frowned. "You don't have to stay with me. I'm sure I'll be fine."

He shrugged. "Where am I going to go? Our excuse is sightseeing together. Besides, it gives me a chance to relax. I'll beg a cappuccino and some breakfast off Luciano." He held out his strong hands to her. "I've already had a cup and not one shake," he said smugly.

She looked at him, making a face. She started toward the front door. As they walked out on to the porch, she looked around. "Where's Sophia?"

He grinned. "I left her in her crate. Precautionary measure. Marco promised to get her out and feed her when he gets up."

Mike drove up just as they got to the bottom stair. "Morning, boss," he said, getting out to open the door. He gave Ellie's ponytail a tweak. "Kiddo."

"Hey, Mike, I haven't seen you. Where have you been?" Ellie asked.

"Oh, here and there. You know, the life of security people," he said nonchalantly. "I had to go with a couple of my guys to chaperone on Marco's yacht last night. She sure is a beauty." He whistled. "You guys had a lot of fun."

Lucca grinned. "Yeah, that was a good night."

Mike pulled up to the venue now. "I'll put this behind in the parking lot. You guys go in. Do you need me this morning?"

Lucca shook his head. "No thanks, Mike. Go back to your planning."

"What's he planning?" she asked as she slid out of the car door Lucca was holding.

"Oh, just how things are going to work in Tuscany. No worries. Come on, let's go in."

They entered the venue and went straight to the kitchen. Luciano was there, putting finishing touches on some canapes. He told them Marco was flying in additional chefs to help him for the cocktail hour and wedding dinner, but he still wanted to do as much prep as possible. He pointed toward the side of the kitchen. "You can have that end of the kitchen—where the pastry chef usually is. I won't get in your way."

She grabbed a cart and swung it into the walk-in. She was pleased she had Lucca with her just for this part. He'd come in handy. He helped her load each cooler on to the cart, one by one, and take them out to the work area. Luciano had gotten out the cooling board the cake was to rest on. He pointed toward the doorway. "Don't worry, this cart fits in the walk-in. We'll cover the sides with table clothes and make sure it looks great before we bring out the cake. We do weddings all the time. Not as important as this one, mind you."

She nodded, relieved she had all she needed. She grabbed the bag Brigid had packed for her with all her tools. Rolling it out, Lucca's eyes widened. "Wow, now it's your turn. Are you operating?"

She laughed. "I'm as queasy as if I am."

Lucca eyed her for a second. "I think it's time to breathe, Ellie. I've seen that look before."

She stared at him. How did he always seem to know what she was thinking? "You're right. My heart is hammering," she admitted.

He smiled gently at her and grabbed a chair, pushing her into it. "Okay, let's go!" He took her through the series of breathing exercises—a little more complex than the ones they had done on the plane. She closed her eyes and followed his instructions obediently. She knew she needed to relax.

"Open your eyes, Ellie." She felt his breath near her ear. She opened her eyes to see his concerned blue ones just inches from hers. She felt her heart start to beat fast again. "Um, I'm okay now. Thanks, Lucca," she stammered. "I think it's just been all the waiting around for this moment."

"Tell me what I can do to help," he said simply.

With Lucca's assistance, and sometimes also with Luciano pitching in, they were able to put each round piece on top of one another. They stood back admiring the five tiers.

"Do they look straight?" Ellie said nervously.

"*Perfetto*," said Luciano, and Lucca nodded. "I wouldn't adjust anything. You and Brigid nailed it."

"Oh no, that was all Brigid." Ellie laughed. "I don't bake. I just decorate!"

Lucca went to sit on a bar stool as she began laying out all her tools. She went back in the walk-in to get the smaller cooler with her frosting. Lucca watched her choose a tip and fill a pastry bag. She had laid out her notes and looked over them one more time.

Ellie looked at him for a second. "I can't do this if you watch me."

"Oh, sorry, I won't look, I promise. I just find it all fascinating."

"I get it, but I'm nervous enough."

He walked away to get his cappuccino, and she took a big breath. She rationally told herself anything she did at this point could be fixed. It was only frosting, not superglue. She began to pipe.

"DO YOU WANT TO TAKE A BREAK?"

Lucca tried again, clearing his throat. "Herbal tea? Water? Lemonade?"

Ellie continued piping, not answering. It was then he saw the earbuds in her ears. He hadn't seen her put them in. She was definitely in the zone, adding beads of frosting in perfect formation and size. She kept going, concentrating fully. She was completely unaware he was even in the room.

Lucca took a moment to ponder that. When was the last time he had ever had a woman in a room with him who was not competing for his attention? Well, never, he acknowledged.

He watched Ellie's silky ponytail shake a little as she bounced her head with the music. Despite that movement, her hands were steady. She was humming, too, slightly off-key. He smiled. He admired the view of her slender frame as she moved lithely around the cake. He had noticed that before—she was well-toned and moved with such grace. He wondered if she had ballet lessons growing up. She moved like a dancer, even as she used the small step stool.

Last night had been fun, he thought. The guys had been ribbing him about Ellie a lot, though, mostly because they hadn't seen him with a woman since he was a teenager. He had never even thought about bringing anyone to meet his family. No one had ever come close to the high bar he had set.

Marco had finally put a stop to it all, giving Lucca a sympathetic look. Lucca had told him later it was fine. In a way, he had enjoyed the teasing. He envied Marco so much. Finding someone you could trust and love unconditionally seemed like such an unobtainable goal for him.

Ellie was standing up straight, stretching. She wiped a hand across her face, instantly smearing frosting. She had donned an apron before she started and now wiped her hands on that. She suddenly turned, meeting his eyes. He waited for the blast about not watching her. Instead, she gave him a rare, wide smile.

"What do you think?"

He looked up from his script. He had glanced down as she was stretching, carefully hiding the fact that he had been intently watching her for the last few hours.

"I think it looks fantastic."

"You didn't even look at it," she protested.

He couldn't tell her he had watched her every move. He got up then and made a show of looking at all of it. "Still looks fantastic." He smiled at her. "Ellie, you're really good at this!"

She laughed, and he saw her face turning pink. She averted her eyes from him. Why did she look so guilty?

"I'm just going to add the edible pearls and a few of the other details and then I guess I'm done till tomorrow."

"What's left then?"

"Oh, just the flowers I pre-made and the fresh flowers. And just a little last piping. Oh and of course, the little bride and groom for the top," she answered absentmindedly, already picking up her frosting bag and sitting down on her stool.

Lucca laughed. "No, my cousin did not insist on the little bride and groom."

"Of course! It's old-school!"

He continued to chuckle. "He's so in love."

She looked at him indignantly. "What's wrong with that?"

He looked at her, a little surprised. "I didn't think you'd be a romantic."

"Really? What do you think I am? Please tell me," she said curtly, frowning at him.

Lucca struggled to find the words. He didn't really know what he assumed Ellie to be. She was so cool and capable. She hadn't really seemed even the least bit interested in him. He realized now maybe his own ego had hoped that she wasn't romantic just for that reason. The truth was staring him in the face. He swallowed hard. It could just be him that didn't interest her.

"I'm sorry, Ellie," he said sincerely. "I didn't mean anything bad. I guess you just seem pretty matter-of-fact all the time. I don't think of you as soft-hearted."

"Well, I am," she said. "I think it's wonderful Marco and Kate are so in love."

"Have you ever been in love—like really in love?" he asked softly. He hoped she'd say no. He didn't know what it was—he wanted to believe she had led the life of a spinster up until now.

She looked at him as if she was deciding what to say. "I thought I was a couple of times. But no, I guess not. In the end, it wasn't the all-consuming love that you see in movies or read about in books. I wasn't sure that was really a thing until I saw Marco and Kate."

She spun away from him and picked up the pastry bag. Just as quickly, she turned back around on her stool and faced him again. "What about you?"

He looked at her now steadily. "No. Not even a smidge."

"Oh, come on, you must have thought you were at one time or another. You've been out with most of Hollywood."

His eyes widened. "I think that's a slight exaggeration. Yes, I have dated. But no, I have not been in love since Carla McKellahan."

"Was she beautiful?" Ellie asked.

He nodded, a glint in his eye. "Oh definitely. She could run faster than any girl I'd ever seen. She baked amazing chocolate chip cookies, and when she got her braces off, I thought she was stunning."

Ellie frowned at him now. "And you and Carla were…"

"In the sixth grade."

She smiled then, shaking her head at him.

He laughed, before turning serious. "As I told you, my parents' divorce was horrendous. I honestly am not sure I will ever be able to commit to someone."

"But that's so sad."

He looked at her steadily. "Go ahead and finish. It's getting late."

She stared at him intently and then swiveled around to face the cake. Using tweezers, she began putting the pearls on the cake delicately and with precision.

He felt bad now. She was actually having a conversation with him, but he shut her down. He had never talked about his parents' divorce with anyone outside the family. He felt like he already said too much. She glanced back and met his eyes.

"Stop watching me," she said with a small, grudging smile.

He gave her a steady look. He sighed then. "Ellie, I can't."

LATER THAT EVENING, Ellie watched Kate walk down the aisle on the arm of her dad, Finn Malone. She had met Finn as they all gathered in the entry hall earlier. He was a sweet Irish man, who obviously had the gift of gab. Margherita had been right about that part. Now he was already wiping his eyes at the rehearsal—Ellie wondered what he would be like for the actual wedding.

They had traveled in several cars to Positano and then taken the golf carts again down to the Church of Santa Maria Assunta for the rehearsal. She remembered it from visiting with her parents and was happy to see the stunning church again. Right before leaving, Ellie had tried to say she didn't need to be a part of it, but was immediately shouted down by the family. They were all so warm and welcoming. She played with the folds of her bright blue sundress. While it was simple, with its tight bodice and full skirt, it made the most of her shape. It was new, and she hadn't worn it yet. Now she adjusted the spaghetti straps a little. She had been relieved when Kate told her that dinner afterward was at Marco's villa and would be very casual.

"It's a beautiful church, isn't it?"

Ellie turned to see Lucca sliding into the pew next to her. "Aren't you supposed to be up there doing your best man duties?"

"Nah, I got it. First take." He grinned at her, nudging her a little with his elbow.

She smiled. "I think it's sweet you're the best man."

"He couldn't pick a brother. He had to pick me. I'm the default best man," Lucca said with a laugh. "But you're right—we are a close family, and I'm honored to be here for Marco."

"Who is that other groomsman? I haven't seen him before." She pointed to a young man in his early twenties. He had a big head of black curls and an even bigger smile.

"That's Alfonso. He's like another cousin to all of us, but he's not technically related. Marco lived with him and his parents for a time, helping them at their ceramics store. I'll introduce you to him later." His expression suddenly turned serious. "My father can't be here tomorrow. He's on his honeymoon. He got remarried finally after all these years. My parents divorced when I was almost ten."

"Lucca, it's okay. You don't have to tell me. I wasn't trying to pry earlier."

He gave her a sad smile. "I'm sorry if I shut you down. I just don't normally talk about it. I guess I should have my attorney give you an NDA first."

Ellie made a small face. "I *definitely* promise not to sell it to the tabloids."

He looked away from her, speaking quietly. "It was an ugly divorce. My mom eventually took me to the U.S., and we got a place in Brooklyn. She told me a lot of things about him that I eventually learned weren't really true. I could never figure it out —he didn't appear to be the low-life she described. But I spent years avoiding him. It was easier." He shrugged.

"Zia Rita urged me to get to know him. So several years ago, I finally spent some time with him at his vineyard. And I really liked him—in fact, I loved him. I realized I had always loved him. Since then, we've spent a lot of time together. It's just hard, you know? I don't understand why my mother said those things. I lost a lot of time with him—time I'll never get back."

"At least you have him now," Ellie said softly.

He nodded. "You're right. And I'm grateful for that. And he married a really nice woman. I like her, and I'm glad he's happy. I just think he and my mom didn't have much in common."

"Have you ever asked your mom why she told you all that stuff that wasn't true?"

He shook his head. "Maybe someday. It's never seemed worth it. We aren't that close. As soon as I was old enough, I moved to Los Angeles. She was completely against it. Told me I was just like my father, and so we don't talk much."

Ellie smiled sadly. "I think you should go see her sometime. It sounds like you need to discover what she intended. Or at least let her talk about it."

"I'm not sure she would. She hates the fact that my father and I reconciled."

"Parents can really screw up their kids." Ellie shook her head.

"What about your parents? Are you close?"

Ellie hesitated. "I guess so. As close as we can be given our lifestyles," she said carefully. Here was her opening, she realized. She'd just tell him. It was a perfect time.

"My parents are..."

"Lucca, we need you up here!" a cheerful Marco yelled suddenly from the altar.

"Whoops, I'm being summoned! Save my seat." Lucca looked at her intently. As he walked away, he turned and gave her a lopsided grin. Her heart turned over.

eleven

Ellie stared at herself in the mirror. When she was done with this dress, she may ask Meara to buy it from her. She absolutely loved it. It was so well-designed and flowy. She felt wonderful in it. Though she had assumed, the label confirmed it was couture. It probably cost a fortune, but it was worth it. Ellie hadn't been shopping—well, that kind of shopping—in a few years, much to her mother's dismay.

She wondered if Lucca would say when he saw her. She immediately made a face in the mirror. "Stop it!" she said to the silent room. The last thing she needed to do was be sidetracked by Lucca. He would only be a passing fling. He had made that very clear.

She was relieved that they had been interrupted, and she hadn't been able to tell him about her parents. When the rehearsal had ended, she was swooped up into the family fold and laughingly deposited in a car with Stefano and Nico. They enjoyed needling Lucca and demanded she go with them to the dinner. They had driven, twisting and turning to a breathtaking villa built into the hill. The dinner had been outside—long tables put together and, of course, flowers everywhere. Ellie had laughed when she saw a chef making pizzas with the stone wood-fired pizza oven at the side of the patio near the infinity pool. She had already heard of the couple's love of pizza. The guests had dined on a multitude of different kinds of pizza and a variety of salads at the tables overlooking Positano. Ellie had loved watching the pastel houses across from them glow during dusk, the lights illuminating the hills. There had been a lot of toasts and joking, and Ellie had laughed so hard her sides hurt. She had never expected to have so much fun.

She was very conscious of Lucca sitting next to her. And though he slung an arm around her shoulders casually and once or twice whispered in her ear, he made no romantic overtures. She had found herself disappointed—but yet, she was a mixture of emotions. Maybe a fling would be worth it?

That morning, he had traveled up the hill with her just like the day prior, and she had carefully put the flowers on the cake. Luciano had given her the real flowers the florist had dropped off, and she had draped them across the tiers diagonally, securing them. She took the porcelain bride and groom that Marco had left with Luciano and climbed the stepladder holding her breath. She then looked over to see Lucca watching her intently. He came over and held on to her so she could place it on top, ensuring its pins were stuck in and that it wouldn't move.

They had stood and admired it for several minutes. Lucca had told her the cake topper was the same one Kate's parents had used. Ellie was touched. She did one last thing on her to-do list and that was to pipe *Sempre Insieme* on the side of the bottom tier of the cake. "Always together." She wanted their forever after to be prominent on the cake.

She had finished in time to come down to the house and get ready. The other women had stayed at a nearby hotel and spa and were getting ready there. They had invited her, but she had politely declined, wanting them to have their own time together. She had put up with their gentle teasing that she wanted to remain with Lucca.

Ellie had taken a quick shower, and then after drying her hair, she used a curling iron, before pulling part of her hair back to the crown of her head. Evaluating herself critically, she was pleased—it transformed her face for some reason. She then carefully applied make-up, applying more than usual. The dress called for a more glamorous look, and for some reason, tonight she wanted that.

Her phone buzzed.

You are amazing! It looks incredible!

She smiled. She had taken photos and videos and texted them to Brigid for her to see when she woke up.

Are you sure? It's not too late for me to go up and fix anything. Seriously.

I wouldn't fix a thing. And oh my God, you made me cry with the engraving. Was that your idea?

Yes—I checked with Lucca, and that's our surprise for Marco.

It's perfect.

Ellie felt herself relax. She quickly texted back: *Have to run but will try to call you later.*

Have fun!

Ellie went down the stairs carefully. She definitely wasn't used to wearing this high of heels. Good thing Lucca was so tall, or else she'd tower over him like she did most men. She bit her lip. There he was again. She mentally tried to shake him off.

She was happy to see Sergio waiting, and she received his praise with a smile. Marco and the groomsmen had left earlier because they were getting dressed at the church and taking photos. Sergio drove carefully to Positano, and a golf cart was waiting to take them to the church. She sighed in relief, thankful she didn't have to descend on cobblestones in the heels. As they pulled up to the staircase leading to the church, she saw Mike was standing outside with a couple of his security men.

"There you are, Ellie. Wow, you clean up nice."

She smiled widely at him as Sergio took her arm. "Let's go take our seats."

"Oh, I'm just going to sit in the back," Ellie explained.

Sergio frowned. "I have strict instructions you are to sit with me."

"Oh, but…"

"Let us go take our seats," he answered firmly.

And with that, Ellie found herself in the first pew next to Sergio, who would be sitting with Margherita. She looked around wildly. She shouldn't be in the front row!

Music started somewhere in the church, and the groomsmen walked out. Lucca's eyes traveled past her and then darted back again. His gaze met hers, and his eyes widened. He didn't smile; instead, he stared at her with such intensity, she felt her entire body tingle. She stared back, a small nervous smile on her face. Slowly, his smile widened, showing his deep dimples. It warmed her, and she felt herself beginning to flush.

It was only after Marco escorted Margherita to her place in their pew that Ellie broke the stare. She watched the bridesmaids come down the aisle and then stood with the rest of the congregation for the bride. She glanced back at Lucca, and he had put an arm on Marco, as if to steady him. She saw tears forming in Marco's eyes. What a softie he was. Her heart melted. Then she saw Lucca dabbing at his eyes. He looked more emotional than Marco. She smiled, remembering his recommendation about crying. She swiveled back to see Kate, looking confident and serene, walking down the aisle on Finn's arm.

The rest of the ceremony was a blur. She couldn't take her eyes off Lucca, so handsome in his dark gray suit and light gray tie. She could see the blue of his eyes even from the pew. Soon Marco was hauling Kate into his arms for their first kiss before the priest even proclaimed them married. The crowd laughed and cheered. She found herself beaming at Lucca. The bride and groom walked down the aisle to the thunderous applause, smiling at each other. They could have been by themselves and not even noticed.

The rest of the wedding party filed out. Sergio was getting ready to escort Margherita, and Ellie stood to follow them when she felt an arm slide around her shoulder.

"Ellie, you're breathtaking," Lucca whispered in her ear, sending chills down her spine. He had come up the side aisle to escort her. She felt her heart pounding again. She smiled shyly at him. He crooked his arm, and she allowed him to escort her down the aisle. She saw appreciative stares from some of the other women in the church. She didn't care. He was escorting her, and for that one moment, she soaked it in. He turned to her now and looked at her with such an intensity, she almost had to look away. Something had changed since the moment when he first saw her.

He held her hand now as they climbed into one of the golf carts shuttling guests. "I came with Sergio," she said abruptly, looking over her shoulder for the man.

"I know, but you're leaving with me," Lucca said firmly, nudging her into the cart. They got to the top of the cobblestone hill where a discreet parking lot held many of the guests' cars. Ellie glanced over her shoulder and saw Mike and a couple of his men following them. One was standing at the entrance of the parking garage.

"I'm driving myself, Mike."

"Boss, I don't think that's a good idea."

"I'm driving myself, Mike," Lucca repeated. He turned and whispered something in Mike's ear. Mike finally nodded grudgingly. "We'll see you there."

She found herself being ushered into the passenger side of a black Ferrari. "Whose car is this?"

"Marco's. I know it sounds silly, but I'm so tired of being driven around. Tonight, I want to drive to the reception. And I want you by my side."

She found herself flushing. He had started the car, but was looking at her intently. "Is that okay? Just for tonight, Ellie?"

She smiled, feeling overwhelmed. "Just for tonight," she agreed softly.

LUCCA DROVE through the hills with ease. He'd driven this way a million times. He could probably drive it in his sleep, which was a good thing—he was having difficulty concentrating on anything but Ellie. He had practically fallen off the altar when he located her in the church. He had looked past her before focusing on her. She was gorgeous. The thing was, he had always thought she was pretty in her natural way. It wasn't the make-up or even her hair this afternoon, he decided. It was the way she was carrying herself. She looked like she belonged on the red carpet. She walked with such a regal air. And God, that dress. It fit her like a glove. He glanced sideways. The neckline was deeply cut in the front. She shifted in her seat, and he could see one shapely long leg from the high slit. He swallowed hard.

Something had changed between them. He knew exactly when. She had looked at him in the church with the same intensity he was feeling. His heart was still pounding. Was it fair to start something with her? They began their relationship as a lie—should he take it any further? He knew deep in his heart he didn't care. He had been waiting for this moment without realizing it. He was going to seize this time.

This morning, he had watched her put the finishing touches on the cake. He knew she put her heart into it, and he felt such pride. When he had steadied her on the stepladder, he had gripped on to her waist. It was then he wanted to lift her down and kiss her until neither of them could think too hard about anything.

Tonight, he would wait for the perfect moment, and then he would kiss her. And if she was agreeable, many more kisses would occur after that. He snuck a look at her now. She was staring out the window, looking like she was avoiding his eyes. Her perfect teeth were biting her pink lips, just as they had done while she piped the cake. Tonight, he would taste those lips. He hit the accelerator of the powerful car. It was going to be a magical evening.

ELLIE HAD to admit Lucca had been right about how stunning the outside area was. After the cocktail hour, they had walked out to the most spectacular scene she had ever seen. There was something so simple, yet exquisite, about it. The lights at dusk were everywhere, reflecting off the white linen, the sparkling glasses, the Italian-made white place settings, and the silver. She looked up in awe at the intricately woven lemon trees through the pergola.

While she admired everything, she knew she couldn't relax until the cake came out. She had checked it twice so far. It was all loaded and ready to be brought out. Still, she was anxious.

She drank the prosecco the waiter had just poured for her and listened to the toasts. All were funny and poignant. Lucca had grabbed his napkin to dab his eyes before he started. For an actor, he wasn't good at hiding his emotions. She realized that she had found his Achilles heel—his family. He was so happy with them.

She looked up to watch him gather himself, and it was only appropriate that he quoted a popular old movie: "When you realize you want to spend the rest of your life with somebody, you want the rest of your life to start as soon as possible." He had looked down at Ellie warmly, and she had felt herself growing pink. She had glanced over and caught Margherita's eye. The older woman gave her a knowing smile. Ellie quickly looked away. Was she being so obvious? Suddenly, she wanted to be alone with Lucca in the worst way. She had never in her life felt like this. Her heart was thudding. Every time he whispered in her ear, stroked her hand, or casually put his arm around her to introduce her to yet another cousin, she wanted to grab him and take him somewhere—anywhere where they could be together without prying eyes.

He turned now and gave her a smile. The dinner was almost over—course after course had been brought out. She had thought she was full with all the canapes and appetizers they had eaten during the cocktail hour and had looked alarmingly at the printed menu at her plate. Now she had eaten her way through prosciutto and melon, ravioli with fresh crab and lemon, a perfectly grilled steak with fresh vegetables, a lemon-mint sorbet, and then cheese and nuts. It was nearing time for dessert. She turned to Lucca, but he was already anticipating her move. She stood, pretending she was going to the bathroom.

"Can I help at all?" he whispered anxiously.

"No thanks. I'm just going to go tell them in the kitchen it's time. You talk to Teresa." She winked. Teresa had been sitting on the other side of Lucca. Though she had behaved herself, Ellie had once in a while looked over and hid a smile at Teresa's glassy-eyed stare. In fact, Ellie had almost burst out laughing when Lucca had to ask Teresa twice to pass the parmesan.

As Ellie walked past Marco, he gave her a subtle nod. She smiled just a little, trying not to be obvious. She heard clinking of the glasses and the crowd shouting *"Evviva gli sposi!"*

She smiled, glancing back and watching Marco and Kate kiss yet again. She sighed, not sure why.

When she walked into the kitchen, she took a deep breath. She went to the alcove in the kitchen. It was perfect. She gave the nod to Luciano. He spoke in rapid Italian, and two waiters came to gently wheel it out. They carefully loaded large sparklers into the chutes at the corners of the table.

"I hope they will be careful," Ellie said nervously.

"*Si.* We do this all the time," Luciano answered reassuringly.

She smiled and nodded. "I better go sit down so I can see Kate's face."

She slipped back to her seat, and Lucca grabbed her hand. She held it in her lap, clutching it tightly, and waited. The palms of her hand were sweaty—she gave Lucca a grateful smile.

With the sparklers lit and shooting amber fountains, the waiters brought out the cake, and everyone shouted and applauded. Marco led Kate over to it. They were laughing and kissing and then cut the cake with the intricate silver knife. Gently, Marco fed Kate a bite. Kate's eyes visibly widened, and she turned sharply to him. She then glanced around hurriedly, as if looking for someone. Even from where Ellie sat, she saw tears forming in Kate's eyes. Marco whispered to her then, and she put a hand over her mouth briefly. She looked back toward the table until she found Ellie. "Thank you," she mouthed. Ellie found tears in her eyes. She dabbed at her eyes. Why was she so emotional?

She turned to meet Lucca's gaze. He was smiling but staring at her intently. She felt an impulse running through her body— her adrenaline was so high. She leaned over and kissed him, a soft sweet kiss. It was so unlike her, but she couldn't resist. He began kissing her back. She leaned into him. The people around them disappeared in her mind. It was she and Lucca alone—at last.

"Don't worry! I caught the whole thing on video," a female voice said.

She caught us kissing on video? Ellie had drawn away from Lucca, looking at him with wide eyes, still shocked she had just kissed him.

"I'll send it to Brigid right now," said Meara, who had moved to stand behind them. She leaned down. "Marco spilled the beans somewhere around the third course. He didn't want to bother you, but he knew Brigid would want to see Kate's reaction. I made sure I got the whole thing. Katie was really surprised!"

Ellie smiled weakly.

"So you decorated the whole thing?" Meara was asking.

Ellie nodded. Lucca was looking at her now, his face impassive. Was he regretting the kiss? Did it not have the same effect on him?

Guests were getting up from the tables, walking over to look at the cake and the adjacent dessert table of a large variety of Italian cookies and cups of gelato. Lucca stood and held out his hand to her.

"Let's go see if Kate liked it," he said with a smile.

Ellie stood automatically, but then panicked. "Let's give her a moment. I don't want to intrude," she said shyly. Suddenly she felt nervous—not of just hearing Kate's reaction, but being with Lucca.

"Marco is waving us over. Come on, Ellie."

She let Lucca pull her through the crowd. Suddenly, Kate flew at Ellie, a flash of white coming at her so fast. Ellie returned Kate's tight hug.

"Oh my God, Ellie. Marco said you decorated the whole thing! I can't believe you did this for me. You have no idea how much this means to me. There is no cake like this in the world, I swear. And to think Brigid made it for me. I know she couldn't be here, so I was so confused. And it looks so amazing—and with my parents' cake topper, too. It must have taken you hours and hours!"

Ellie smiled. "It was worth every second. You were so surprised!"

Kate looked back at Marco with loving eyes. "I was. It truly was the best surprise—that and half the congregation that Marco surprised me with. He flew in so many of my friends and family!"

She gave Ellie another hug. "I really can't thank you enough." She turned then, giving Lucca a hug. "And what's crazy is how you and Lucca ended up dating on top of it. It's all so perfect. Did you meet him at the bakery?"

Marco opened his mouth, and Ellie saw Lucca put his hand on his arm and shake his head slightly.

"No, we met at my house when your husband decided to send me a cake to bribe me to fly it over," explained Lucca, putting his arm around Ellie. "It was a little rough there for a while, but yes, that's how we got together," he said.

Ellie turned to look at him. His blue eyes were daring her to argue. She would let it ride. Explaining to the bride this was all a farce seemed awkward. She found herself nodding and felt herself blushing under Marco's narrowed gaze.

"If you don't mind me saying so, I think the two of you should dance," Lucca suggested dryly. At their confused look, he continued, "That way the rest of us can," he hinted.

Marco slapped him on the back. "Once in a while, *mio cugino*, you have a great idea."

And with that, he led Kate on to the dance floor.

LUCCA TIGHTENED his arms around Ellie. He had danced with her for most of the evening, with the occasional cut in by one of his cousins. Nico and Stefano were messing with him, as always. Even Alfonso had tried, but had slunk away at Lucca's glare.

He wanted this night to go on forever. Once it ended, he and Ellie would have to face reality, and he wasn't certain how she was feeling. To say he had been shocked when she kissed him was an understatement. He hoped it was not just because of the high-intensity of the moment when the cake had been brought out. Maybe she was finally through with her strong feelings about him being an actor. He grudgingly withdrew his arms from the silkiness of her dress. The music had stopped. He looked around and saw the crowd was thinning.

"Do you want to take a walk?" he whispered.

She nodded, her eyes huge. She could feel the magic, too. He was certain of it. He pulled out his phone for a second and texted Mike. His security team had stayed on the perimeter. He hadn't wanted anyone to notice the heightened security or ask questions. He had promised Mike he'd tell him if he left the venue, though.

He escorted Ellie down the stairs and toward a path that wound around to a white gazebo. He remembered Zio Angelo building it when he was young. He knew it well. It was lit with fairy lights all around. He heard Ellie sigh.

"This is beautiful."

"*You* are beautiful, Ellie. I didn't want to keep telling you tonight. I thought you'd take a swing at me."

She smiled but looked down.

He put his hand on her chin so her gaze would meet his. "You're always gorgeous. I don't want you to think it's only tonight. It's just that in the church, you took my breath away, and I haven't been able to breathe very well since."

She smiled gently at him. "Do we need to do some box breathing?"

He smiled a little, putting his forehead against hers.

"Or was that a line from one of your movies?" she asked quietly.

"No, please, Ellie. Tonight, you are Ellie, and I am Lucca. It's not about acting or cake decorating. It's about us."

He put a hand on either side of her face. He wanted her to see his eyes and the sincerity he hoped shone through. He could see the moment of acceptance. The moment he had waited for. But instead of him kissing her, it was Ellie, again, who leaned up and took his lips in a searing kiss. He quickly took over, continuing to kiss her, afraid if he stopped, the moment would be lost. His lips only left hers to travel her jawline and back again to capture her sweet lips again. His hands slid down the silkiness of her back, grabbing her hips and hauling her closer. His arms circled her again tightly.

They kissed for some time after that. All time seemed to cease, and they were the only two people in the world. He wasn't sure later how eventually they got to the bench that was on the side of the gazebo. He spoke to her softly in Italian as his lips traveled her jaw and back to her ear, confident he could be honest about what he was feeling, and she wouldn't understand. He poured out how much he already cared for her, his hopes that maybe this was the start of something bigger than he could hope for. He told her how amazing she was and how much he wanted to take this further. He told her he hadn't felt like this with any other woman, and he was afraid he could almost fall in love with her.

Finally, he nestled her neck. "Ellie, we've been here for a long time," he said in English this time. He listened closely. He could only hear a few voices. "I think it's just us and the staff cleaning up." He stood, looking reluctant. "I better take you back." He kissed her again long and lingeringly, his arms holding her tight again. She was quiet as he grabbed her hand tightly. They walked back up and around the side of the venue, avoiding the staff.

They both stayed silent, as if they didn't want to break the spell. He drove up in front of the house, going to her side of the car. He helped her out, his eyes searching hers in the inky night. There was enough light coming from the house that he could see the mix of emotions in her expression. He led her inside and upstairs to her bedroom. At the doorway, he kissed her several times, his hands cupping her face, before pulling away roughly.

"We'll talk tomorrow, *cara*, okay? We'll go do something fun."

She nodded, her eyes wide as she closed the door softly.

Lucca began to walk away. He wasn't sure why, but as he glanced back, he had a sense of dread.

twelve

Lucca ran down the stairs toward the kitchen. It was a clear, sunny day, and his negative premonition last night seemed a thing of the past. He was up early with a desire to do something romantic. Maybe he would pack a picnic and take Ellie out to a special spot. They could finally be alone and talk. He sensed she was still holding back from him. Yesterday had changed everything, though. Despite his uneasiness about relationships, he wanted to see where this would go. He knew she had come to trust him a little, and now it was time to take it to the next level. He felt confident and had a sense of calm—the happiest he'd been in months.

He walked quickly into the kitchen, thinking about last night. He knew he probably had a silly grin on his face. He came face to face with Margherita, who had just made herself a cappuccino from the big red machine. She was looking at her phone, and then glanced up at him over her readers. Unexpectedly, a blast of Italian came at him.

He raised his eyebrows. "Zia, what is the matter?" He automatically switched to Italian.

"What did you do?" she asked curtly.

"What do you mean?"

"Lucca, tell me right now what you did to that lovely woman!"

Lucca felt the sense of doom return instantly. He raised his eyebrows at her tone. "I haven't the slightest idea what you are talking about," he answered honestly.

"Ellie! She's gone! What did you say to her? Or better, yet," she added, narrowing her eyes, "What did you *do*?"

"Ellie? Gone?" he found himself repeating her words dumbly. "No, she's not gone. She's probably still asleep!"

Margherita pointed to a piece of paper on the island that he hadn't noticed. "No, she's definitely gone. I don't know what time, but she left this."

He scanned the note quickly—a huge thank you to Margherita, perfect wedding, blah blah blah, and that was it. He turned it over stupidly. It was blank. There was nothing addressed to him. He turned and jogged out to the front terrace. Mike had just driven up and was getting out of the car.

"What's up, boss?"

"Ellie! She's left."

Mike looked at him steadily for a moment. He had his usual sunglasses on, but Lucca could almost feel his suspicious look. Why was everyone blaming him?

Mike spoke into his phone for a minute and hung up.

"One of the men stationed at the front gate said she appeared there around six this morning. She had called for a driver, and he picked her up on the main road." He glanced at his watch. "She's long gone now."

Lucca ran his hand through his hair. "Any idea where?"

Mike shook his head. "I know she talked about Tuscany, but I have no idea where in the region."

He took off his glasses now, his eyes thoughtful. "Lucca, this is what Ellie does. She runs when things get...too much for her," he finally finished. "You need to just let her be."

"What if I can't? What if I want more?" Lucca asked angrily.

"Won't work. She's as stubborn as a mule that one. Always has been. She might come around, but it has to be on her terms."

Lucca was the one to look at him suspiciously now. "You seem to know a lot about her, Mike."

He nodded. "I do. But it's not my story to tell." He stepped back now, looking like the cool security agent he had hired. "What time do you want to leave?"

ELLIE DROVE SLOWLY through the hills of Tuscany in the white convertible BMW she had rented in Florence. She had hired a driver to take her to the Naples Train Station, and then grabbed a fast train to Florence. There had just been a quick stop at an art store to buy some of her favorite paints, including an important color: Naples Yellow. It was definitely needed to paint the hills.

She felt at peace and a sense of belonging in Tuscany. It brought back her art school days and how normal it had been for her. No one had treated her differently or had any idea who she was—or, more importantly, who her parents were. She had been accepted and only judged for her art. It had been a wonderful time in her life. So freeing.

Ellie felt a sudden surge of enormous guilt wash over her. Last night after Lucca left, she had sat on the bed in shock. What he had said to her in Italian had panicked her, pure and simple. Of course, he had no idea she spoke fluent Italian. She had been so spellbound when he told her about how much he wanted to be with her, stay with her, and what she already meant to him. It had stunned her. Was he just in the moment or had really felt that way?

It was obvious now that Lucca was not like most actors she had met. He was truly a good, sincere person. Her heart skipped beats just thinking about last night. She couldn't fall for him. She just couldn't. Even if he wasn't like the others, she couldn't get sucked into that lifestyle again. She had spent her entire childhood and teen years in it and had finally dug out as an adult. The last thing she wanted was to have anything to do with the industry anymore. She loved her parents and knew they had done what they could to protect her, but it was the nature of the business.

Driving up to the villa's gates, Ellie entered the code that Madeleine had given her. The gates swung open and she drove past the rows of vines—luscious grapes hanging from them. A large villa sat on the hill, but to the right of it, she spotted the guesthouse Madeleine had said would be waiting for her. She pulled her car to the side of it and glanced at her phone for the code to open the door. It looked like it had been built more recently, and it was charming inside. Ellie breathed a sigh of relief. The living room was full of big comfortable furniture—a modern kitchen stood next to it, almost a part of the room. It featured numerous sparkling windows. She could feel the day's heat already and went to turn on the central air.

There were three bedrooms, and a back primary bedroom held a massive bed with a colorful comforter. An adjacent modern bathroom had everything she needed. She wandered into the next room and almost cried out in delight. Madeleine had filled it with easels, a palette box, custom canvases and linen panels. If she couldn't be creative here, then her talent was completely gone. Ellie went to quickly unload. This was going to be home for a while. Madeleine had said she and her new husband wouldn't be home for at least a couple more weeks, and she could stay as long as she liked. Ellie was looking forward to the peace and quiet.

～

HOURS LATER, Ellie admitted to herself she was already getting tired of the peace and quiet. Unloading her suitcase and backpack, she tried to give herself the idea that this was now home. She had stopped on her way and picked up food at a market and now she made herself a quick sandwich.

The silence was eerie after being surrounded by Lucca's family the last few days. It was odd because she usually never minded being by herself. She went out on to the deck, looking at the vast acreage of vineyards and the villa—its mustard-colored stone walls reflected the sun. It featured lots of windows, black wrought-iron balconies, and a bell tower jutted out from the back.

All this quiet was giving her too much time to think. How could she miss Lucca? She had only left this morning, though it already seemed a long time ago. On top of that, she'd only known him for a short time. Yet, he was just so...solid. She smiled, remembering his breathing techniques. He had been quieter than she had thought he would be—a steady presence. Her assumption that he would be showy was wrong. He wasn't one of those people who needed to be the life of the party. He was comfortable in the spotlight, but didn't seek it. It was hard to admit she liked having him with her when she decorated the cake. She even loved when he teased her, though she made a show of pretending she didn't.

Ellie acknowledged she had acted poorly. The right thing to do would have been to stay and explain to Lucca that while she really did like him, any kind of relationship wasn't going to go anywhere for either of them. She wouldn't get involved with anyone in the industry, and she certainly wasn't going to live in California anymore. Just these last few days in Italy had felt so right. If Madeleine's husband was as nice as she was, maybe they wouldn't mind if she hung out at the guesthouse for a while. Or she could always ask her parents if their villa was free, though it was often lent to friends. The thought of rattling around in that massive place by herself was not appealing. This new guesthouse was perfect, despite the quiet.

Pouring herself a glass of white wine, Ellie felt the gentle breeze from the window she had opened. What was Lucca doing? He was probably laughing with his cousins. He had relaxed from the time he had arrived at the lemon grove. What was causing him so much stress in California? He had seemed so tense there and tightly wound. That's what the industry does to people. She shrugged and knew she'd never find out. Even if she saw him again, he'd probably never talk to her. She hadn't even left him a note. Though she thought about texting him several times, she struggled with what to say. She didn't want him to think she had taken last night that seriously. The truth was she had, especially after his emotional words, but he didn't need to know that she had actually understood him. If she was honest, she'd acknowledge it was probably just the start of a small fling. A fling with the likes of Lucca wouldn't necessarily be so bad, but it would be a distraction from her art. She furrowed her brow. It could also be a lethal blow to her heart.

Ellie didn't want to think about what could have been. She was already distracted and walked back into the house determinedly. Earlier, she had unpacked her canvas roll with her brushes and had gotten everything ready to paint. She sat down in front of an empty canvas and looked at it. Her idea was to just paint in the coming days and not worry about anything specific for Madeleine, but just see what unfolded. Get her mind warmed up again. If things started flowing, she would then focus on a piece for Madeleine and her husband. In the meantime, she grabbed her sketch pad and smiled, looking at her initial drawings of Lucca. She put down her glass of wine and ran a fingertip down his jawline. All those nice angles. It would be fun to paint him. Ellie began to finish the sketch now, drawing from memory, since she had a lot of time to study him. Maybe she could turn this into a painting, otherwise she'd never capture those eyes.

Who would believe the color of his eyes was real? It was often assumed he wore contacts.

Ellie finished the sketch and walked back outside, restless and distracted. Tomorrow would be better.

LUCCA WASN'T LAUGHING with his cousins. He clicked off his phone, frustrated. Brigid didn't have a clue where in Tuscany Ellie was headed. He had waited for Brigid to check with a couple of friends. That, too, came up empty. He could text Ellie, but what would that do? She hadn't even bothered to leave him a note. He knew he had to see her in person to even have a chance.

Every time he had walked near his aunt, she raised an eyebrow. She was sure he had done something to drive Ellie away. Maybe he had. Ellie might have thought he was moving too fast. He didn't care—he wouldn't take last night back for anything. It had been magical and everything he imagined. He was falling for Ellie—he had even told her last night—in Italian, of course. At least she didn't know how badly he wanted her. Now he wanted to be with her—at the very least, to plead his case. Emotions this strong should be given a shot. He ran his hands through his hair. He had never felt like this and it had shaken him, but he was also determined to see her.

It was time to head north like he planned. If he was at least in the same region, he had a better chance of finding her. He had arranged to take Marco's helicopter, but Mike had balked. He wanted the whole team together and insisted they go by caravan. Lucca had opened his mouth to argue, but one look at Mike's steely gaze and he knew he wouldn't win this one. He decided they'd leave in the morning—the quicker he got up there, the better. He would hire a private investigator if he had to, but he would find her.

thirteen

Ellie woke up disoriented. She slept so heavily she didn't even remember where she was for a minute. Then it all came rushing back. Lying in the luxurious bed for a long time, her mind continued to race. She'd be a fool if she didn't admit she had been way too impulsive leaving like that. There was nothing she could do about it now.

It had been nice to hear from Brigid, though she had texted her the night before that Lucca was looking for her. Brigid had sincerely been able to tell him she had no idea. Ellie let her know she was outside of Siena, but that's all she passed along to her friend. They had texted for a while longer, mostly about Kate and the wedding. Brigid had loved seeing the videos Meara sent. Brigid asked a few leading questions about Lucca, but Ellie chose to sidestep them. She told her she'd fill her in by phone soon.

Finally getting up, she drank a cappuccino before going to the studio. Picking up an easel and canvas, she went out to the deck. This morning she would paint outside and try to capture the fields below. She was starting early and knew she would have to work fast to lock in her composition with the changing light. She put in her ear buds and blasted her tried-and-true music. It always made her feel creative. A few hours later, she had the beginnings of a painting, but her shoulders sagged. She was better than this.

The sun was high up in the sky and she stretched. It had been a long time since she had painted for this many hours straight. She could do with a little yoga or something. She squinted up at the villa, and remembered Madeleine telling her to use the pool anytime she wanted. It sounded like a fantastic idea. It would be great to cool off, stretch out her muscles and come back invigorated.

Ellie put on her swimsuit and cover-up and grabbed some sandals. Traveling quickly up the landscaped garden, she soon saw the long, exquisite pool. The water was so clear, and it looked inviting. She dove in quickly and began swimming laps. The cool water felt so good against her skin.

It was during her third lap that Ellie heard voices. Landscapers? Madeleine had said there would be staff in and out. Swimming to the edge, she looked around. Some workmen were in a field down the way. She turned and started another lap and then definitely heard shouting.

"Stop! Trespasser! You in the water—stop!"

Ellie swam to the wall, grabbing onto it. She squinted up directly into the sun, and put a hand over her eyes trying to see the source of the shouting. Mike's angry face came into view. And running right behind him and stopping abruptly was Lucca.

ELLIE PUSHED herself away from the wall and treaded water, squinting up into the sun. Mike was now shaking off his shoes that she had inadvertently splashed.

"Uh, sorry, Mike."

Mike seemed incapable of words. His face was beet red, sweat was beginning to show on his button-down shirt. He yelled now into his radio that the cameras were triggered by a false alarm. Ellie glanced around to see some of the security men who had come from all directions, snickering and walking away. Sophia was even turning and running—she seemed to know it was smart to get away from the situation.

"Lucca, I told you to stay in the house," barked Mike.

Lucca was ignoring him. He was staring at Ellie as if she wasn't real.

Ellie continued to tread water and glanced toward Lucca, but she didn't meet his eyes.

"Get out of the pool, Ellie, and get in the house," commanded Mike quietly. She nodded. When he spoke to her like that, she was back to being sixteen years old and breaking her curfew yet again. Swimming to the stone stairs, she climbed out.

Lucca was still rooted to the same spot, and she felt his eyes on her. Clad in her old black one-piece swimsuit, she was probably a sight. Grabbing her cover up on the chaise where she had left it, she put it on without waiting to get dry. She sunk her face into her towel before finally raising her head. She slipped her sandals on quickly.

Mike was waiting for her impatiently and led the way up the path to a massive stone patio filled with an array of patio furniture. Lucca was behind her. She didn't dare glance around. They entered the house through French doors, and Mike indicated a gigantic table off the modernized farmhouse kitchen. "Sit."

Ellie sat down tentatively in one of the wooden chairs. She used the towel to dry her hair. "Mike, I'm dripping all over everything."

"It's fine. You're not going to ruin anything."

He was pacing now. "Ellie, what the hell? What are you doing here? Did you break into this house? This is a major security breach. I've never had anything like this happen."

Lucca had sat down across from her. He was staring at her, his face impassive. "Ellie, did you follow me?" he accused.

"Follow you? What are you talking about? I left before you! How could I follow you?"

Lucca shook his head as if he was still trying to figure the situation out. "Yes, I obviously know you left. Though I heard that from Zia and not you." His voice was dangerously quiet and it unnerved her.

Ellie looked down, feeling her face flush.

She felt Lucca's eyes on her. "First you showed up at my house in California, and now you're at my family home in Tuscany. Don't you think that's a little weird?"

"I went to your house in California to deliver a cake. That's it. And I was invited here," she said. "This house isn't yours!"

"I didn't say it was mine. I said it was my family's home."

Mike made an impatient sound. "Lucca, she's not your stalker."

Ellie's eyes widened. "You have a stalker? She glanced around for the security, but they had disappeared discretely. "That's why you hired Mike and his team?"

Lucca looked uncomfortable. "We can talk about that later. First, I need to know what you are doing here."

"Madeleine invited me here. She's the mother of my college roommate. I moved into the guesthouse for a while. Now you tell me what *you're* doing here."

Lucca stared at her intently. "Madeleine just married my father."

"But that can't be." Ellie glanced at him, confusion registering. She had never asked Madeleine who her new husband was. And now that she thought about it, Madeleine had never referred to him by name. A sick feeling in her stomach started to spread. A premonition was coming on.

"She married Bruno Benedetto Delarosa. And he is my father."

And Ellie felt the wind knocked out of her.

"ELLIE, BREATHE," Lucca was saying. She could hear his voice from somewhere in the room. She must still have water in her ears—the sound was muffled. She felt his breath now and his hand on her back. He began counting, and she breathed as he instructed. Her anxiety began creeping away.

She looked up at Mike, who was frowning at them. "It's time for the two of you to talk. I'm done with both of you. Talk!" he said roughly as he stalked out of the room.

Lucca moved back across the table. He stared at her. "Let me get you some water."

He filled two glasses from the refrigerator and brought them back to the table, sitting down.

Ellie sipped the water, glad for the reprieve. He was staring at her in such a way that it unsettled her. "Why did my father's name make you react like that?"

"I didn't know that was his last name. I only knew him by Bruno Benedetto," she said quietly, still shaken. "And I had absolutely no idea that's who Madeleine married, so it's a double shock."

"He dropped our last name when he went into the art world. He told me once he wanted to maintain his family's privacy."

Ellie was shaking her head. "I just can't believe he's your father. I never guessed. Not for one second."

"I look more like my mother's side," said Lucca dryly. "Ellie, you're freaking me out. Why did his name send you into a full-blown panic attack?"

Ellie took another sip. She suddenly focused on the wall behind Lucca and smiled a little. He had kept it. Bruno had kept it. She pointed to the painting on the wall.

"That's mine."

Lucca looked at the painting and back at her, confused. "No, that's my father's. It's hung there for years."

Ellie smiled at the memory. "I gave it to your father. I painted it."

～

LUCCA STARED AT ELLIE, feeling stunned. He walked over and looked at the painting closely. He glanced back at her. He looked at her signature *EJ* at the bottom.

He approached her, giving her an odd stare. "My father once told me if the house was burning down, he would run back in and save this painting. It means that much to him."

Suddenly, he had a terrible thought. "Did you have a relationship with my father?" he squeaked out.

She looked horrified. "No! Absolutely not! Oh my God. No! He was my mentor. He encouraged me, pushed me to do better. He introduced me to the art world, and he hosted my first show. He made introductions to New York art dealers. I would be nothing in the art world without your father. I love him with all my heart."

He sat down quickly, weak with relief. For a moment, he was going to be sick. Now that feeling had passed. "And this painting?"

"It was my first one that I sold. I was so proud at that moment. Someone actually wanted to pay money for my art. It was a couple of years later that I went back and made the buyer a ridiculous offer. I gave it to Bruno as a thank you. I felt like it was a small present compared to what he gave me—total belief in my talent."

Lucca nodded absentmindedly. "He gave me the same gift. Always encouraging me. It all makes sense now. Oh my God, I thought you worked in a bakery!" He laughed.

"Well, I do—I mean I did," admitted Ellie. "I've been struggling artistically. I don't know exactly when it was, but suddenly I just couldn't paint. Nothing. I was honest with Madeleine about that when she convinced me to take this retreat. She told me I could stay as long as I wanted and come back to my roots. I went to art school in Tuscany. That time meant everything to me. That's how I first met your father. He mentored many of the students and knew our instructors."

Lucca nodded. "He donates money to the school for scholarships as well. Did you know that? He loves art so much. Since I didn't see that much of him as a teenager, I didn't get exposed to it. I honestly don't know much about art. You'd laugh at me if you knew how little I know. He's tried to teach me, but it's literally like starting at square one." He looked sad, shaking his head.

"Your father is a genius in the art world. And people listen to him. If he likes something, it's a precursor to an amazing career. She sat up. "Wait a minute. Rita's brother. Oh my God, it's all coming together. She shook her head. "This is freaky. I was going to look him up if I had the nerve while I was here."

"What do you mean if you had the nerve?"

"I don't know. I guess I felt like he'd be disappointed in me. I haven't had a show in more than a year. Time is going fast, and I'm a washed-up artist at 29."

"That's ridiculous. So you've had some off time. That's normal for a creative person. Look at how many actors go years between movies—or singers who don't have hit songs."

Ellie nodded sadly. "I know. It's just been really difficult to not be able to do something I love so much."

She looked down at her hands for a minute. "So you have your answers. Now tell me about this stalker, Lucca. I knew you were hiding something."

He looked uneasy. "I didn't want you to be frightened. You weren't in any danger," he rushed to tell her.

"It started a few months before we met. Just threatening letters and random texts, even when I changed my number. But it ramped up with deliveries to my house, and the letters got more frequent and more threatening. I left for a while—just completely went off the grid and went to Africa. I finally realized I couldn't just hide anymore, and I came home to Italy. That's when I met Kate and went to the shareholders' dinner. I avoided the limelight successfully that night, thank goodness."

"But when I returned home, I met with the police. Everything had stopped while I was out of the country, which was even more peculiar if you think about it. That meant the person involved somehow was in my inner circle and knew I wasn't in L.A. I went over it and over it with the police. There were so few people who knew my plans."

"Things were quiet for a very short time, and I was getting hopeful that it was somehow just a twisted lark. But then it began to escalate. My car windows were shattered when I was running an errand. A note was inside. I don't even want to tell you what it said." Lucca looked uneasy. "Obviously, I was being watched."

"Shortly after, there was a burglary at my home—they made a mess of my house. But nothing was taken that we could tell. There was another note, and this one was even worse. That's why I acted the way I did when you came to deliver the cake. I thought my security was adequate, but obviously it was lacking. I found out only a few of my security cameras were even working. I fired that firm and then hired Mike and his team. He came with the highest recommendations. He has a lot of friends in law enforcement, and they are working on it. We hope to have a break soon."

"Have you had any threats while you have been in Italy?"

"Well, yes and no."

She raised her eyebrows.

"Okay, the good news is not in Italy. I was very careful. Only an extremely tight circle knew I was coming here. Of course, with the wedding, more people saw me. That's another reason I wanted to get out of the Amalfi Coast and move around. I thought I'd stay here while, hopefully, the police figure this out."

"And now the bad news?"

"They found a suspicious package at my home in California. They detonated it, and it was an explosive device—enough to destroy my house, at the very least. Or me," he added grimly. "That means whoever this is keeps intensifying."

Her eyes widened. "So today, I must have tripped some alarm."

"Yes, the cameras were all going off that a person was near the house. We knew there was staff in the field, but no one was supposed to be up here."

She smiled weakly. "And there I was, just minding my own business, swimming away."

He laughed. "I didn't think the person threatening me would want to come to Italy for a swim, but for Mike, it was that someone had breached his security. They were in the midst of sealing the property when it happened. I'm sure they hadn't gotten to the guesthouse yet."

"Well, thank God. They would have scared me to death."

He looked serious now. "Ellie, I'm sorry. I'm like kryptonite right now. I thought maybe it was going to go away, but it hasn't. Do you feel safe staying here now? We should talk to Mike."

She rushed to reassure him, but he was already texting Mike to come back to discuss the situation with them.

The older man walked in, still looking harassed. "I think we're all clear. I've got the entire property covered. Everyone who *should* be here is accounted for. And I got a man putting up more cameras." He eyed them both. "You two get everything worked out?"

"Well, sort of. Ellie is supposed to be staying at the guest-house, but I just wanted your opinion about if that's a good idea."

"In a word, no," Mike said firmly. "Look, we obviously have a person who wants to make a statement. Having you down at the guesthouse gives me two locations to worry about," Mike said.

"You need to be in the villa. I could use the guesthouse anyway for overflow security details to rest. I'm adding more people since the device was found."

"Well, my word is no, too," Ellie said roughly. "I'm here to paint. I can't be here with all of you roaming around. I can't work that way. I came here for a retreat—not to be held hostage."

"Ellie, you know me. I'm doing all I can to resolve this situation. We have a lot of people looking for the suspect—now the FBI is involved. It's not long term. I'm just asking you to give it a shot for a few days. This place is enormous. I'm sure there's some nook or cranny you can have where no one will bother you."

She wanted to scream. Mike was being reasonable, but all her emotions from seeing Lucca again were bubbling to the surface, and now having her plans altered was just sending her over the edge. She stood abruptly. "Lucca, where should I move my stuff?"

"I'll help you."

"That's not necessary," she said roughly, sending him a dark look.

Mike took charge. "Ellie, you go down and get organized. When you're ready, text me, and I'll have a couple of my men come down to help. I assume you have canvases and art supplies to move?"

At her nod, he made a little snort. "You two are going to have to get along. I can't manage you both and the security at the same time. So just figure it out."

Mike stomped out, and Lucca gave her a mocking smile. "Daddy is mad at you."

Ellie, who had felt tears of frustration coming on, found laughter bubbling up.

"No, he's mad at *you*."

Lucca stared at her for a second. "Go get your stuff," he said gruffly and walked out.

fourteen

Ellie stared at the blank canvas. She hadn't made a lot of progress since moving into the villa a few days prior. Progress in any area, really. She furrowed her brow. Her art was at a standstill, and her relationship with Lucca was—well, nonexistent. Ellie had seen very little of him since he had shown her to the third floor. Her vast corner bedroom, with its enormous mahogany bed frame and pure white comforter, stood in the center. Walking over to the multiple windows, she looked out over the pool and vineyards. She had run her hands over the solid antique furniture. How old was the house? She wanted to ask him. There was a bell tower, for goodness' sake. Who has a bell tower?

Care had obviously been taken to modernize some parts of the house but ensure the character wasn't compromised. A room next door that served as a default storage room was cleared, and Ellie's art supplies were moved there. It had fantastic light. She painted sometimes there or on the patio overlooking the hills and fields. She hadn't seen Lucca, with the exception of a chance meeting in the kitchen. He had been polite, but quickly excused himself. She knew she only had herself to blame and should have told him about her painting a long time ago. Her biggest regret was taking off after their night together. Yet, she firmly believed they would have still ended up in the same relationship standoff.

She was restless and wished she could go somewhere—into Siena or just for a drive. When Ellie had officially moved in, Mike had come up and talked to her, outlining his rules. She had accepted them—so meekly that he had given her a second look, as if assessing they would be followed. Ellie quietly agreed—she didn't want to cause any more trouble for Mike, his team, or even for Lucca.

Ellie grabbed her sketch pad. Maybe she'd go out to the grounds and find some inspiration. She went back to her room and looked in the mirror. Wearing a pair of jean shorts and a white T-shirt, with her hair in a ponytail, she shrugged at her reflection.

Walking down the stairs, the first thing she noticed was the eerie quiet. She poked her head in a few rooms to just satisfy her curiosity. An expansive living room with comfortable modern furniture mixed with antique wood pieces looked inviting.

"What are you looking for?"

Ellie jumped at the sudden voice. Turning, she put a hand over her heart. "Oh my God, Lucca, you scared me."

He stood there staring at her. Dressed in a cargo shorts and a T-shirt that had seen better days, he was just as casual as she was. He looked like he hadn't shaved in days, his black beard heavy on his jaw line. He had dark shadows under his eyes. Her heart softened.

"Not enough to get tossed to the ground, I guess. You must be off," he said dryly.

She decided to let him have that victory and smiled slightly. "I apologize for snooping. I was just kind of looking around. I haven't seen much of the villa. How old is it?"

"15th Century—not as old as some in the area," Lucca

shrugged. "It's been handed down in my family every generation since. And everyone was raised here—well, except me of course," he said, bitterly. "Sometimes when I'm here I feel like I'm home and then other times, it seems very foreign to me."

Ellie stared at him. She wasn't sure what to say. He seemed really vulnerable—not the self-assured Lucca she had come to know. He'd probably hate it if she pitied him or tried to comfort him. He stood gazing at her, his arms crossed, clearly keeping his distance. She wasn't sure what to say.

He stared at her, as if contemplating what to do next. "Would you like a tour?"

"Um, sure. If you want to. I don't want to pry or anything. I just love old houses."

He nodded. "Actually, so do I. Did you see this piece on the wall?"

Ellie turned behind her, her eyes widened. "Lucca, oh my God, that's amazing." She rattled off the 19th century impressionist's works and how valuable they were. His response was to shrug. "I told you—I don't know a lot about art. Come on, I'll show you the other wing."

For the next hour, Ellie found herself on a stunning tour of the house. It was breathtaking for her at least to see the valuable art from famed painters and sculptors. She took a long time admiring each piece, with .Lucca standing patiently. She explained details and tried to get him to understand the skill in the artists' techniques. She explained the differences in paint— what was ground and what was done later when paint became available in tubes. He nodded, but she couldn't tell if he was truly engaged. He seemed preoccupied.

Finally, the tour ended in the kitchen. Ellie's shoulders slumped. While it had been as much fun as going through a special exhibition at a museum, she now felt even more challenged.

Lucca hopped on a counter to sit and was staring at her. He took a sip out of his water bottle. "What's wrong?"

She looked at him, startled. This man had a way of reading her emotions.

"How am I supposed to paint something that will hang in this place? It's like walking into a museum and plunking my painting on a wall next to a Picasso or Rembrandt."

Lucca stared at her for a minute before pointing to her own painting behind her. "You're already here, sweetheart," he said sarcastically.

She grimaced at his unfamiliar tone. He was still staring at her. He looked away and seemed to take a breath. "You've already done it. So you'll do it again."

She stared down at her hands, still grasping her sketch pad. "I can't, Lucca. I'm completely blocked."

He looked out the window now, not meeting her eyes. "I'm sure it doesn't help that you're locked up with me of all people and you can't go anywhere. You probably need some inspiration."

Ellie flopped into a chair and slapped her sketch pad on to the farmhouse table. "What do you mean you of all people?" It was time for them to talk. She swallowed hard.

"Obviously, you didn't want to have anything else to do with me. Not even a note, Ellie," he said, running his hands in his hair. "I deserved better."

She felt a lump rising in her throat. She could only nod. "I'm sorry," she finally whispered. "Things just got a little intense, I guess." She felt his stare, but she couldn't meet his eyes.

Lucca looked uncomfortable. "Can we call some kind of temporary truce?" he asked softly. "We're locked up here together. Mike's right. Let's make the best of it and just move on. Right now, you need some inspiration to paint."

She looked at him, a grateful smile coming to her face. If possible, she felt her heart giving in a little to him. She knew it was dangerous territory. This vulnerable Lucca, forgiving her for not her finest moment touched her.

She shrugged. "I don't know what will help."

He gave her a small smile. "I read somewhere that doing something creative unrelated to your work can help get the juices flowing. I know writers have told me that anyway."

She looked at him, drawing her eyebrows together and then laughed weakly. "Oh, so I should decorate another cake?"

He shook his head with a small laugh. "No, hopefully we're done with cakes. But you may be on to something." He gestured toward the kitchen. "What about cooking? Do you cook?"

She smiled. "I love cooking. I haven't for a long time, though. When you live by yourself, you end up just eating what's easiest."

"Are you any good at it?"

She looked indignant. "Yes, I'm good at it! For a while, I thought I might want to go to culinary school."

He suddenly brightened up, sitting up straighter.

"Then I have an idea. What if we cook dinner for Mike and some of his team? They can take turns eating. It would be something nice to do for them. They've been great and have worked hard."

Ellie looked at him now, eyes narrowed.

"I have a better idea. You cook something, and I'll cook something. I'm not someone's sous chef," she retorted.

He raised his eyebrows. "Hmmm, are we talking a competition?"

She smiled. This could be fun. "Yep. They'll be our judges."

He looked at her speculatively. "What does the winner get?"

She paused, giving it some thought. "When we can leave— dinner out in Siena. My favorite city, and I know the restaurant you can take me to. I'll order everything!"

He smiled. "You seem pretty sure of yourself."

She stuck out her hand. "Deal, Hollywood?"

He grabbed it, and she felt the electricity shoot through her body. He looked her straight in the eyes. "Deal, Ellie James, Artist Extraordinaire."

ELLIE POURED the flour on to the old wooden island in the kitchen. She was sure it was reserved for pasta making and pasta making only. It had the well-scrubbed look of an old Italian ravioli-making table, just like the one in Florence where she had taken cooking classes. She made a well in the flour and cracked eggs into it. Whipping the eggs, she began to blend it with the flour. She turned around to see her arrabbiata sauce bubbling. It smelled delicious.

The dough blended, she began to knead with all she had. She had put an apron on before they started, and she wiped her hands on it, resting for a second.

Lucca was at a counter with the mixer. His brow was furrowed, and he was concentrating. He was also measuring flour and adding it to the mixer. She frowned. He better not be copying her!

"Whatcha making?" Ellie asked casually.

"Wouldn't you like to know?" he answered without looking at her.

"It better not be pasta."

He looked over at her. "You can't own pasta. You didn't call it."

"I called it! Well, maybe not out loud, but it's kind of obvious what I'm doing over here."

Lucca rolled his eyes. "If you think you'll lose going head-to-head with me on pasta, then that's your problem."

She frowned. She went back to kneading, pretending the dough was Lucca's head. She rolled and folded as hard as she could.

He laughed suddenly, and she looked up. His eyes glinted as if he guessed what she had been thinking. "Hey, Ellie."

"What?" She looked up, running the back of a flour-covered hand over her forehead.

His dimples were deep now. "I'm making pizza."

"That's fine. Pasta, pizza, I really don't care," she said casually, going back to her kneading. Secretly, she was very pleased. Pizza was so ordinary. She would wow them with her tagliatelle.

She folded the dough into a ball and put it aside to rest. She went to wash her hands, scraping the dough off. She glanced over her shoulder, and Lucca had now turned on the mixer. A little flour cloud floated up, hitting him square in the face. She heard a blast of Italian. She turned back around so he couldn't see her grin.

She wasn't sure how they had gotten themselves into this cooking competition, but she had to admit it was fun. He seemed more relaxed, and hopefully he wasn't concentrating on his troubles. She hadn't even thought about painting. This creative journey might not help, but at least she was having a good time. She stirred her sauce for a minute.

He looked over at her, his eyebrows raised. "Can I ask what sauce you made, or would that be some trade secret?"

She smiled proudly. "Arrabbiata."

"I should have known," he said mockingly. "You know what it translates to, right? Angry."

"I'm not angry!"

"Your sauce is!" He laughed.

She went back to stirring. True, it was a spicy red sauce, but it would be delicious. "What kind of pizza are you making?"

"Not sure yet. I'm letting my creative process unwind." He grinned at her. She smiled back, and for a moment, they were back. The magic was there. Her heart gave a funny somersault. She didn't know how she felt about it.

"Wow, you two are sure hard at work." Mike came walking

through the doorway, sniffing appreciatively. "Thanks for doing this. My team is excited for a home-cooked meal."

Ellie looked away from Lucca. The spell was broken. She sweetly smiled at Mike. "Well, your team will have a delicious dinner from me, but I can't speak for what you're going to get from him. But it's okay—I'll make a lot."

"At least you two can't kill each other while you cook." Mike looked around. "On second thought, maybe hand me those knives, Ellie," he said with a laugh. She swatted him with a nearby kitchen towel, and he hurried out, shaking his head.

Ellie began to roll out her dough, not looking at Lucca. He was cutting up vegetables and fruit and seemed completely unaware of her presence. She concentrated on feeding the dough through the pasta machine, gently grabbing the thick strands as they came out.

"Did you grow up cooking?" he asked suddenly.

"Oh no, not at all!" she said with a laugh before she could even think about it. While her mother hired a long line of decorated chefs over the years, her parents also liked to cook. She had usually avoided the kitchen during those times, or else they would suck her into clean-up. They had a habit of using every pan in the house and were too embarrassed to ask their staff to clean up their catastrophic messes.

She bit her lip. "My mother was sort of in charge of the kitchen. You?"

He smiled, looking up briefly before going back to cutting.

"I used to cook for my mom while she worked. And then, summers in Italy when I was down at the lemon grove, sometimes I would cook with Zia Rita."

"What did your mom do?"

"She went back to school, and she became a CPA. She is a partner in a large accounting firm and does very well."

"Wow, I had no idea."

"Very boring stuff, mostly tax auditing, but she loves it."

"That's interesting," Ellie said and then instantly regretted it. "What?"

She made a face. "Sorry, none of my business. I just can't see Bruno with an unartistic type of person. He's just so creative."

"Well, maybe that was one of their problems. I have no idea. I stay out of it," he said bitterly.

"Lucca," she said softly.

He looked up.

"I'm sorry. I should just keep my opinions to myself."

He looked like he wanted to say more, but shook his head, as if to change the mood. He smiled a little. "You're going to have a whole lot to say when you taste this pizza!"

LUCCA POKED AT THE FIRE, getting it just right. He should have started it sooner. Now he was probably going to cook his pizzas too fast. Not to mention that he had paid little attention to even what he had put on them. He had been so distracted in the kitchen watching Ellie work. She had put her heart into it. He loved watching the expressions on her face. He could read her like a book.

He admitted he really didn't care if he won or not. Competitive, he liked to win, but this was already a win-win in his book. Either way, he got to spend time with Ellie.

He didn't have a clue to why that made him so happy. He had avoided her the last few days on purpose. Part of him just wanted to give her the space she wanted. The other reason was harder to admit. He still struggled with the feeling he had when Zia Rita told him Ellie had just left. No note. No anything. Was it her? Was it him? He thought they had really come to a different place the night of the wedding. Now he realized he was the only one feeling they could become something together. She must have just gotten swayed by all the romance in the air at the wedding.

After she had time to think about it, she clearly wasn't interested. She had told him that over and over, in fact. He had wanted to press her and ask her when the subject came up today, but he let it go. He hated confrontation, and he admitted to himself he didn't want to hear her tell him the truth—that she didn't share his feelings. Seeing her so down about her craft, though, had melted the hard façade he wanted to have with her.

If he were honest, the competitive streak in him wanted to win her, too. At least win her over. He didn't know about anything long term, but he had to admit he had never been rejected. Even now, hearing that she was a renowned artist didn't really explain why she was so against dating an actor. If anything, she should understand fame a little better.

If he were being completely honest with himself, he'd admit he was deeply attracted to her. She was so natural—look at her now; she was just wearing shorts and a top, no make-up—her hair up. She did nothing to try to attract his attention. He loved that. He realized just being around her made him relax. He let down his guard with her, that's for sure. He had never talked about his parents' divorce or his relationship with them to anyone outside the family. He frowned. He really had over-shared. He knew deep down that Ellie would not betray his trust and gossip about it. Still, it left him feeling a little vulnerable. He knew so little about her.

Lucca also understood he couldn't even trust his emotions right now. He had glossed over it with Ellie, but the last few months had taken its toll. He had never had this kind of darkness in his life. It was a fact the stalker was escalating, and someone would get hurt. That's why he had ordered all his staff to stay home—even the groundskeepers. He couldn't take the thought that someone would inadvertently get hurt by this clearly unstable person.

And now, here they sat cooped up in a villa. If he and Ellie were a couple, this clearly would not be a hardship, but obviously she did not want that to happen. The other reason he had left her alone was because he didn't trust himself to not reach out and grab her. He would kiss her until she admitted she returned his feelings. He highly doubted she would appreciate those caveman tactics.

Lucca invented this cooking competition as a game to distract her. He could tell how the painter's block was affecting her. It was the one time she didn't seem confident, and that was jarring to him. He was used to the self-assured Ellie, who seemed like she could do anything.

Feeding his pizzas into the oven now, he realized she might just win this one. And he'd enjoy this loss more than anything.

fifteen

Ellie knew she wasn't at the top of her game. Lucca was distracting in the kitchen, for sure. She found herself busy watching his movements. She forgot to put water on to boil for her pasta and add the last-minute ingredients to her sauce. It was only after he went outside to cook his pizzas in the wood-fired oven that she got her head out of the clouds. She scrambled, barely getting her food on the table at the same time as Lucca's. They took a helping of each dish and decided to go outside, where there were tables and chairs on the stone patio. Lucca left for a minute and came back with a bottle of red wine and a couple of glasses.

Instead of sitting across from her, he moved next to her at the round table. He poured their wine and held up his glass, "*Ai cuochi!*" To the cooks. She smiled.

She bit into his pizza while he took a bite of her pasta. She moaned. "I think you're going to win."

He laughed. "Why, Ellie, I think that's the nicest thing you've ever said to me."

She giggled. "You're probably right, but oh my God, Lucca,

what did you put on this pizza? The pears and the gorgonzola really work. But what is the sauce?"

"Wouldn't you like to know?" He smiled smugly.

"It's the best pizza I have ever had in my life!"

"I highly doubt that," he said dryly.

He took a bite of her pasta and sighed after swallowing. "Ellie, this is really amazing! You added something to this. It doesn't taste like any other arrabbiata I have had. You're going to win. What is it?"

She rolled her eyes. "You don't have to say it cause I said it. And you're never going to get my secret ingredient out of me!"

"Yeah, because filling you with false compliments is what I do. I'm serious. You nailed the pasta, too. You rival Stefano, and he makes the best pasta I know. I don't know how anyone can eat boxed pasta after they have had fresh."

She laughed. "Well, I can. I mean, if I'm home by myself, I'm not whipping up a batch of fresh pasta dough. You probably just have your chef do it."

"I don't have a chef."

"Really? I thought it was mandatory for any Hollywood type."

He shook his head. "I have a very small staff when I am home—which is not often. I wasn't raised with a lot of people around. You saw how little staff Zia Rita has in her home. I'm just not comfortable surrounded by a lot of people. It's a pain anyway. You have to have them backgrounded and sign NDAs and all that stuff. Then you still find stuff in the tabloids about you."

She put down her pizza and stared at her plate, her expression serious. "I might have misjudged you."

"Do you think?"

She continued to look down, and he reached over and tweaked her hair, which had long fallen out of its ponytail. "I might regret this, but what did you think of me?"

She grimaced. "I imagined you were a Hollywood spoiled type. The typical leading man with any number of women in his life, giant staff, humongous ego, arrogant, no ability to laugh at himself..." She trailed off suddenly, not sure if she had said too much.

"Wow, that's quite a laundry list. Who have you been hanging around? Okay, I admit there's been some women—well, maybe a few more than that, if I'm being honest. My ego is probably large, but don't know about humongous. We covered the staff. Yes, on the arrogance, I'm sure. But I *can* laugh at myself."

"I'm sorry, Lucca. It wasn't fair. I put you in a box. I hate when people do that to me." She shrugged. "And I do know nice people in Hollywood. Really nice people. I just hate most of what goes with it."

He looked at her seriously now. "I agree. I never sought fame. I just loved the idea of entertaining people. But as you said, then came the dark side. I've had fake stories written about me, pulled fans out of my hotel rooms—legally went after people who wanted to use my likeness to sell stuff. It seems like I talk to my attorneys more than I do my agent these days. And now there's this sicko who apparently has some kind of warped obsession with me. I know you probably don't really understand all of it— you have to kind of live it to fully get it."

She looked away from him toward the vineyards. Now would be a good time to tell him. She knew there was no future with Lucca, but she generally liked him and she wanted to be honest with him. She opened her mouth.

"Lucca..."

"Hey, boss, I have great news!"

"I WON!" Lucca stood, raising his fists in the air.

Mike looked at him, confused. "Oh yeah, the cooking competition. No, sorry, we haven't voted yet. I just got a call. My friends at the FBI had a lead a few days ago. I didn't want to say anything in case it went nowhere. They are working with LAPD —we think we got our stalker."

Lucca sat down, looking at Mike, stunned. "You're serious?" He threw his head back in relief. "Are you sure? How can you be sure?"

"Pulling it up for you now. Just a second." Mike was bent over his tablet. "Your neighbor's camera showed a man with a bag—probably the device. Not great footage, and we saw he had a hoodie on with an emblem. We traced it to a private school in New York. Then they found a partial piece of DNA on the device that they ran. It matched to an ancestry site. They did some interviews with some of the people associated with him on the site and his former classmates, and that was enough for a search warrant. They found the suspect's cell phone pinged a tower near your home repeatedly. Then they found evidence on his computer. It's him."

"Who?" Lucca asked, his eyes narrowing.

Mike showed him the tablet, staying silent.

Lucca's face drained of all color. "I know him."

"I bet you do," said Mike, shaking your head. "He's your stunt double."

LUCCA STOOD QUICKLY and walked away to the edge of the patio. He looked out over the vineyards below. His mind was swirling. He turned around. "I don't understand. Why would he want to hurt me? He'd be out of work!"

Mike shrugged. "It's hard to say. I've seen it all. Could have been jealousy. Could have been that he thought if something happened to you, he could step into your shoes. Sometimes it can start as a small idea, but he definitely escalated. They found an airline ticket in his email. He was booked on a flight to Italy this week."

Lucca's eyes widened. He turned around again. He was shaken, and he didn't want Mike and Ellie to see him this way.

Ellie got up and took Mike's tablet. She closed it sand handed it back to him. "Mike, can you give us a minute?"

"Sure. I'll be inside if you need me."

Lucca nodded without turning around. He swallowed the lump in his throat. How was it possible to be so angry and yet want to cry at the same time? He felt Ellie's presence next to him, not touching him. Out of the corner of his eye, he saw her rock back on her heels.

"Soooo, it's over."

He nodded, not trusting himself to speak.

"How are you feeling?"

He shook his head. "I don't know. Kind of stuns me. I spent a lot of time with Andrew. I thought he was a good friend."

"I've had friends betray me. Not to this level, but it sucks."

He turned his head and looked at her. "I thought it was a woman."

She didn't look fazed. "Makes sense. I mean, half of the female population is in love with you. I thought it was, too."

He felt a smile come on grudgingly. "I don't think that's correct. I'd say at least three-quarters."

She elbowed him. "There's my arrogant, Hollywood."

"You know I'm kidding, right?" he asked quietly.

She grinned. "If you say so!"

He laughed, putting an arm around her. He wanted to talk to her, find out the real reasons she had run away. He wanted to see what her true feelings were. Now that their secrets were out in the open, he suddenly felt free. Maybe they could start over. He gave her a kiss on the cheek to see her reaction. She simply smiled up at him. "It's over, Lucca. They found him."

He shook his head. "I still can't believe it. There's a part of me that worries they're wrong. You know, if this was a movie, in the next act, the real stalker would surface."

She rolled her eyes. "Well, as far as I can tell, it is definitely not a movie. I trust Mike. Let's go in and learn more."

"Okay, okay. I believe you. Let's go open some prosecco and celebrate with Mike and the team."

Her eyes narrowed. "Oh no, you don't. You're not going to be all Mr. Charming and ply them with alcohol. We are taking a vote before you do that, my friend!"

"We can take all the votes you want. I remain confident in my pizza," he said smugly.

"Yeah, well, let's see!" She started to walk toward the doors.

He suddenly desperately wanted another minute alone with her. He grabbed her hand, pulling her back. "Hey, Ellie."

She looked at him. Her hair was completely in disarray, her face shiny from the hot kitchen. She still had some flour on her forehead. He smiled at her gently, rubbing it off. "You have flour on your face."

She continued staring at him, clearly waiting for him. He kissed her, a long lingering kiss. He slowly put his arms around her, still being cautious. She was kissing him back. He took that as a good sign. He pulled away and smiled. "I just want to say thank you."

"For what?"

"Distracting me this afternoon. Being here now. Making me laugh. I don't know. A long list. It's been nice."

She nodded, her eyes apprehensive. "Anytime, Hollywood."

ELLIE WASN'T SURPRISED by Mike's briefing when they had gone into the house. She knew he was thorough and professional. He had more information by the time they had walked in, quickly going through the highlights of the report. Andrew had been committed to a mental hospital at one time. He had used his dead brother's social security number and assumed his identity to get jobs in Hollywood. His real name was Henry. They believed he had sent threatening letters to others in the industry in the past. They were running DNA on an old case in New York involving significant kidnapping threats toward a Broadway star —so intense, the actor was still in hiding with his family. Federal authorities were putting together a strong case, crossing state lines, and Mike believed the suspect would probably be committed or do some serious time. Lucca slapped him on the back before shaking his hand.

"I can't thank you enough, Mike."

"Hey, I've been relaxing here in Italy while these guys did the work," he said with modesty.

"You helped find the right people to take the case. I'm sure it would have probably gotten lost in a giant pile of threats against celebrities if you hadn't been involved."

Mike inclined his head. "Thanks, boss. I felt like this one was different. It rang very serious to me. I'm happy we got the guy."

Lucca had walked over to the massive wine cooler, getting out several bottles of prosecco. Opening them now, they had a quick toast. Mike's team all took a sip, but Ellie noticed they quickly put their glasses down.

"We're going to keep operations up for the next couple of days," Mike was saying. "We'll talk tomorrow about the level of security you should maintain, but probably just a small footprint while you're here in Italy. For now, everyone's going to keep working."

As the men prepared to leave, Lucca stopped them. "Mike, we have a serious question for you," he said, his eyes dancing. "Who won?"

Mike looked uncomfortable. He went over to the paper on the table now. "Well, everyone voted," he said slowly.

Ellie smiled sweetly at Mike. "It was me, wasn't it? It's okay. I know you work for him, but Lucca can take it like a man."

Mike handed Lucca the paper. "Congratulations, the pizza

won!" Then he playfully darted past Ellie, as if he was afraid of her.

She looked at Lucca now, her eyes narrowed. "I want a recount."

144

sixteen

Ellie's brush had a mind of its own. She painted with carefree abandon, and her heart felt light. She had been at it since dawn this morning, only stopping to grab some water. She smiled, admiring her work. It felt so great and freeing to paint. She was so happy to be producing something, only this was nothing that she'd ever be able to give Madeleine. Lucca was coming to life on canvas, and she found she couldn't stop. She studied the sketches some more and kept going. He was a fascinating model. She couldn't resist painting him and bringing his character to life. Sitting back, she frowned. While it felt good to paint, this was not what she had imagined herself painting. She had never thought she could paint portraits—and had long given up trying.

The fact that this could be a mistake suddenly dawned on her. The one portrait she had tried in years was of Lucca, who she was desperately trying to avoid. After going to bed the night before, she had lain awake thinking about their time together. She had two roads she could take: fend him off and keep him at arm's length or go for it and spend time with him. The latter meant having to walk away, most certainly with her heart shattered. Ellie had never fully given her heart to anyone. This was who she was going to start with? He was in the center of everything she had fought so long to leave behind.

Still, she could be assuming too much. Maybe he didn't want to continue anything with her. She felt he still desired her. It had been in his eyes. But realistically, now that his stalker was caught, he could return to Los Angeles any time he wanted. He had never said how long he was going to stay in Italy.

Ellie had mentioned moving back to the guesthouse, but Mike had stalled her, asking for a few more days while they transitioned operations. Running a hand over her hot forehead, she stretched her shoulders and neck that were tight from remaining in the same position. Deciding to go grab lunch and take a break, she closed the door, being extra paranoid, even though Lucca had never come near her studio. She stopped in her room to wash her face and re-tie her hair in a ponytail and went down to the empty kitchen. Making herself a quick sandwich, she was lost in her thoughts.

"You going to grill that?"

She jumped. "Lucca, for the love of God and all that is holy, would you stop sneaking up on me?"

His eyes widened, and he held up his hands. "Down, Ellie. I simply walked into the kitchen. I only asked cause grilled paninis are my specialty."

He was looking at her arrogantly, and she frowned. "Is that your way of reminding me of your win again?"

He grinned, looking innocent. "Oh, that's right. I had forgotten. Slipped my mind completely."

She automatically got out two more slices of bread to make another sandwich. She looked at him and rolled her eyes. "Yeah, I bet, Hollywood. What expensive restaurant are you choosing?"

"I'll have to think about it, but I thought we'd go tonight if you're free?"

She took her time in answering. "I guess that would be fine. I might as well get it over with."

"That's what most women say when I ask them out," he commented dryly.

"But you're not asking me out. This isn't a date. It's just..."

He was looking at her intently. "Paying a debt? Restitution? I'm so flattered. Whatever you want to call it, we're going to have a good time. You'll see."

Ellie chose not to look at him. She brushed the bread now with olive oil and put them on the nearby grill.

His eyes widened. "Are you extra hungry, or did you just make me a sandwich?"

She sighed in defeat.

~

LUCCA SMILED, watching Ellie cut his sandwich. She was trying so hard not to like him, but he had to admit he was feeling pretty likable. Wait until she saw his next surprise. He was excited to show her.

"So, how's the painting going?"

Ellie was blushing for some reason, handing him his plate. They carried them to the table before she answered. "Um, I started this morning—again. It's actually some good work. It's not for Madeleine, but at least I'm painting."

He nodded. "That's good. Maybe the cooking helped!" He laughed. "But seriously, a lot of the writers I work with say they switch it up and write something completely different than the screenplay they are supposed to be working on. Eventually, they're able to switch over, and it starts flowing again."

Ellie seemed to accept that and began to talk about painting a little and how she looked for inspiration. He was fascinated at the way her mind seemed to narrow in on the small details—things he would never think were worth capturing. He listened intently and tried to ask intelligent questions, even though he knew so little about art. He should have listened to his dad a little more, but up until now, he had never had that much interest. He just knew what he liked.

She was staring at him, and he realized she had asked him a question.

"Sorry, I was distracted for a second."

She frowned at him. "I asked where Sophia was. I haven't seen her much at all. Did you lock her up or something?"

Lucca grinned. "Hardly. In fact, I have a surprise to show you after you're finished."

Ellie looked at him questioningly. "I'm finished now."

He smiled. "Then let's go!"

ELLIE FOLLOWED Lucca onto the patio. What could he possibly have to show her? She had to admit he was a wonderful companion at lunch. He had listened to her and even though his questions were basic, and it was obvious he did not know much about art, he at least was trying to understand. She seldom talked about her art, let alone her process, and it had felt good. If he only knew what her inspiration had been this morning!

He stopped now on the expansive lawn and looked at her. She couldn't see his eyes because he had put his sunglasses on, but he had a smile. She jumped when he put his fingers in his mouth and whistled sharply.

Sophia came bounding from some hidden spot, directly for Lucca. As usual, the puppy was excited to see him. She saw Ellie and changed course, but Lucca gave the command to stay and Sophia stopped in her tracks. She wagged her tail now, looking at Ellie expectantly.

"Good girl!" Ellie said, rubbing the dog's head enthusiastically. "That's my good girl."

Lucca came up and gave her a treat from his pocket.

"Watch this. Sit, Sophia." Sophia dutifully sat, and Lucca supplied a treat.

"Down, Sophia." Sophia laid down and got her treat.

"Stand, Sophia," Lucca raised his hand, and she stood.

He grinned at her. Ellie was standing with her mouth open. She dropped to her knees and hugged the dog. "There's our smart girl! Sophia, you're amazing."

She heard a throat clearing. She glanced up at Lucca, who had taken off his glasses and was now the one looking at her expectantly.

"Those are called puppy pushups," he said proudly.

"I know! But how…? I'm so confused."

He shrugged. "I was bored. I lost interest in the scripts and so I watched some videos online and started working with her."

"What else can she do?"

Lucca rolled his eyes. "Seriously? We just showed you all that and you want more?"

Ellie laughed. "No, sorry, I was just wondering. I think you got the basics down. I mean, she's still a puppy. There's more, of course."

He nodded. "I'm working on having her go to her bed next. Sophia, place. Place." Ellie looked around and saw a dog bed on the patio. Sophia ran into the flower beds instead, calmly chewing on a branch of a rose bush.

"Sophia, stop! Stop! Oh man, the gardeners are going to hate me," Lucca waved Sophia off, and she bounded down the grass.

"We should get her some more dog toys," Ellie commented.

"She has some, but I want some balls for her to fetch. Maybe we should go early tonight and walk around Siena and look at the shops before dinner. I haven't been there in many years—I'd love for you to show me more of the city."

She agreed happily. She loved Siena, and she wouldn't pass up the opportunity. It held a special place in her heart. She tapped down the small part of her that realized walking around her favorite city with Lucca was a dream. She was going to put it down to just having a good time. Why not have a wonderful evening with Lucca? She pushed aside her doubts and gave him a bright smile.

seventeen

Ellie was still smiling as they rode in the gray Lamborghini convertible Lucca had backed out of the garage. They were winding their way through the gorgeous Tuscan region on their way to Siena, and she soaked in the scenery around them. They drove down a straight road lined with cypress trees. Ellie looked off into the distant fields of sunflowers, white cows—a rare and ancient breed that are found in Tuscany. She mentioned this to Lucca—a fun fact she had read somewhere.

He gave her a quick smile, his hair blowing gently in the wind, his eyes hidden by sunglasses. It was still late afternoon, but it had cooled down nicely. Ellie had secretly admired Lucca's gray chinos and blue-and-white striped shirt, the sleeves rolled up. He had leaned over to help her find the seat belt buckle when they first had gotten in the car, and he smelled good. She had breathed in his spicy cologne.

Ellie was glad she had made an effort with her appearance on their "non-date." Digging out a sundress she hadn't worn yet that was a pretty shade of cream, she had decided it was simple and elegant. She thought it went well with the slight tan she had gotten from her walks around the property every day. Ellie had even blow dried her hair and styled it a little. Adding a little make-up, she was pleased with the final look. Settling into the comfortable leather upholstery, they listened to soft music. She smiled. "I love this car, Lucca."

"Thanks, it's actually mine. I ended up buying something to keep at my dad's. It just made sense. I felt like I was a teenager always asking him to borrow a car!"

Ellie laughed. "It makes sense, and Tuscany is so much fun to drive around. It just seems like there's adventures around every corner."

"Did you explore much when you were in art school, or were you a starving artist?"

Ellie bit her lip. She thought about telling him now about her parents, but that would lead to the whole story and Lucca possibly being upset with her for not saying anything sooner. She was secretly looking forward to this evening, and she didn't want it ruined. She vowed to tell him soon.

"Well, not exactly starving. We got around a lot. There was always a new town to explore and lots of wine tasting, that's for sure. And just so much inspiration. The architecture, the flowers, the fields. It's truly lovely."

"I agree. I've often thought about buying my own place in Tuscany. I realize how much I relax here."

Ellie nodded happily. "Me, too."

They arrived near Siena, and Lucca drove neatly into a parking spot by a hotel.

"I don't think you can park here," Ellie said hesitantly.

"Mike called ahead and squared it with them. It's fine. We can walk into the old city from here."

Ellie looked behind her. She had almost forgotten his security. After negotiating with Mike, they had agreed on two of his security team following them discreetly. Mike was much more relaxed now that he continued to get information on the suspect. Ellie knew the reason Mike was so good at his job was that he was cautious. He warned Lucca he would relax a little, but not completely let his guard down yet. And then, they should talk about his security long term. Ellie had slid away during this discussion, seeing the look cross Lucca's face. He was obviously not pleased with it all.

She realized Lucca was holding the door open for her and smiled up at him. She took her hair out of the ponytail she had put it in when she saw the convertible and slid the hair tie into her bag. She shook out her long hair now and combed her fingers through it. Lucca stared at her.

She looked at him. "What?"

"Oh, uh nothing. You just look like a girl tonight."

She frowned at him. "As opposed to what?"

Lucca smiled at her, his deep dimples now on display. "A cake decorator? Artist? Chef? Let me pull my foot out of my mouth so I can eat that fabulous dinner you're buying me later."

Ellie laughed despite herself, and he must have been encouraged because he suddenly grabbed her by the hand. "Let's go explore."

The next couple of hours were everything Ellie had hoped. A thought crossed her mind that she would remember this time with Lucca forever. There was nothing unique about it except, she admitted, she was with Lucca. They had formed a camaraderie, and it was relaxing and fun. They started at the edge of the city and moved through the shops. He proudly showed her some of his family's products on display—lemon candles, soap, limoncello, and olive oil. She was familiar with the brand but hadn't realized how vast their operation was.

They moved to a sweets shop and watched the chocolatier at work. They couldn't resist buying a small bag and sharing it as they walked along. Once in a while, they held hands, especially when Lucca got excited and wanted to pull her into a new shop to look around.

"It's been a long time since I was here," he told her enthusiastically. She willfully allowed him to set the pace and let him poke around the shops. They argued over soft toys and balls for Sophia and ended up buying several at a small pet shop.

She looked behind them a couple times, and Mike's detail had stuck with them but remained discreet. In fact, Ellie had been shocked that so far not one person had even approached Lucca. She had waited for the fans to rush up, but so far no one had even glanced their way. She wasn't sure if it was the sunglasses or just the fact that everyone seemed so relaxed. Of course, he blended in far more in Italy than he did in the states, she realized. There were certainly many good-looking Italian men walking around, she acknowledged, though none were half as handsome as he was.

They stopped at every street when they saw the symbol of each *contrada*. Animals or mythical creatures were on banners, lampposts and flags waved, representing their area. Ellie told Lucca about how the *contradas*—basically a district in which people lived or were from—were a big part of the lives of the Sienese people.

They were just leaving a shop when Lucca grabbed Ellie's shoulders, pressing her toward a wall. A crowd of people were coming at them. Lucca's security detail was near them but couldn't get to them in a crunch. People were waving flags and banners and shouting.

"What's the date?" She shouted at Lucca. When he told her, she smiled. "Tomorrow is Il Palio!" He looked at her quizzically but waited for the crush to be over. The crowd moved through shouting and chanting and were gone almost as quickly as they came.

Smiling reassuringly, Lucca grabbed her hand to lead her down the street toward the Siena Cathedral. They stopped and bought some lemonade and carried it to a nearby bench.

"So, Il Palio—it's a horse race, right?" he asked.

"Not just any horse race—like the world's wildest horse race.

It's twice a year—July and August. It's going to be crazy here. But you must know all about it."

A sad look crossed Lucca's face. "You have to remember that I didn't really grow up here. I visited, but it wasn't the same as living here."

Ellie reached out and stroked his arm. "I'm sorry, Lucca. I shouldn't have said that so flippantly. I forgot."

He gave her a small smile. "It's fine. You can tell me about it at dinner."

Ellie nodded, looking at the cathedral. "This is one of my favorite," Ellie remarked, changing the subject. "I took a tour here years ago. There are so many masterpieces in there—from painters to sculptors. From all different centuries, too. I was overwhelmed. And you should see the floor. It's this marble mosaic. I could look at it all day."

He smiled at her enthusiasm. "I feel like I can learn so much from you."

She rolled her eyes. "I'm hardly up to your dad's knowledge. I'm like a kindergarten teacher, and he's like a college professor."

"But you are much prettier," he said quietly.

She narrowed her eyes at him. "Stop it, Lucca. You don't have to give me compliments. I'm sure I don't look like most of the women you spend time with."

He took off his sunglasses now and put them in his pocket. "You're right, Ellie. You don't at all. And that's what I like about you."

He stood suddenly. "Are you finished? I want to find out if we can at least go inside for a few minutes so I can see some of what you talked about."

For the next hour, they walked slowly through the cathedral. It was an abbreviated tour, but it was perfect for the day. They stopped frequently so Ellie could point out a sculpture, painting, the floor, the stained glass. She had been right—there was so much to look at.

As they left, she looked at him sheepishly. "Oh my God, I just bored you to death, didn't I?"

"Not at all. I enjoyed it. You have such an eye for every detail. I see a whole different world when I'm with you," he said, staring at her intently. She returned his gaze and tripped over a stone as they were walking. His arms shot out to steady her. "Don't fall," he said softly.

"Oh, I won't," she returned sharply.

He acknowledged her remark with a serious nod but didn't break his gaze.

"What time are our reservations?" she asked nervously.

He finally looked at his watch. "We have some time. Shall we find a place and go for an *aperitivo*?"

Ellie nodded happily. She had loved going out for an *aperitivo* when she lived in Italy. The Italian version of a happy hour was fun for college students. They sought out the more elaborate ones and often used it as dinner, with their companions who were struggling financially.

They sat down at a table outside of a café on a side street, and Lucca murmured to the waiter in Italian, who promptly scurried away.

"I told him we were here for *aperitivo* and asked for a wine list unless you'd like a cocktail," Lucca told her.

Ellie shook her head, but bit her lip. She had never told Lucca that she spoke fluent Italian. "Lucca..."

They were interrupted by the waiter coming back with menus and wine glasses and a wide array of snacks. After consulting with her, Lucca ordered a bottle of wine, and they munched on homemade potato chips and cheese and crackers.

"I used to dream about these potato chips when I was in America," said Ellie. "I don't know if there is a giant potato chip factory in Italy or what, but they are served at so many places."

He nodded. "I know what you mean. And these little crackers." He held up a small round cracker that looked almost like a tiny donut. "Someone makes these, too."

She laughed. "They are called *Taralli Pugliese*. I love them."

They talked more about the cathedral as they sipped their wine. She glanced around the street. People walked by without even giving him a glance.

"Lucca, why do you think you don't get recognized here?" she asked suddenly.

He shrugged. "I'm not sure. I think people expect me to be in some sort of costume or something. Maybe it's this lush beard," he stroked his face with a laugh. I'm usually clean-shaven for movies."

She looked at his piercing blue eyes. "But your eyes," she said softly.

He looked startled. "What about them?"

"Oh, I just mean they are pretty distinct," she stammered.

"A lot of people have blue eyes. My mother's are the same shade," he said nonchalantly, obviously not wanting the attention.

"Well, yes, but not that particular shade."

He shrugged. "I don't know. They just allow me to see, thank goodness." He glanced at his watch now. "I am a boring topic. Let's go to the restaurant so I can see what you were raving about."

She smiled. "I can't wait."

LUCCA LOOKED over the menu on the pretense of caring what he ate. He had no appetite at all, and it wasn't because of the *aperitivo*. He realized with a sinking heart he was falling harder for Ellie, even after he had warned himself not to. They had such a great day together. He had relaxed completely. He couldn't imagine a more perfect day and yet, he could tell she held herself in check. She wasn't going to let herself feel anything for him.

They were sitting outside at what she said was her favorite restaurant. He had conceded they could go there, even though he was the victor. He didn't know any restaurants in Siena anyway.

He had purposely ensured with a discreet large amount of cash to the hostess that they were shown to a table outside in the corner. He had been so happy no one had approached him today. He didn't want to admit to Ellie he had seen his security reach out a couple times to an incoming fan. He was hopeful they hadn't been rude, but he was relieved they had stopped them. He just wanted this time to be a regular guy on a date with his girl. His girl. That gave him pause. He realized that's what he wanted all along, looking at Ellie in the evening light, a candle flickering over her face. Her dark lashes covered her eyes as she looked at the menu, and she was making the face she always made while concentrating. He had seen that look while she decorated the wedding cake.

He took a sip of the white wine he had ordered, enjoying the view. "I should translate the menu for you," he offered.

"Lucca..."

"Ellie!" Suddenly a man was swooping in, grabbing Ellie out of her chair and clutching her in an embrace, pulling back to kiss her on each cheek before wrapping her back up in a bear hug.

Lucca saw his security detail move quickly, but he held up his hand and waved them off. Ellie was laughing. They quietly retreated, but he could tell they were on high alert. He watched Ellie finally untangle herself from the man's embrace. He was talking to her in rapid Italian, excitedly waving his hands, stopping every so often to hug her again.

She looked nervously at Lucca before answering him in perfect Italian. Lucca's eyes widened listening to their conversation. She was telling him about coming back to the area and that it was only temporary while she painted. They seemed to be catching up on their lives. He finally heard his name, and that snapped him back to the conversation. He held his hand out to the man at Ellie's introduction.

"Lucca, Tomas, our chef for the evening."

The man seemed to size him up, but then his face lit up and he gave Lucca an enthusiastic hug. "It's an honor to meet you and cook for you."

He turned to Ellie once more, asking her several more questions. Just by listening, Lucca was learning more about her time in L.A. and her desire to regain her artistry while in Tuscany. She was talking with him effortlessly, and Lucca realized with a sinking heart that he wasn't on that level with her. He knew she kept him at a distance, but now it was hitting him smack in the face.

Tomas backed away with the excuse he was needed in the kitchen. He swept up their menus, telling them they were not needed. He would simply cook for them. He bowed slightly and skirted the tables to get back to the kitchen.

They sat back down, and Ellie began twirling her wine glass around, avoiding his eyes. Now that the menu was gone, she couldn't hide behind it. She looked up, a guilty look on her face.

"Please don't look at me that way, Lucca," she said quietly.

He tried to steel his face into an impassive expression. He was an actor, after all. He was finding it difficult, though. He knew he probably looked angry—hell, he was feeling so jealous of Tomas right now he couldn't think straight. He tried the innocent approach. "Look at you how?"

She made a face. "You look like you want to either wring my neck or pull a stunt knife on me again." She smiled weakly. "I should have told you I speak Italian. I knew we'd probably run into Tomas, but I didn't think it through."

His eyes widened. She thought that's why he was so angry!

He wanted to slap his forehead with his stupidity. Obviously, if she had studied in the region for some time, he should have realized that she would have learned to speak the language at least a little. From what he'd heard, she was fluent, though.

"Ellie..."

"No, let me talk. I should have told you. I'm sorry. I was embarrassed because I figured you didn't want me to know what you said—you know, the night of the wedding." She looked at him now, color rising in her cheeks.

He stared at her, completely confused. Then he felt a rushing in his ears as his mind began piecing it all together. The night in the gazebo. What had he even said? He remembered being so caught up in the moment, feeling so many emotions and telling her how much he wanted to be with her. He felt a pit in his stomach. She clearly remembered. Telling her he was swept up in the moment would make it sound like he didn't mean it, but he knew deep down he had meant every word he had said. He just hadn't wanted to acknowledge it.

"So that's why you left," he stated, looking directly into her eyes.

She looked away but nodded.

He decided this was a good time for deflection. "Ellie, I don't know about you, but I had a really good time today. And with the exception of the chef coming out and putting his hands all over you, I'm having a good time tonight. What do you say if we just file that away for now? It's a topic for another day. Let's just continue to have fun."

She looked at him seriously. "I had a good time today, too, Lucca." She paused. "But just one thing—Tomas and his wife," she added succinctly, "are old friends. I helped them out from time to time with their *children*."

Lucca grinned. "Well, that's excellent news."

He lifted his glass. "To new beginnings."

She gave him a reluctant smile, raising her own glass and clinking it with his. "To new beginnings...again."

They both sipped their wine for a minute.

He couldn't resist. "Any other languages you speak that you want to tell me about?"

She smiled. "French."

"I'll remember that."

~

ELLIE LEANED back in her chair, putting her spoon down in her bowl with a clank. "Oh my God, I'm so full." She put her hand on her stomach. "I don't think I've eaten this much since the last time I was here."

Lucca agreed. "Your friend Tomas is an amazing chef."

They had dined on fresh burrata with olive oil and crusty bread, pici with truffles, and grilled pork with a vegetable tart. They had waved off the more sophisticated deserts and settled on a flight of gelato—tasting each flavor, giving a detailed critique of them.

"Even though I'm full, that gelato went down pretty easily," Lucca admitted.

"Tomas has worked really hard to build the restaurant up. I wonder where Elisabetta is. She usually is here for a while in the evening."

"Who helps with the kids now that you're not here?"

Ellie smiled. "Probably his mother-in-law. She is quite the character. But here he is, so let's ask him."

Tomas drew up a chair now that the dinner service had died down. He had brought a glass of chianti, and they toasted him, praising him lavishly for the amazing meal. He acknowledged their kind words with a simple nod, but it obviously pleased him very much.

He sipped his wine, answering Ellie's questions. Elisabetta

had a bad cold and was home, he explained. He looked sad for a moment. He pointed to the banner hanging on a nearby building.

"Tomorrow is Il Palio, and we will be unable to attend. I think it's the first one we've missed since our daughter was born," he said.

"Lucca and I were talking about that earlier. I've never been," Ellie said with a smile.

Tomas shook his head laughing. "It is a war. A true battle," he explained, glancing at Lucca. "One that must have a *capitano*—a captain. My madre in law is a *capitano*, and she is one of only a dozen women in its history. It's a big honor. She hires the jockey, decides how much to pay him and many more duties—whatever it takes to win—some of which we don't talk about because they concern a little corruption if you understand," he said with amusement.

"Ellie said there are many *contradas*. Do all of them race?" Lucca asked.

"There's seventeen, but just ten participate in the race. They rotate," answered Tomas. "It is from the medieval times where a *contrada* related to their professions such as tailors, butchers, and other things. They use to fight for the territory, for the size of their territory. No matter what, it is a battle."

Lucca's eyebrows raised. "What do they win?"

"The *Drappellone*," responded Tomas matter-of-factly.

At Lucca's confused look, Ellie laughed. "It's a banner of painted silk. An artist paints one each year. It's a huge process for the selected artist. There's all kinds of requirements about what has to be included on it—such as religious symbols— because of its historical significance. I learned all about it when I was here."

"What is your *contrada's* symbol?" Lucca asked Tomas.

"We are the panther. We have won many times but we must beat the eagle. It is a huge rivalry."

Tomas looked at them, suddenly excited. "Why don't you two go in our place? Our mamma would love it! To think that she could watch it with Lucca Delarosa. She would be bragging for months."

Ellie looked uneasy. "Tomas, thank you so much. But Lucca isn't really into the crowds and the fame. Too many people might recognize him, and that could be a nightmare in that crush."

"But you've always wanted to go, Ellie. You told me so! This is your chance. You don't have to be in the big crowd—we watch from a private balcony—it shouldn't be too difficult for you."

Lucca frowned at Ellie, raising his eyebrows as if asking her what the problem was. "Ellie, we can go. I think it sounds fun. I've never been. I can wear a baseball cap and sunglasses. I'll blend in!"

Ellie frowned at him. Did he really think he could ever blend in? She couldn't imagine it.

Lucca still staring at her, his face determined. "If you don't want to go, then we won't. But don't say no because of me."

She glanced back at the security detail. "Let's just check with Mike. If he's okay with it, then we'll go."

Lucca's big grin was the only answer she needed.

eighteen

Ellie walked down the street, holding Lucca's hand tightly. If she lost him in this crowd, she would never find him. He had been right, though. There were so many people, no one was really looking at them. She had dressed casually, wearing white jean shorts and a simple navy top. Lucca was in a pair of gray shorts and a black short-sleeved shirt that said *Italia* on it. He had smirked at her—telling her his plan was to look like a tourist. Ellie told him with his baseball cap on he looked like a college kid *and* a tourist.

Tomas had given them instructions the night before on which shop to go to outside the Piazza del Campo. The balcony of the shop overlooked the Piazza, where the race was run.

"I think this is it," Lucca said, stopping suddenly. They approached the doorway, and it was whisked open for them and abruptly shut and locked just as fast.

"Ellie!" An older woman with curly bright red hair—definitely not a shade in nature—grabbed Ellie, almost picking her up. Ellie laughed, hugging her.

"Vittoria! So good to see you! This is Lucca..."

"I know who he is. Come here!" Vittoria kissed him soundly.

Lucca's eyes widened in alarm, but Ellie smirked. She had warned him.

Vittoria went on an extended monologue of Lucca's movie titles. It seemed important to her that he know how big of a fan she was. He smiled kindly. Finally, he gently nudged her about the race.

"I am so happy you are here for the win!" she stated confidently. Pointing to herself, she smiled. "Vittoria means victory. How can we lose?" she asked with a shrug. She then urged them to continue walking through the wine shop and out to the balcony.

Ellie's eyes widened, looking at the massive crowd in the piazza. "Wow. I always imagined this, but I can't believe it. There's a sea of people."

Lucca laughed and told her he heard it was called "the pit" during the race. "Thank God we aren't down there."

Vittoria nodded. "People start coming in the morning, and they keep coming. It's a crush. And emotions run high. You would not want to be there."

"Thank you so much for having us," Ellie turned, smiling at her. "I can't wait to watch."

Vittoria fussed around them, pouring a glass of wine. "We will relax for a while. It will not start for some time." She left to go let in some other friends, who crowded out to the balcony. Vittoria brought out cheese, meats, crackers, and olives. The wine kept coming—she was the ultimate hostess. While everyone shook hands and kissed cheeks, no one seemingly cared who Lucca was.

Ellie smiled, waiting for the event to start. Vittoria brought out handkerchiefs that held the coat of arms and colors of their *contrada*. She explained the *fazzoletto* was to be worn around their neck. Ellie tied hers loosely around her shoulders, but then tied Lucca's. He frowned and told Ellie he probably looked ridiculous. She gave him a big smile, agreeing.

They heard excitement buzzing through the crowd, and Vittoria explained the pageant was about to start. They watched the flag throwers, drummers, and people in medieval costumes with amusement, but Lucca was more interested in watching Ellie's face. Her eyes were huge, and she was clapping and screaming with the rest of the crowd, watching people on horseback wielding swords. They were galloping around the track, stirring up excitement. Ellie was yelling, urging them on. He smiled, watching her animated face. He felt like he could watch that all day. He didn't need to be at *Il Palio* for excitement.

Ellie was taking as many photos as possible. It was unfortunate that one of the guests rushed forward to take some photos as well and bumped into Ellie. They both watched in horror as her phone flew in slow motion out of her hands, off the balcony, landing on the ground.

"My phone!" Ellie yelled.

Lucca looked down, seeing it lying on the sand. He guessed it was badly damaged but wanted to get it for her. "I can run and get it."

The words were hardly out of his mouth when they watched in horror as the crowd stepped over it and it became lost in the sea of people.

Ellie turned wide eyes to him, and then she did something remarkable. She burst out laughing. He was forced to laugh with her. She was so amazing. He thought of the many women who would let something material like that ruin the day.

"It's just a phone," she said and shrugged. "Everything will be backed up. Give me yours so I can take photos."

He shook his head. "I think not, butter fingers. I'll take the photos."

She frowned but let him have his way, frequently pointing out things for him to take a photo of.

Soon it was time for the race, and they all jumped as the explosion to start echoed through the piazza. They screamed with the rest of the crowd as they watched the jockeys riding the horses bareback. They whipped around the piazza three times. The horse representing the panther was second, nose to nose with another horse. They had learned the real loser in the race was the horse that came in second, not last. Ellie turned to Lucca, her eyes concerned. They were nearly on the final lap. He joined her in screaming support after glancing over at Vittoria, whose hands were clasped over her mouth, her eyes worried. The horse must have heard them, or divine intervention kicked in because suddenly in the last several yards, the panther moved quickly and crossed the finish line first!

"We won!" Ellie turned to Lucca, throwing her arms around him. He laughed, lifting her up and twirling her around, as much as he could in their confined space. The crowd was roaring, and the sound was deafening. He set her down on her feet but stood smiling down at her. It was Ellie that leaned up and kissed him, and he took it. The kiss went on and on. He slid his arms around her and held her tight. He forgot where he was for a minute. A tap on his shoulder brought him down to earth.

Vittoria was jumping up and down. "I'm next!"

He threw his head back and laughed but gave her a smack and twirled her around for good measure.

ELLIE WAS ENJOYING DRINKING prosecco and celebrating with the group. Pandemonium was breaking out in the crowd. Thank God they were still up in the balcony. She was glad Lucca kept an arm casually around her—it gave her a feeling of safety. It was fun to celebrate with the others, and she was so happy for Vittoria. Everyone was talking about marching through the streets together to their district.

She looked up at Lucca's face. He looked apprehensive. She sensed he didn't want to disappoint her but was also thinking about the crowds. She leaned up to whisper in his ear, and he bent his head down toward her. "It's okay. We've been to the race. We don't have to march in the streets." She took the opportunity to take a deep breath. She was so close to him. She wanted to reach up and kiss him again.

He turned his head, his eyes searching hers. "Are you sure? It's been the most spectacular day."

She smiled. "It has. But I've heard before it can get—well, *emotional* out there. We can't have that famous face of yours marred or anything." She laughed, trying to make light of it all.

He smirked. "Oh yes, the moneymaker." He continued to assess her now more seriously. "Okay, let's stay here for a little bit, and then we'll work our way opposite of the crowd. Maybe take a drive. Go somewhere outside Siena for a late dinner?"

She smiled. "I'd like that."

They looked at each other for a second, before one of the guests came to interrupt to ask if they were going to follow them outside. The spell broken, they both shook their heads and watched them leave. They turned to survey the now thinning crowd. They walked slowly back the way they came through the shop, thanking Vittoria, who was locking up to go join the *contrada's* march.

Lucca's security detail was waiting right outside, and he spoke quietly with them about the plan. There still was a large amount of people in the streets. They had to stop several times, their backs up against store fronts to let the crowds go by.

"Maybe this wasn't such a good idea," Lucca said in her ear. "I feel like we're going upstream."

She looked around. There was no end in sight to all the people. "What if we go with the crowd for a few blocks and then cut through one of the side streets and back track? It might be easier."

He nodded and jerked his head toward the security detail, who were staying close. They turned around and joined the throngs of people as they were marching and chanting through the streets. The crowd seemed to envelop them, and Ellie was glad Lucca kept a tight grip on her hand. Occasionally, they would hear shouting and start to see a fight break out. Lucca looked stern as he shouldered through the mass of people.

Ellie glanced behind her. "I think we lost the security," she shouted. Lucca turned to look, but the crowd was pushing.

"They'll just have to meet us at the car," he shouted back. The crowd continued pushing, and finally they made it toward a side street that would take them away from the march. They paused for a minute to let people pass so they could duck into the narrow street.

"Wait!" Lucca shouted. He was looking up at a balcony. Two children—a boy and a girl—both very young—were on the balcony by themselves. They were standing on planters, hanging over the rails, transfixed by the crowd.

"I don't see an adult up there." Lucca looked at Ellie, his eyes concerned.

They watched both kids leaning further over the balcony. "Stay here," he shouted. "Right here, Ellie. Don't move. I'll be back."

With that, he waded into the mob, with Ellie shouting after him to be careful. She watched as he muscled his way through people in a straight line toward the balcony. She held her breath. The children leaned over farther. They were waving and laughing, trying to get the attention of the flag-bearing crowd. The boy was now climbing up higher, dipping lower over the rail.

"*Aiuto*! Help!" Ellie began screaming. People around her looked at her, but continued marching. She pointed to the balcony, screaming for help. It was drowned out. She started making her way through the march. She couldn't watch this! She had to get below the balcony just in case. Just as she was getting closer, she glanced over to see Lucca catching the boy as he toppled over the balcony. The little girl shrunk back down, her eyes wide. People began screaming, and several people stopped to help.

Two police officers emerged from somewhere and grabbed Lucca and the boy, taking them inside the building. Ellie tried to follow, but she couldn't get there. She was pushed forward several yards before she could stop and wait. Finally, she saw an opening and was able to double back and duck into the building. She figured Lucca had gone upstairs with the police, so she waited where she was.

After several minutes, Lucca descended the stairs with a police officer who was patting him on the back. Lucca stopped to shake hands with the man, his face grim.

"Ellie, thank God. We were coming back to find you. Are you okay?"

"Of course. Is the little boy alright?"

"Yes, perfect. I was right. There is no adult in the apartment." He looked concerned. "Do you mind if we wait for a little bit? I just want to know they are okay."

Ellie agreed and they stood there for a few more minutes before seeing a woman with a baby, pushing through the crowd, looking very upset. The police officer stopped her to talk with her, and Ellie and Lucca leaned in to hear the conversation. Yes, they were her children. She had run out of diapers and had to go to a pharmacy, leaving the children inside. She thought they couldn't unlock the door to the balcony. It was her brother's apartment, and she was just staying there temporarily while she got on her feet after her husband's recent death. She didn't mean to be gone so long, but there were so many people in the streets. She was openly crying now.

Lucca moved away from Ellie, telling her he would be right back. He touched the woman's shoulder and walked several yards away with her, his face close to hers, talking quietly. He ushered her inside and was gone several minutes before emerging. The other police officers had also exited, talking enthusiastically, and Lucca kindly took a selfie with them all.

He grabbed her hand. "Come on, let's try this again." As they got to a quieter street, they were able to relax a bit and stroll. Ellie stopped, her hand still in his. She looked at him seriously. "What did you say to her?"

He shrugged. "I just told her that life had not been fair to her, and she was doing her best."

She looked at him suspiciously. "You gave her money, didn't you?"

He stared at her. "Ellie, you need to mind your own business."

She laughed. "Well, sorry, but remember, I was right there, so it *is* my business. You gave her money, didn't you? It's tough to have to think about money when you're grieving, but she obviously needed it."

He smiled sadly. "It's just a small gesture. Anyone can do that. It hardly fixes everything for her." He looked at her steadily. "If you must know, I also gave her a card. I'll have someone find her a job if that's what she needs or childcare."

Ellie smiled gently at him. "It won't bring her husband back, but I'm sure that will help. And not everyone would do that."

He shrugged, and she gave him a nudge with her shoulder. "You're a nice guy, Lucca Delarosa." They stared at each other in the dim light of a lamppost. He looked embarrassed. "Let's get to the car," he finally said roughly.

When they finally made it back to the parking lot, the security detail was there, looking harassed. "Thank God! We were worried we were going to have to call Mike," one of them said.

"Not this time, fellas. But listen…" Lucca approached them and spoke quietly. They looked at him apprehensively and then at Ellie. Lucca was continuing to talk to them, and they finally nodded, getting into their car.

Lucca approached his car, grinning at Ellie.

She looked at him curiously. "What did you tell them?"

He shrugged. "I told them to go home. I told them I was taking my girl out for a late snack, and we'd get home before curfew."

Ellie raised her eyebrows. She wasn't sure what she should address first—the "my girl" or the curfew.

"Not a word, Ellie. Just get in the car," he said softly, opening the door. He walked around and got in, starting the powerful engine. They began to drive out of Siena into the hills before pulling into a small restaurant near the town of Greve.

There was nothing but silence when he parked the car. "There's so many stars tonight," she said, looking at the inky sky with its glittering stars.

He gave her a funny look.

She laughed. "I mean the ones up there, by the way—not next to me."

He made a small face at her. "Let's find the brightest one tonight."

Something changed after *Il Palio,* and Ellie couldn't put her finger on it. Sure, they had both enjoyed it and the event had been crazy, wild and fun, all wrapped into one. Her heart felt lighter, and she wasn't sure why. Maybe she had thrust caution to the wind when she had thrown her arms around Lucca. They had driven through the hills of Tuscany, enjoying the serenity after the crowds of the race and celebration. It had felt wonderful to breathe and relax. They had been content to be silent, listening to soft music.

The restaurant Lucca took her to was run by a family, its warmth and charm evident. The owner had greeted Lucca like a long-lost relative and promised them a wonderful dinner, which he delivered, small plate after small plate. Ellie and Lucca had talked quietly over candlelight and laughed about the day. When they had finally left and pulled in front of the villa, Lucca shut off the car and turned to look at Ellie. She stared back at him, and they had both moved together. They had kissed for a long time until finally Lucca told her hoarsely to go inside, and he would put the car away. She had looked inquiringly at him, but he almost shoved her out of the car. She heard the car roar to life and quietly went to bed. Certainly, their night of kissing had helped dispel any notion in her head that he was no longer interested.

She sat before her canvas now, painting with an ease she hadn't felt for some time. For the last two days, she had been almost locked up, painting scenes of Siena and the countryside around it. Every so often, she picked up the one she had started of Lucca. It needed work, but for now, she quickly stashed it out of sight.

While she felt her old artistic self coming alive, she still didn't feel any of the paintings were worthy of hanging in Bruno's villa. She tried not to think about it. Lucca had been right when he told her to just paint what she felt and not think so hard. She had just painted for hours, letting it flow.

Her earbuds in, she swayed with the music as she continued painting the Tuscan fields she loved. She felt a slight swish on her back. Swiping it away, she assumed it was fly. But it came back—light as a feather on her shoulder. She thrust at it again. This time, it tapped. She turned abruptly to see Lucca standing in the doorway holding a long mop handle with a what looked like a rag cut up into strips at the end. He grinned at her, looking innocent.

She took her earbuds out. "What the heck, Lucca?"

"I didn't want to get too close in case you took a swing." He pointedly touched his face.

Ellie tried to keep serious. "What is that?"

"It's a flirty pole."

"Excuse me?" She looked at him, confused. "You're flirting with me?"

He laughed. "Now that's a loaded question! I promise to show you later what it does. So how's it going?"

She smiled. "Actually, not bad. I took your advice."

He raised his eyebrows. "No, seriously? Let's mark this day on the calendar! That anyone—anyone—took my advice."

She laughed. "Lucca, you don't give yourself enough credit. You are a great listener, and I think you probably give out a lot of good advice."

"No one"—he enunciated the words—"comes to me for advice."

She looked at him thoughtfully. "I don't think that's true. I'd come to you for advice."

He stared at her for a minute. "That may be the nicest thing you've ever said to me, Ellie James."

She frowned at the use of her name. It had been weighing on her for the last several days.

"Lucca…"

"Okay, I know. I'm sorry. I shouldn't have bothered you. I truly have tried not to come in here. I know you need to focus. So that's why I'm no farther than the doorway. And I didn't even want to interrupt you in case it was really flowing. It's just that it's afternoon, and I was going to see if you wanted something to eat.

Ellie looked at her watch then. "Wow, I really have been up here a long time." Her stomach grumbled. "And I'm starving!"

She stretched. "I could definitely eat. And honestly, it's okay. I think I'm done for the day. Sometimes I have to make myself stop, or else I'm tapped out creatively but don't realize it. And the next day I come in and the colors are all muddled."

He grinned. "Are you sure?"

She nodded, rubbing her neck. "Yes. I had a teacher who once told me you always need a reason to touch your canvas— whatever it is—fixing an edge, adjusting a value, changing a color or correcting a hue." She looked back at the canvas. "I'm definitely finished for today. Have you eaten?"

"No, and I have a great idea," he said with an even wider grin.

∾

"THIS REALLY *WAS* A GOOD IDEA," Ellie said, leaning back on her elbows on the blanket. After changing into a casual sundress, they had thrown together an eclectic picnic of sorts. Lucca had kept some of the local chefs busy. Ellie had remarked every time she opened the refrigerator, she found more and more food. He protested that he needed it for the security team, even as Mike had scaled back. They had chosen an assortment of salads, Italian meats and cheeses, and, of course, some crusty Italian bread for their picnic. Lucca had been excited to discover some fried eggplant and threw that in, as well as some fruit and cookies.

Ellie balanced her stemless wine glass on the grass next to her, taking in the view below. "I could look at this forever," she said with a sigh.

"Remember it and paint it later," he said, giving her a lazy smile. He stared at her for a minute, before leaning over and giving her a lingering kiss. What he intended on being a small kiss was now turning into something more as she put her hand on his neck and drew him down. He continued kissing her now, using every bit of knowledge he had in this area to ensure she knew how much he loved kissing her. He finally drew back and looked at her intently. He could still see some wariness, despite how far they had come. He forced himself to stop and laid down next to her, grabbing her hand.

"Ellie…"

"Shhh," she said. "Don't say it, Lucca. Don't say anything. It's a perfect day. Let's just lie here and enjoy Tuscany."

He got up on one elbow to look at her. Her eyes were closed, her mouth in a small smile.

"Ellie…"

"You talk too much, Lucca."

He frowned at her. They needed to lay their cards on the table and figure out where this was going. He had thrust her out of the car last night, as things were getting too heated. They shouldn't move forward until they figured out what this was between them. He needed to talk to her about his plans and figure out how long she intended on staying in Italy.

They had to talk about the future, but he knew if he even brought it up, she would wave him off. He wasn't sure what a future meant with her. They had to spend more time together to even see what this was. Meanwhile, she wasn't into the L.A. scene, but he wasn't sure where she wanted to live. On the other hand, he could live anywhere, and he was at a point in his career where he could work as little or as much as he wanted.

He hadn't even told her that he had a movie to film soon. He had long committed to it and couldn't back out now. The director/writer was a long-time friend. Lucca was playing a psychologist in the movie, and it was a much more serious role than he was used to. He was actually looking forward to it as it would allow him to stretch himself artistically—something he hadn't done in a very long time.

"What are you thinking about?" She was still lying down with her eyes shut. "I can feel your thoughts almost like picnic ants marching across the blanket," she said and smiled.

He smiled gently at her. "I thought you didn't want me to talk."

"I didn't, but now I realize you need to. I'm listening," she said, still not moving.

He laid down now, looking at the sky. "I think I'm have an artistic crisis of my own."

"Crisis, huh? Do tell."

"Well, it probably will sound so ridiculous to you, but I'm just not feeling the acting thing right now. I've been feeling like this for a while—going through the motions."

"But you were so amazing in *Heroes at Dawn*."

He laughed. "What's funny about that is I didn't feel like that was my best work. It felt so weird to even be at the Oscars."

She opened her eyes now, turning on her elbow, lying on her

side toward him. She had a glint in her eye. "But you didn't give it back."

He grinned, still staring up at the sky. "Well, no, I'm not stupid. But it still felt weird."

"Well, what would you like to do instead?"

"Produce, direct—something behind the camera. It's what I've always wanted to do."

Her eyes widened. "Really? Why didn't you?"

He turned now on his side to face her. He wanted her to see he was serious. "You promise not to laugh?"

She nodded, her eyes sincere.

"No one took me seriously. I joke about my looks, but it's what got me into acting, and it's what has made me stay. Those with power want me in front of the camera. I'd much rather be behind it."

"Lucca, you're more than just looks. You have to know that. You are very talented. I know talent when I see it."

He raised his eyebrows. Did she know people in the industry? What was she referring to? Before he could ask, she continued. "Maybe that was what you had to do to break into Hollywood, and maybe that's what you've had to do to stay on top. We both know you can call the shots now."

He looked away from her gaze. She seemed to be eying him very intently. He sat up to avoid her stare.

"Do you want my opinion?"

He nodded, still not looking at her.

"I think it's probably scary to do something you've never done. Look, acting is known to you. You haven't had to stretch yourself that much. Maybe take on a role that really taxes you. But also start thinking about what you want to do behind the camera."

He finally turned to meet her gaze. "What if I fail?"

She smiled. "I'm not going to lie to you. The industry is

brutal. But you have to try. I think you'll be upset with yourself if you don't."

"Ellie, I'm not saying this to brag. But I have a lot of money— I've earned millions over the years. My last movie netted me a fortune. And I have even more money if you count my shares in Oro Industries."

She frowned. "Why are you telling me this? What does money have to do with it?"

"Just that I don't need to do anything. I could buy a villa here in Tuscany and just retire forever. Sometimes I wonder if I'm just feeding my ego."

She laughed. "Retire? And then what? Go on picnics every day? You would be sooooo bored."

She sat up and touched his arm. "I don't think it's feeding your ego to find something that fulfills you creatively. And you would never know, would you?" she asked softly.

She was staring at him. Her face was so lovely and sincere he couldn't resist. He reached over and kissed her now, hoping that his feelings were coming through in his kiss. He wanted to show her how much she meant to him already. He had never confided any of his professional desires to anyone but Marco. Even then, he had hedged a little bit.

She was kissing him back, and together they sank back on the blanket. He took his time, kissing her lips, tasting her sweetness, running his lips down her jaw to her ear. His hands were traveling down her sides to her hips. He heard a soft moan escape her, and he smiled. He finally pulled away. He had to stop before this got completely out of control. He gently ran his hand over her hair, tucking it behind an ear.

He gave her a little smile. "Thank you."

He didn't explain for what, but she seemed to sense his relief at talking to someone. She abruptly stood and he realized maybe he had taken things to far. But she smiled at him. "Come on, Hollywood. Too much talking. Let's go back to the villa."

twenty

Ellie hummed to the song coming through her ear buds as she cleaned her brushes with solvent. She finished painting for the day early and was going to go see if Lucca was ready to go on an adventure. They had fallen into a pattern of her painting from sunrise until around noon. Somedays she lugged her easel and palette box out to a hillside and other days she holed up in her studio. When she finished, she would seek him out and they would do something together. Yesterday had been a short bike ride, and then they had gone for a drive, looking at the exterior of a few nearby villas. Lucca had confessed to her he really wanted to buy something of his own in the area no matter what his future held. A real estate agent had sent him a list of properties for sale. None really excited him, but it was fun to drive around and at least take a peek. She didn't care if they were looking at shacks and had to admit that every day, she was enjoying his company more. He was so easy to talk to. They still sparred over stuff, but overall, she was discovering they had the same interests in books, music, and even movies.

At night, they either raided the refrigerator or cooked something together. Last night, she had wowed him with her special salmon recipe, and he promised to make her a steak tonight. They had stayed up late watching a movie they both had wanted to see. She had purposely exaggerated her admiration for the male lead until Lucca had grabbed the remote, hit pause and turned to her with his eyebrows raised and a ferocious look on his face. She couldn't hold it in—grabbing a pillow, she laughed into it. He seized another pillow and swatted her with it, saying a few chosen words in Italian.

They usually ended the night on the patio, sipping wine and gazing at the stars. It was her favorite time of day. It was when she could pretend this was their world. She didn't want to stop and think about any of it. She was trying to go with the flow for the first time, just like her artwork. She found her painting improving almost to the point of confidence.

"Hey, Ellie?"

Ellie jumped and turned around. "Mike! Don't sneak up on me!"

He was leaning on the doorframe just as Lucca had done the day before. "Sorry, kiddo. I just came up here because I wanted to tell you that I'm sending most of my team home. I will keep a small footprint here until I know what Lucca wants us to do."

She smiled. "I'm so glad, Mike. I trust you, and I'm sure you wouldn't do that if you sensed any issues."

He continued eying her seriously.

Ellie looked at him thoughtfully. "So why exactly are you telling me?"

He looked nervous—she wasn't sure she'd ever seen him like this. He was staring at his feet now as if his shoes were of deep interest. "Well, uh..."

"Mike, spit it out. What's the matter?"

He looked at her now, his eyes almost regretful. "You can move back to the guesthouse now, if you want."

She felt the color rising in her face. "Oh right. Of course." She turned around, pretending to tend to her brushes. "Thanks for telling me. I'll do that."

"Ellie, he's a nice guy. I've seen the way he looks at you. He's the real deal."

She turned back around and looked at him, swallowing the lump she felt rising in her throat. Mike strode toward her and put his arms around her. He felt so good and so comforting. Suddenly, she was back being the fifteen-year-old awkward kid whose face was splashed all over the tabloids kissing a boy—a boy she later found out had only bet his friends he could get her to kiss him. She still felt the mortification of it all.

She drew back to look at him. "I don't know, Mike. He's told me how he'll never commit to anyone. And would I even want one? It's all so scary."

He nodded and wrapped his big arms around her again. "I know, honey. I know."

He gave her one last squeeze and promised to send some guys up to move her canvases, paints and equipment back to the guesthouse. She went to her room, washed her face, and sat on the bed for a few minutes. She should go find Lucca—he was probably waiting for her. Ellie had promised they could go explore another town in Tuscany. It had sounded so fun yesterday. She squared her shoulders. This was ridiculous and nothing had changed. She was in her head too much. Before she could think anymore, she got up and put some make-up on, and brushed her long hair, keeping it straight and hanging down her back. Purposely donning the sundress she had worn the first night with Lucca's family felt good, as he said he liked it. After putting some tennis shoes on, she ran down the stairs. Lucca was just coming in the door with Sophia. He was holding the stick from yesterday. "Ellie, you look nice."

She grinned at him. "Why, thank you, sir. Are you still up for some exploring?"

He nodded, still staring at her.

She bent down now to pet Sophia, who was lying at her feet. "She's not jumping on me anymore!"

He smiled smugly. "I know. We've been working on that."

She looked over at the stick that Lucca had tossed. "You never showed me what you're doing with that."

He laughed. "I'll show you when we get back. Let me go change and get pretty like you. I'll be right back."

She gave him a small smile, watching him run up the stairs. "But the thing is, you're almost prettier than me," she muttered.

She sat down on the bottom step now and petted Sophia. Sophia rolled over for a tummy scratch, making Ellie laugh. She wondered what Lucca was going to do with Sophia—she really was the sweetest dog. Originally, he talked about her being temporary, but now she could tell he was attached. He had to keep her.

Ellie reached into her pocket for her phone to take a photo of Sophia and almost laughed at herself. Of course, she didn't have her phone. She probably missed some calls from friends or even her parents. She had borrowed Lucca's phone to text Brigid, who she knew would be trying to get a hold of her. She stopped short of texting her parents on Lucca's phone, but realized she should replace hers soon. If she took the day off tomorrow, she could go to Florence. Would Lucca want to go with her?

"I'm ready!"

She turned around to see him running down the stairs. He wore khaki pants and an untucked white shirt. He looked casual, yet sophisticated somehow. His hair was freshly combed and a little wet.

"Did you take a shower?"

"Yeah, why?"

"You were gone like five minutes!"

He shrugged. "Sorry, I said I would be quick."

She shook her head. Five minutes, and he came out looking so startlingly handsome.

He was staring at her. "What's the matter?"

She grinned. "Nothing, nothing. Where are we going?"

He smirked. "One of my favorite towns."

WHEN THEY PULLED into the town of Lucca, Ellie rolled her eyes, but then giggled. She had seen it on the map near Pisa but had never been.

"Look, they named a town after me!" he said, giving her a quick smile.

She made a face at him, pointing to the medieval walls. "I think the town was here a little before you."

"Yeah, okay, but it was one of the inspirations for my parents when they named me."

He pulled into a parking space and came over to her side of the car to grab her hand. They walked slowly through the town, which was soaking in history. Once again, she found herself pointing out the art, even the natural art, all around them. Lucca indulgently smiled, pulling her along the cobblestones. At his persuasion, she agreed to climb the Torre Guinigi, a 14th century tower. They admired the small garden at the top, and then strolled around, taking in the surrounding mountains and the view of the city. He leaned over and gave her a quick kiss, his eyes amused.

"What's that for?" she asked, giving him a shy smile.

He grinned. "Seemed like you ought to be kissing Lucca in Lucca."

"You're not letting this go, are you?"

"Do you like Lucca?" He eyed her mischievously.

"You are killing me," she grumbled, rolling her eyes again. She had to laugh despite it, grabbing his hand to descend the tower. They leisurely walked through the streets, poking through the little shops. They stopped at a street vendor, where he insisted on buying her a straw hat with a black ribbon. She smiled, thinking how many women all over Tuscany wore them. Still, this one was from Lucca. She put it on, and he stared at her intently. Finally, he leaned down to tap the brim and give her a quick kiss.

They finally settled on a restaurant for lunch where they dined outside, enjoying two different types of pizza and a salad. "The pizza wasn't as award-winning as yours," Ellie remarked with a smile. He flashed a grin at her.

Afterward, they sat in the piazza and ate gelato and watched people milling about. It was a casual, carefree day, and she was loving it.

Ellie was intrigued by how well Lucca blended in. Mike and another security officer had followed them at a distance. She forgot they were even there. Lucca had said Mike wasn't ready to relinquish his duties quite yet. The fact was, most celebrities of his caliber employed security all the time anyway. Lucca wasn't sure he could get used to it but had told her on the way how fond he was of Mike. She had agreed but bit her tongue. She wanted to tell him why she loved Mike, but that was a longer story. She would tell him tonight under the stars when they wouldn't be interrupted.

They talked about so many things. He told her more about his father and how much progress they had made getting to really know each other. He had shared how at first he had been angry and belligerent to his dad. It was only after Zia Rita had practically smacked him on the head and urged him to give his dad a chance that he actually had. They had stayed at the villa together, cooking and playing chess for days, Lucca told her. He had found the courage to finally confront his father about some of the things his mother had been told him over the years, only to find out most of it was untrue. His father sincerely admitted his mistakes, but also denied some of the bigger, more egregious tales, and Lucca believed him.

For the first time in a long time, Ellie felt blessed to have grown up with both her parents in a loving marriage. They were such an oddity in their world. Maybe that's why the press was so enthralled with them. Either way, they had been good parents. She felt a little guilty now, not communicating with them as much as she should. They only wanted the best for her and she vowed to do better.

Lucca pulled into the gates of the villa and traveled up the hill. He had been silent on the drive home. Possibly bringing up all the past was weighing on him. Ellie desperately wanted to lighten the mood. "Hey, I really like Lucca," she said, giving him a quick smile.

He reached over and squeezed her hand, but still seemed preoccupied. She decided to try a different tactic. "It's hot, Hollywood. Why don't we take a swim, and you can show me whatever you're doing with that pole? I'm hoping you're not beating Sophia with it!"

Lucca's serious face now looked amused. "That's a fantastic idea. I'll meet you at the pool in fifteen!"

Ellie ran up and changed into a bright pink bikini instead of the one-piece Lucca had seen her in. For some reason, this time, she wanted to distract him even further. She winced a little, tugging the bottoms down. Maybe this wasn't such a good idea. She rarely wore this one, feeling a little exposed. Before she could think too much, she threw her white cover-up on and ran down to meet him.

Sure enough, Lucca was already by the pool, taking his shirt off. Good God, the man was fine. He was wearing simple black swim trunks, but that body made her swallow hard. His muscles gleamed and his abdomen was toned. She knew he worked out every morning dutifully. She had even seen the workout room in the villa one day—carefully avoiding it. The last thing she needed was to be in that tight space watching Lucca sweat. Even now, she averted her eyes.

"What's the matter?"

She feigned innocence. "Oh nothing. I was just thinking we haven't used the pool enough. It's so wonderful out here."

"I agree. Today it's going to feel great after walking around in the heat. Come on!" With that, he dove in and began swimming laps.

She was relieved that he wasn't going to stare at her while she took her cover-up off. She unzipped it and tossed it and her flip flops on a lounge chair before using the stairs to climb into the pool. The refreshing water felt amazing. She stopped to tie her hair up in a high ponytail with the hair tie on her wrist. She began a steady crawl toward the edge where Lucca was waiting. She barely got to him when he pushed off. "Race you!"

"Lucca!" Instead of complaining, she took off after him. She was an excellent swimmer. She'd show him! Of course, this pool would be extra long and she was gasping for breath when she arrived at the side. He was already there, pretending to lounge in the sun.

She treaded water. "You're such a cheater."

"Am not!"

"You took off before you even told me it was a race."

He grinned. "Okay, catch your breath, and we'll try it again."

"I don't need to catch my breath."

He raised an eyebrow, and she laughed. "Fine, just a second."

He smirked, and she flung some water at him. That led to a splashing contest for the next several minutes.

"Stop! Lucca, stop!"

"You started it."

"Oh my God, what are you, five?" she accused giggling.

"I am not!"

"Yes, you are!"

They both were laughing. Ellie finally turned and thrust herself back toward the opposite side, and Lucca swam with her

—leisurely this time. After a few laps, they both stopped, breathing hard.

"I think I've had enough of you right now." She heaved herself onto the pool deck. Her hair tie had come loose, and she flung her wet hair behind her back.

He was staring at her.

She narrowed her eyes. "What?"

"Nothing."

"Okay what? You're staring."

He smiled. "You just take my breath away."

"You're nuts."

He shook his head. "I'm not."

He was staring at her so intently. She decided to change the subject. "So are you going to show me what the stick was for?"

He grinned. "Oh, yeah. Wait till you see this."

They walked over to the lawn, and Sophia, who had been dozing, got up excitedly. Lucca waved the stick toward her on the ground, letting her almost get it. He then told her to sit. She did and then he began waving it around and near her, but a little out of her reach. She finally successfully grabbed the end. He let her pull for a minute before telling her to release. She sat again. He repeated this several times.

"This is amazing! She's doing so well!" Ellie cried.

"I watched some online videos. It helps with impulse control and gives her a good workout at the same time."

She grinned. "Can I try?"

He came over and held the stick out to her. "Sure, just dangle it a little bit."

"Sophia," Ellie yelled. She didn't need to bother. Sophia came running, jumping for the stick. Ellie commanded her to release, and she did and sat.

Ellie turned to him, still showing her surprise. "You've done a great job, Lucca. Really, she's coming along. You're going to keep her, aren't you?"

"Of course!" he said. "I couldn't imagine not keeping her. Besides, we still have work to do."

Sophia had been sitting, looking at them. She now seemed to sense Lucca's words and ran toward the pool. She stopped suddenly, noticing Ellie's flip flops that she had put on top of her cover-up.

"Sophia, no," Ellie shouted in vain.

The dog grabbed a flip-flop, thinking it was her new toy. She wrestled with it, and in the process, the coverup was also in her grip.

Lucca ran toward her and, sensing that he was going to take her new toy away, Sophia dove into the pool.

"Oh God, wet dog!" Lucca said and grimaced.

They both had to laugh, watching Sophia try to paddle in the pool.

"Come on, I'll help you," Ellie volunteered.

They got back in the pool, and between the two of them, they were able to get Sophia over to the stone stairs to climb out. Ellie grabbed her cover up and one flip-flop and threw them out of the pool as well.

"You, my friend, are going to dry off in the sun and think about your behavior," Lucca told Sophia, who was sitting with her tongue out, smiling at them. Chastised, she obediently laid down in the shade of a nearby tree.

He shrugged. "I guess we have work to do. Sorry about your stuff."

Ellie laughed. "Oh, it's fine. I'll go change."

He smiled. "Don't on my account. I got some food ready. Let me go get it, and we can have a glass of wine on the patio."

She rolled her eyes. "I'm not going to stay and eat like this."

His eyes roved over her appreciatively. "As I said, don't change for me." He smiled. He tossed her his T-shirt. "But if you'd rather, put this on. We'll have an *aperitivo* and then you can go change before I cook you an amazing dinner."

She grabbed the T-shirt and pulled it over her head. It hit her at the top of her thigh. Well, at least she didn't feel so exposed. She followed Lucca to the patio and sat down while he went through the doors shortly to return with a charcuterie tray. He put it on the table and came back with a bottle of wine and two glasses.

"Wow, full service." She smiled up happily at him. She was hungry after their swim.

He flopped into a chair next to her and poured her some crisp white wine.

She raised an eyebrow at him. "So, how many videos did you have to watch to get the hang of this latest training?"

"A lot," he said and then laughed. "All this is more difficult than you think! I also need to up my treat game. I think she's starting to want more incentive."

"Ha, I know the feeling," Ellie said, grabbing a piece of cheese.

"Oh, really. Do I need to up my treat game with *you*, too?"

She smiled. "Maybe. I was wondering if you'd like to go to Florence with me tomorrow. It's probably time I replace my phone. We could have lunch and maybe go to a museum or something. Continue your art lessons."

He looked a little uncomfortable, and she rushed to say, "If you'd rather not, that's fine. It's only an idea. I can totally go by myself."

"It's not that, Ellie. I'd love to go. But Florence is a bigger city with a lot of tourists. I may get recognized. We've been able to move pretty freely about."

"Oh, I didn't think about that," she said, looking off in the distance. She took a sip of her wine, thinking for a minute. "Well, if you are willing to try, I am."

"Really? I thought you hated all the attention and stuff."

She looked at him seriously. "I do. You have no idea."

"Ellie, are you ever going to tell me what makes you so negative about the whole movie industry or L.A. or whatever it is? I feel like there's something more to the story."

She turned her head away from his gaze, sipping her wine, stalling. She knew it was time—she had promised herself it would be tonight. This talk should have happened long ago.

He leaned over now and turned her face toward him. "You know you can tell me anything. I'm not going to judge."

He kissed her softly, and it sent tingles down her spine. She put her hand around his neck and kissed him again, this time deepening the kiss. He ran his hands through her now drying, tousled hair. The kiss went on and on. Ellie felt herself melting. She ran her hands through his hair as well, feeling the silky feel. His beard was scratching her face a little, but she didn't care. She found herself moving onto his lap, running her hands over his beautiful chest. She wanted to get closer.

"Ellie!"

She broke away from Lucca with a start. Mike had run out on to the patio, and instead of looking his cool self, he was disheveled and anxious.

"Oh, hi, Mike." She swept her hair back from her face, feeling herself flush. She quickly got off Lucca's lap.

Right then, she saw a familiar car coming up the drive below them. She squinted. The hairs on her neck stood up. Oh God, it couldn't be!

"Mike," she said anxiously. "Is that…"

"Security called from the gate. Ellie, your parents are here," he said quietly.

twenty-one

Lucca looked at Ellie. She had a wild look in her eyes, and guilt was rushing over her face. He glanced at Mike, who was clearly uncomfortable.

"Your parents are here? Well, that's a surprise!" He shrugged. "So what? I'd like to meet them," he said, clearly oblivious to the drama that was about to unfold.

"Lucca, I need to tell you something quickly. I probably should have told you before."

Mike interrupted. "Ellie, maybe you better go get dressed. Your clothes are still here in the house. We only moved your painting stuff. I can go stall."

"You moved your painting stuff out? Why?" demanded Lucca. "I told you to stay in the villa. You even told me the light was better!"

She was anxious now. "There isn't time to explain. Mike's right. Let me go and at least throw some shorts on."

She ran toward the French doors and got within a few feet before they were thrust open. She stopped dead in her tracks.

"Ellie, honey!"

"Hi, Dad." She could barely get it out before he grabbed her in a big bear hug, lifting her up—his usual greeting. In his sixties, he still had bulging biceps, and loomed over Ellie. His full head of gray hair and craggy face was comforting to her now, she realized. She had always been proud of him—he was the type of man who looked debonair in a tuxedo but just as good in the casual shorts and shirt he was wearing now. And most of all, he was very kind and told bad dad jokes. She loved him immensely. She hugged him back tightly, realizing how much she had missed him.

"Emerson, put her down! It's my turn," her mom was saying.

Ellie found herself in a tight embrace with her mom, who pulled back to kiss her several times on the cheek. It was her usual greeting. She looked at her mom, shorter than her. she was also thin but had more curves than Ellie could ever wish for. Her signature platinum hair was mostly real, a study in some great genetics. It was pulled back in a chignon. She had brown sparkling eyes and deep dimples. She was the most photographed women in the world—called by most of America as the girl next door when she had been younger. She aged remarkably well, only having a small amount of plastic surgery to nip and tuck. Her face was still youthful, despite approaching sixty herself.

"Honey, let me look at you." Her mom's gaze traveled over Ellie as if to ensure she was okay. Ellie wiggled away. "Mom, I'm fine."

Ellie's mom raised an eyebrow. "I didn't know you were a hard rock fan."

"What?" Ellie looked down at her T-shirt that displayed an old 80s band. "Oh yeah, um..."

She looked back at Lucca, who was standing, frozen a few feet behind her. His face was paling, and he was staring at the three of them, clearly in shock.

"Lucca, I'd like you to meet my parents, Emerson and Miranda Montgomery. Mom and Daddy, this is my *friend*, Lucca Delarosa."

He frowned at her for a second. Well, what else was she going to call him? They hadn't talked about any kind of relationship.

Her father was the first to recover. He held his strong hand out to Lucca, shaking it enthusiastically. "Delarosa, nice to meet you. I'm an admirer of your work. Call me Monty," he said with a wink. "Everyone does."

Lucca nodded, turning his wide eyes to Ellie's mom. "Mrs. Montgomery, it's nice to meet you as well," he croaked out, his voice not sounding like his usual rich baritone.

Miranda looked at Ellie, taking in her wildly tousled hair and flushing face. She glanced back to Lucca, still standing there in his swim trunks, his gorgeous olive skin chest on full display. His hair was still damp, but wavy and looked great on him. Ellie almost rolled her eyes. She watched as Miranda gave him a wide smile. "Lucca, it's *very* nice to meet you. I think we have a lot to talk about."

ELLIE SAT at the table outside and examined her nails. She might as well stay silent, since she could barely get a word in edgewise. She had gotten changed after making the introductions, putting on a faded pair of jeans and a casual top. Her hair was in its usual ponytail and she had not bothered with make-up. Ellie had hurried downstairs, trying to beat Lucca who had gone to change, too. She was desperate to beat him downstairs and not have him interrogated by her parents.

In the end, they both arrived down to the kitchen at the same time. He stared at her without saying a word, his face lacking expression. She silently helped him carry more wine glasses and snacks out to the patio. Now Lucca and her parents were busy discussing the industry and the latest news. She had zero interest in their gossip that included who was starring in what movie or who was producing what.

"Ellie, honey, sorry we are talking shop. I know you don't care. Tell us what you've been doing?" Monty boomed out in his signature gravelly voice.

Ellie smiled. That voice. People knew it everywhere. She remembered times when her father had tried to go incognito and yet, that voice always gave him away.

"Oh, Dad, it's a long story."

"You painting?"

She nodded slowly. "Yes, it's coming back a little. It's not where I want it, but it's flowing better."

"Ellie is an exceptional artist," Monty bragged, reaching over to put an arm around her. "Quite well thought of in the art world. I'm sure she told you all about it, Delarosa."

"Dad, his name is Lucca."

Lucca put up a hand. "You can call me whatever you want, Mr. Montgomery. I'm still in awe. I'm a big fan of both of your work."

Miranda had gone strangely silent. She appeared to be studying Lucca and Ellie. They had been careful not to touch each other and hadn't even made eye contact.

"That's real nice to hear," Miranda said in her familiar Texas drawl. "We appreciate that." She turned to Ellie abruptly. "Ellie, are you living here?"

Ellie felt herself flush. What her mother was asking was if she was living with Lucca.

"Well, it's a long story."

"Isn't it nice? We have a lot of time." Miranda smiled, putting her chin in her hands. Her voice held a warning note to Ellie.

Ellie told her about meeting Lucca and decorating the cake

for the wedding. She drew out the story until she got to the guesthouse and then explained Lucca's stalker.

Monty stood abruptly. His eyes narrowed, his hands fisted. "Are you sure it's taken care of? You're safe?"

Lucca nodded. "Yes, Mr. Montgomery. I wouldn't have put Ellie in any kind of danger. We were perfectly safe at my family's home at the lemon grove. I had no idea Ellie was coming here—to this property. It was just a weird coincidence."

"Emerson, sit down. We'll talk to Mike later. You know he's always taken care of Ellie."

Lucca's eyebrows went up and he turned to Ellie. "Wait a minute. *That's* how you know Mike?"

She looked down at her hands again, feeling guilty. "Mike was my security officer for years," she said quietly. She looked up to see Lucca's careful expression. He wasn't showing much emotion, but she could see something in his face—a quiet anger was growing. The muscle in his jaw was twitching violently and his hand tightened around his wine glass. Any minute he was going to snap it.

"Mike is like family," said Miranda, looking at Lucca and then at Ellie. "Eleanor Montgomery, did you not tell Lucca who your parents were? Are you that embarrassed of us?"

Ellie rolled her eyes. "Of course not, Mom. But you know I never tell people right away."

"Right away? You're living with this man!"

"We are not living together," argued Ellie, avoiding Lucca's eyes. "Well, not in that way."

Ellie's mom pursed her lips as if she was going to say more, but Monty chimed in. "Say, I'm getting a little hungry. These snacks were nice, but how about some dinner? Anyone want to go find a restaurant?"

Ellie couldn't keep from turning to her dad with an aston-ished expression. "You want me to go out with the three of you?

Oh my God, can you imagine the commotion you'd cause? We probably couldn't even get through an appetizer!"

Miranda smiled, patting her daughter's hand gently, calming her. "She's right, Emerson. How about you and I go in and see what we can find for dinner and rustle something up and let these kids talk?"

Lucca interrupted. "Mrs. Montgomery, I can't allow you to do that. I'll cook something, or we have a lot of food that some of the local chefs have brought in. I haven't had a chef up here since we were tight with security."

Miranda was already standing, gathering the snack trays. "No, no, Emerson and I will cook. You sit here, enjoy your wine and *talk*," she said, emphasizing the word.

Monty stood, taking the trays from his wife. "If you got any meat, I'm excellent at grilling," he said.

"I do—I was planning on cooking steaks tonight in the wood-fired oven. But Mr. Montgomery, really. I can't have you cooking for me. I'll do it," Lucca stood, nervously wiping his hands on his shorts.

Ellie glanced at her father. She had seen this look before. Once he set his mind to it, there was no budging him. She watched him smile remotely at Lucca. "Monty, remember? And sit down, Delarosa. I think my daughter has some things she needs to discuss with you."

So Lucca sat.

AFTER HER PARENTS LEFT, Lucca watched as Ellie carefully looked out in the distance, in order not to meet his eyes.

"Eleanor?" he finally asked mockingly.

She turned then, her eyes glinting. "I *hate* that name."

He shook his head, his eyes wide.

"What?" She looked at him with narrowed eyes.

"All this time, I've been with Eleanor Montgomery."

"You would have known who I was," she stated flatly, not bothering to make it a question.

He stared at her steadily. It was important to be honest with her, but he was trying to tap down his emotions. He stated the obvious. "Of course. I grew up hearing about you. Your parents are the most famous movie stars in the world."

He was beyond frustrated—he was deeply angry. He was hurt, too. Did she not trust him at all?

"Ellie, why didn't you tell me? All this time!" He ran his hands through his hair. "All this time, I've been with Eleanor Montgomery. I feel like an idiot. Were you laughing about it? Did you think it would be funny when I found out later? Here I was confiding in you about the industry. You must have been cracking up—thinking how silly it was that I was explaining to you how things work."

"Of course, I wasn't laughing!" she blurted. She looked away. Were those tears? He had never seen her really cry. He was trying to calm down, but he felt hurt deep down. She must have thought so little of him. He took some calming breaths. Putting his head back, he stared at the sky and counted the white pillowy clouds. "Can you talk to me now and be honest?"

"I didn't mean to lie!" she said, abruptly turning and looking at him for the first time. "Well, I didn't mean to *continue* to lie. Lucca, you should know better than anybody that people treat you differently. Once people find out who I am, they change. I've been burned so many times!"

"And you thought I would burn you, too?" he asked in a dangerously soft voice.

"No, of course not! I didn't tell you at first because I didn't think I'd even be seeing you again. But once we got...we got..." Her face started to turn red.

"Got to know each other?" he finished quietly, taking pity on her.

"Yes. Once we got to know each other and started whatever this is we have between us, I tried to tell you. I started to several times, and then something happened."

"Ellie, do you trust me?"

"Yes, I do." She looked at him now, her eyes wide. "And I don't trust many people."

He decided to take a different tactic. "Then will you tell me a little bit about how you grew up? I can guess, but I think it's important you tell me about it."

She was silent for a few minutes, but then she started talking and it seemed like it was all spilling out. He listened as she told him about the constant attention.

"I often wonder when I first became aware that my parents were different. I mean, I thought that everyone had people taking photos of them when they went everywhere. I thought that constant interruptions were normal," she said bitterly.

"Don't get me wrong. I adore my parents. They were wonderful to me. But do you know they couldn't even take me to Disneyland? I wanted to go so badly. Mike and my nanny finally went with me. They took me most places." She looked at him now sadly. "Then I started growing up, and it became worse because the attention started getting focused on me. The only daughter of Hollywood's most successful couple. I had braces and was this gangly teenager. They loved printing the worst photos of me they could find."

He stared at her unmoving, and she continued. "Any date I went on, they were there. They even captured my first kiss—which turned out not to even be genuine. I found out later it was to get to my parents for some big break."

"That's when I learned quickly that most people wanted to be around me for the exposure. I couldn't trust anyone. I think people are just fascinated that my parents genuinely love each other. All the fake headlines that one of them was cheating on the other—I confronted them, of course, but I knew better. They are devoted to one another. So then it was like the press wanted to find something wrong with me. I remember a side-by-side they printed of me and my mother—asking how I could be her daughter. There were even rumors I wasn't. That I was adopted."

"You're more beautiful than your mother," Lucca told her quietly.

She rolled her eyes. "Please."

"I mean it." He covered her hand with his. "You have no idea. You don't often wear make-up, or when you do, hardly any. You're never fussing with your hair. And yet, you're stunning. Truly. You knocked me out the first time I even saw you."

She smiled a little at the memory. "Well, yeah, I knocked you down."

He shook his head. It was important for him to tell her this. Maybe he should have a long time ago. Suddenly, his anger faded. "Yeah, you definitely kicked my butt. I wasn't talking about that, though. I was talking about how I couldn't take my eyes off of you. I convinced you to come into my home. I wanted you to stay. I couldn't believe this gorgeous woman had shown up at my doorstep and seemingly didn't care who I was."

"You go out with a lot of attractive women."

He nodded. "I'm not going to pretend that's not true. But most of them have on ridiculously long false eyelashes and so much caked on make-up I have no idea what they really look like. Same with the women I've been on set with. I honestly think you're the first woman I've dated who spends the least amount of time on her looks and yet ends up looking stunning."

He leaned over and kissed her. "And it's not all about looks anyway, Ellie. You know that. You're one of the kindest and most thoughtful people I've ever met. I find myself telling you things I've never told anyone. It's a little disconcerting, if I'm going to be honest."

She finally looked at him apprehensively.

He stared at her, willing her to meet his eyes. "I'm sorry you had to go through all that as a kid. And I get why it was hard to tell me. I didn't mean to be angry. I was just caught off guard. You know it's difficult for me to trust, too. Most women are with me because of who I am."

She looked down at her hands. "I didn't even think about that. I'm sorry. Of course, you have some of the same issues." She raised her eyes and stared at him. "I've been so self-absorbed, I never thought about what you go through."

He shrugged. "I'm an adult. When I see stupid headlines or false articles, I can put it aside. I know what kind of person I am. But yeah, look around. I don't have a lot of people close to me for a reason."

He gave her a half smile. "I guess it took your parents coming to finally make us talk." He reached over and grabbed her hand. "Can I ask you something, though? Now that we're getting things out in the open. How are you feeling about me?"

She looked at him directly. "You scare me to death."

His eyes widened. "Well, great. Because I really love to have that effect on a woman who I'm in a relationship with."

"Do we have a relationship? That's just it, Lucca. I haven't really been in a relationship with anyone for a long time." She bit her lip and then met his gaze. "I am falling for you. There, if you want it—there it is. And it scares me beyond belief. So fine. Let's just get it out there. You wanted to rip this bandage off." She took her hands away from his and stood.

He stood quickly; his heart was beating fast. "Ellie, stop."

"I should go see if my parents need anything."

"Not before we finish talking," he said, starting to feel his anger coming back. Why wouldn't she just listen?

She turned and gave him a measured look. "Let's table this until my parents leave."

He grabbed her shoulders. "Ellie..."

"I need to go see what havoc my parents are wreaking on your kitchen. We'll talk later."

He looked at her defiant face, her chin lifting. She had so much pride. He could see the withdrawal, too. She was scared of her feelings. He understood, but he wanted to tell her how he felt —which was also unsettled.

She was right, though. It might be better to wait. He finally slowly dropped his hands and let her go.

twenty-two

"Everything was delicious, Miranda," Lucca said, finally sitting back in his chair in the dining room after devouring a perfectly grilled steak with roasted tomatoes and a fresh pasta with pesto.

Ellie smiled proudly. "I told you. They are amazing cooks. They taught me everything I know."

Miranda beamed, looking at her husband. "It's what helped keep us together, hasn't it, dear?"

Lucca looked at the couple. He had to admit, even he was surprised. They were far more down to earth than he could have ever imagined. "Cooking brings you together?" he asked, smiling a little, remembering his and Ellie's cooking contest.

Miranda nodded. "When we fight, I tell Emerson to get in the kitchen. Something about working together to produce a meal just relaxes us and sometimes we even forget what we were fighting about."

Lucca smiled at them. "You guys met on a film, right?"

Monty laughed, playing with the stem of his wineglass. "Nope. She conked me over the head with a vase."

"Whaaaat? Lucca asked incredulously. He looked from one to another. They were all chuckling.

"This guy was dating my roommate," Miranda said, pointing to Monty and rolling her eyes.

"I wasn't dating her. I went out with her maybe three times," protested Monty.

"The number of times he took her out goes down every time we talk about this," Miranda said with a laugh. "Well, she forgot her key, and they thought I was asleep and they thoughtfully didn't want to wake me up. He broke into my bedroom window, and I hit him over the head with a vase," Miranda said matter-of-factly. "I was still a struggling actress, and we lived in a not-so-nice area. He's lucky I didn't do worse. I think I had a baseball bat under my bed."

Monty rolled his eyes. "Her roommate had a little too much to drink and sent me through the wrong window."

Miranda smiled widely at him, grabbing his hand. "Only it was the right window, Emerson."

He nodded lovingly at his wife. "She's the only one who's allowed to call me Emerson," he said with a glint in his eye. "She captivated me from day one."

Lucca put his arm around Ellie's shoulders lightly. He could feel her stiffen a little, but he was determined to show her parents he had more than just a passing interest in their daughter.

"This story sounds very familiar. The apple doesn't fall far, does it, Ellie?"

Ellie tried to shrug off his arm, but he kept it there. Lucca wisely changed the subject. "How did you make it work all these years in the industry?"

Miranda shrugged. "If I had a dime for every time I have been asked that. The answer is, I honestly don't know. We never consciously did anything. We just loved each other. We tried not to be gone from each other for too long. We like doing the same things. We had a great gift—Ellie—we always wanted to be with her, too."

"Well, you raised a wonderful daughter," Lucca said.

Monty eyed him now, his eyes narrowing. "We did," he acknowledged. "And now I think you and I need to clean up this mess. You ladies go gab or something." He waved toward the patio.

"Dad, um, you and Mom kind of used every pan in the house. I'll help clean up."

Lucca stood and began clearing the table. He glanced around with amusement. Ellie was right—they had virtually destroyed the kitchen.

Monty laughed. "That's okay, honey. Take some wine and go outside. I know your mom is dying to catch up with you."

Ellie looked at Lucca. He smiled at her and gave her a little wave. She remained rooted to the spot. He gave her a bigger smile, walking over. She looked at him speculatively. He reached over and rubbed a thumb over her jawline and then her lips. It was a far more intimate gesture than a kiss—all done right under her mother's watchful eye. Ellie drew away and practically ran out the door.

"GOOD LORD, honey, that man is just about one of the best-looking men I've ever seen in my life. Next to your father," Miranda added slyly. "And he seems *very* nice. Not at all what I expected."

They had been sitting outside, talking for some time. Ellie had been waiting for her mother to finally bring up Lucca. Miranda had instead focused on their travels. She had admonished Ellie for not getting her phone replaced sooner. Now she was finally ready to take on the subject of Lucca.

"What exactly is going on with you and him? Things seem pretty cozy," she said, smiling widely.

Ellie frowned. "Mom, look, don't get ahead of yourself. Lucca and I... well, we haven't really talked about what this is."

"But you're living here with him, honey."

"I'm not living with him," protested Ellie. "I explained that! We're not at that stage, Mom, seriously. We've spent time together, but we haven't discussed any kind of future."

"I have to say, honey, I never thought you'd get involved with an actor."

Ellie rolled her eyes. "Well, that makes two of us. I tried Mom. I really tried."

"What now? Do you go back to L.A. with him?"

"No! I can't. No way. I won't live that lifestyle. Besides, I'm finally starting to paint again. I need to figure that out."

Miranda looked at her daughter, her eyebrows raised. "It seems to me you've been on holiday with this gorgeous man. It's not real, honey. He has to go do his job sooner than later, and then what do you do?"

Ellie stood abruptly. "I don't know! You're asking a lot of questions. I don't have the answers at all. I don't even know how he feels."

Miranda laughed. "I know how he feels! He couldn't keep his eyes off of you! He watched you all through dinner."

Ellie smiled a little. "I know he cares about me. But he's made it very clear to me he's never getting married, and he doesn't want to make a commitment. And I don't want his lifestyle, bouncing around from city to city—film location after film location. And when he's not with me, wondering who he *is* with. We're nowhere," Ellie said sadly. "I tried to avoid this whole thing. And now here I am. I knew it was stupid to spend time with him."

Miranda eyed her daughter thoughtfully. "Honey, I know

growing up as our daughter was difficult. But don't let that lead you to make any rash decisions. Give the man a chance. Promise me you'll at least talk to him and not run away from this relationship. I've seen you run before, Ellie," she finished softly.

Ellie felt the wind knock out of her, finally realizing the depth of her feelings for Lucca. She smiled weakly at her mother, who was watching her thoughtfully. She always knew when to change the subject.

"Now tell me about your painting."

LUCCA CONTINUED TO STACK DISHES, trying not to feel like he was having an out-of-body experience. He was doing dishes with his childhood idol—someone who he modeled his own career after. He didn't have time to be starstruck as he tried to pretend loading a dishwasher was what he did on a regular day. He didn't know if he had done this since he was a teenager. Not only was he doing chores with the legend of Hollywood, he'd been dating his daughter. In fact, he'd been doing a lot of kissing with this man's daughter and wanted to do a whole lot more.

Lucca kept his eyes averted, as if cleaning plates was the most important thing in his life. He'd never been so tongue-tied. Meanwhile, Monty was wrapping up the leftover food carefully.

"Got a project you're working on?" Monty asked suddenly.

"Uh, well yes. In a few weeks—it starts in New York and then takes me to Chicago and Seattle."

"Is it that new Enrique Diaz film?"

"How did you know?"

"I think I must have read about it somewhere," Monty said nonchalantly. "Are you the psychologist?"

"Yeah, I play a psychologist to a sports phenomenon. It is a great script."

The two men continued to talk, with Monty asking detailed questions about the film. As Lucca closed the dishwasher, he saw that Monty was pouring them each a glass of wine. "Leave those pans. Let's sit down for a while. Those two are good for hours," he said, pointing outside. "This was just an excuse for them to talk. Miranda has been missing her peanut."

Lucca smiled, thinking of Ellie being referred to as a peanut. He sat down nervously, taking a big sip of wine. Monty was staring at him, his trademark scowl now evident. "So, what exactly are you doing with my daughter, Delarosa?"

Lucca had been expecting this since Monty's order to clean the kitchen with him. Now he swallowed hard. "To be honest, sir, I have no idea."

Monty smiled. "Ahhh, I see. She's just like her mother. Keeps you guessing, huh?"

Lucca looked away. Ellie's confession that she was falling for him was just hours ago. He hadn't even had a chance to address it. The last thing he was going to do was bring his feelings up with her father before they had an opportunity to talk. "Well, in a sense. But I think where we are now is wondering how we can make this work long term."

"Really? Why is that so difficult?"

Lucca stared at Monty. His eyes were innocent, but Lucca could sense a dangerous gleam. Lucca wasn't about to tell him that he had no intention of ever marrying. All the challenges he and Ellie were facing were difficult to say out loud to this man who was larger-than-life. Monty apparently was going to take pity on him because he began to speak, stating the obvious. "Ellie hates everything about the industry."

At Lucca's nervous nod, Monty continued. "Miranda and I did the best we could, but it was really rough. I have a lot of regret. *We* have a lot of regret. But I'm not sure how we would have changed things. I guess I should have been around more. I know there were times that Mike was almost more of a father to her than me."

Lucca stared at him now—the hero on the movie screen who he had watched save thousands, hurl through fire and explosions and come out unscathed, battle countless enemies and always be the good guy. Now he looked sad and very humble.

"She loves you very much," Lucca said. He wasn't sure what was happening, but he felt the urge to comfort the man. "Sometimes parents make mistakes. I know mine did," he said bitterly. "At least you stayed together and fought for her."

Monty nodded absentmindedly. "I understand your parents divorced when you were pretty young?"

"How did you know?"

"Delarosa, you don't think that we just showed up here having no idea who our daughter was with, do you?"

Lucca's eyes widened. "Um…I'm not sure…"

Monty threw his head back and laughed. "I'm sorry, son. It's too fun to tease you. Did you think I hired a private investigator or something? Ellie would come in here and strangle my neck with her bare hands if that was true. No, I guess her phone broke. We got a little concerned when she didn't answer our calls, so we finally reached out to Brigid, who told us the whole story."

Lucca felt himself sag with relief. Not that a private investigator would be a bad thing. He certainly didn't have anything to hide. He still felt out of his depth, though, and unfortunately, he was not a good enough actor to show it.

"I admire your work," Monty said suddenly.

"You do?" Lucca asked incredulously.

"Of course! You're very talented. Much more than I was at your age. What are your plans after this film?"

Lucca shook his head in wonderment. He found himself repeating some of the things he had told Ellie about wanting to get behind the camera. Monty was nodding and making small comments here and there but letting him talk. It felt good to discuss it with someone who had been in the business so long. Monty finally pushed his chair back and looked at him thoughtfully. "Want some advice?"

"Of course, Mr. Montgomery."

Monty stared at him hard. "Say it one more time, kid, and I'll knock you on your butt like Ellie did. It's Monty." He smiled now. "I've spent all my life as an actor. It's all I ever wanted to do. Miranda and I have been talking lately and I think I might try my hand at Broadway. I've pushed myself often as an actor—but never done much live work. I think I finally have the nerve to do it."

Lucca raised his eyebrows. To hear Emerson Montgomery say he was nervous about anything seemed so surreal.

"I've been offered a few things, and I may decide to actually do it. Miranda and I love New York. Why not?" He shrugged. "So if I can do it—an old dog like me—then you can, too. Don't wait. Someday you're going to wake up and realize the years have gone by and you get...well, stuck, I guess."

Lucca nodded. "That's my biggest fear. I want to keep growing, and the last few roles have been just off. I can't explain it."

"Then go for it," Monty commanded, as he stood. "One more thing," he said, his face serious, but there was a glimmer in his eye. "I feel obligated to let you know that if you hurt my daughter in the slightest, her mother will come after you. Let me assure you that you don't want that. Now I need to go find my wife and kiss my daughter."

ELLIE'S PARENTS didn't stay long after that. They explained to Lucca they had a villa not far away.

"We're actually thinking of selling it," Miranda said. "We use it so seldom. We mostly just let other people use it. Of course, if Ellie wants to live there, we'll hang on to it."

Ellie shook her head. "It's way too big for me, Mom. I love that old house, you know that. But it's fine. I don't even know how long I want to stay in Italy."

Both her parents embraced Ellie multiple times before saying goodbye, telling her to contact them when she got her phone. Miranda had even given Lucca a small kiss, and Monty had all but crushed his hand. Lucca waved at them one last one time before shutting the big mahogany front door.

Ellie walked back into the open kitchen and began to wash the pans that were left. Lucca tried to tell her to leave them for the housekeeper, but she silenced him with a look. Lucca stood beside her with a dish towel to dry them. They worked in silence for a few minutes.

"Ellie..."

She was suddenly focused on the pan, as if scouring it was the most important job. "Lucca, let's not have this conversation now. We're both tired and it's been kind of a draining day."

He remained stubborn. "Ellie, leave the rest. This is ridiculous. Rosa will do them tomorrow when she comes in. We need to talk."

Ellie shut off the water and turned to him. She might as well get it over with. She opened her mouth when suddenly his phone rang, and he took it out of his pocket and frowned at the screen.

"What the hell? Is it Parents' Weekend or something?"

She looked at him, her eyes widening.

He quickly answered it. "*Buonasera, Papa.*"

He walked away, speaking rapidly in Italian. Ellie only listened with half an ear. She didn't want to invade his privacy. Still, he stayed in the room, seemingly not caring if she overheard. She washed the last pan and carefully put it on the counter to dry. Lucca had walked over to the French doors that led to the patio. He was staring out into the yard, talking and laughing. She shifted from foot to foot, wondering what to do. He should catch up with his father.

She started to walk out of the room, and he turned to watch her. She pantomimed going to bed, and he frowned, but she shook her head and mouthed "goodnight." She was conscious of his eyes following her up the stairs.

twenty-three

Ellie dressed with care, knowing instinctively this would be a pivotal day in their relationship. Whatever Lucca had to say, she felt like she could deal with it better, looking her best. She wore a taupe sheath dress that she didn't wear often, but had thrown in her suitcase for some reason. She hadn't worn it yet and now frowned into the mirror, tugging the hem. It was a little shorter than she usually wore. Oh well, it went well with her hair and eyes, and she wanted to look nice. Searching for a pair of flat sandals, she took one last look. Though she thought about tying her hair back, she decided to leave it hanging straight. She even put on some make-up. Lastly, she grabbed the straw hat Lucca had given her.

She walked downstairs and looked around. Mike was on his tablet in the front room. "Hey kiddo. Whoa, look at you! You clean up nice."

Ellie smiled. "Lucca and I are going into Florence for the day, and I thought I might drag him through a couple museums."

Mike nodded. "Yeah, he told me that's the plan. I am staying here—I'm expecting two calls from L.A., and I need to be near a computer. But a couple of my guys will go with you." He held up a hand. "Don't get all annoyed. They'll stay back discreetly."

"I know, Mike," she said agreeably. "Hey, can I ask a huge favor? I packed my suitcase. Could you have someone take it to the guesthouse?"

"You going to move back? I thought you were just going to stay here."

"Nah, I thought I'd move back. That's where I was supposed to be staying. And I'm not sure when Lucca's dad and his wife are expected back. I don't want things to be awkward, you know?"

Mike winced. "Yeah, sorry about yesterday. Were your parents surprised?"

She frowned. "Strangely, they were not. I felt like they knew exactly what they were walking into."

He held up his hands. "I didn't say a word, believe me."

She laughed. "Mike, if I can't trust you by now, I don't know if I ever will. Of course, you didn't. My parents are very good detectives."

He laughed. "That's for sure. Sometimes they have me beat. But sure, we'll get your stuff moved."

"Thanks, it's right there in my room." Ellie didn't add that she didn't bring it down for a reason. She would explain it to Lucca later. If he saw her case, he would undoubtedly ask a bunch of questions. She felt it was necessary now to physically separate herself, and she wasn't sure why.

"*Buongiorno,* Eleanor, are you ready?"

She turned to see Lucca coming through the patio doors, a coffee cup in his hand. He looked breathtakingly handsome in a white button-down shirt and khakis.

"Call me Eleanor one more time, and we won't even be going across the street."

Mike nodded. "I can vouch for that."

Lucca grinned. "Okay, okay. Let's roll, *Ellie*. We'll grab some breakfast in *Firenze*."

She waved to Mike and followed Lucca out to the front of the house where the car waited. Lucca helped her in before running around to his side. He turned to her suddenly. "You look so great today."

She rolled her eyes. "You don't have to say that. Just drive the car."

He shook his head. "When someone gives you a compliment, you just say 'thank you.'"

She gave him a small look, but obediently answered. *"Grazie."*

He smiled slightly at her. "*Prego*. Now let's go. First stop, some breakfast, and then we'll get you a new phone."

They drove out the gates and along the winding roads, talking here and there. It seemed the heaviness of the day prior was in the past, and Ellie felt a sigh of relief. She knew they needed to continue their talk, but Lucca purposely was keeping things light.

She put her straw hat on to shade her eyes in the already sunny day, and he glanced over and smiled at her. She looked at the sunflowers in the distance and the tall cypress trees lining the roads to keep her from staring at his profile. She breathed deeply. She loved Tuscany. She was so lost in thought, she almost didn't hear him.

"Sorry about last night. I had no idea my father was going to call."

She smiled. "Oh, that's okay. I needed some sleep. Did he have anything interesting to say—when are they coming home?"

"He wasn't sure yet. He thinks in a couple of weeks. I told him the whole story about finding you at the villa and I fessed up about the stalker situation. He was understandably upset. He said he never would have let Madeleine invite you if he had known. I assured him that I definitely *did not* regret the move."

She shifted uncomfortably. "You didn't tell him that we..."

He glanced at her with a grin. "Are friends? No. I didn't tell him, Ellie. But thanks for reminding me."

"Lucca, look I know we have a lot left to...discuss. But do you mind if we wait? Can we talk over dinner or later tonight? I just want to have a fun, relaxing day," she said. She knew she was being cagey, but she had put her heart out there, and if Lucca was going to stomp on it, she wanted to have this final day. He wasn't going to intentionally do so, but she understood they were miles apart in what they each envisioned for the future.

"Let's just enjoy ourselves, and we can talk about all that stuff later." She turned to look at him. He was focused on the road, his hair ruffled. The sleeves of his shirt were rolled up, and his gold watch glinted in the sunlight.

He glanced at her quickly, his eyes hidden by his sunglasses. "You really want to wait?"

"Yes—for now."

"I don't want you to think I'm avoiding the conversation, Ellie," he said quietly.

"I know 100 percent that you are not avoiding the conversation. I'm okay with it. Let's agree to table it until later."

"Okay, tabling upon request," he smiled, his eyes on the road still. "So that brings me to my next subject. Just how many museums are on your list?"

IF ELLIE HAD DESIGNED her perfect day, this would have been it. They had grabbed buttery pastries and cappuccinos and sat on a bench near the Florence Duomo to eat them. Lucca had donned a baseball cap, and with his sunglasses on and beard, he blended in well. No one seemed to give him a passing glance. Still, Ellie was uneasy. She'd been on enough outings with her parents where the hat disguise had not worked. At least the day was sunny, so there were many tourists wearing hats and sunglasses.

She tried to put it out of her mind as they went to the phone store where they were able to replace Ellie's phone and download all her info from the cloud. Lucca kept himself busy outside, sitting on a bench and staring down at his phone without looking up. She hated that he had to be so guarded. Inside the store, she was relieved to see all her contacts and texts again. She hadn't realized how disconnected she felt.

Shoving it into her purse, she went outside to greet Lucca, and they took off for their first museum visit. She had teasingly promised only two for the day.

The first museum, the Uffizi Gallery, was one of Ellie's favorites. She knew it was one of the most popular museums in the world, but she still had wonderful memories from her time in art school. She would visit often, sitting there for hours. It was a refuge, a place she could dream and sketch and wonder about the artists themselves. What held them back? What inspired them?

There were a lot of people there, but it almost seemed better that way. They were easily able to blend in and whisper to each other their opinions on the masterpieces. She was surprised a little by the depth of Lucca's questions. Maybe he had held back before, because now he had a steady stream of thoughtful insights. He had a discerning eye, and when she told him so, he only smiled a little sadly. "Could be genetic," he had said with a small shrug.

They walked hand-in-hand past the Duomo, stopping to take a couple of selfies. It was so massive and so intricate. She told Lucca they could visit it another day and maybe walk on the Duomo skywalk. She was embarrassed as soon as the words were out of her mouth. She was acting like there would be another day. Lucca didn't show any expression either way.

She had ruled out the Accademia Gallery and Michelangelo's

David as being too hard to get into since they hadn't bought tickets ahead of time. Instead, they went to the Leonardo Da Vinci Museum, taking their time to really appreciate what a craftsman he was.

When they finally emerged into the bright sunlight, it was getting warm. "Come on, I'll take you to my favorite place for lunch," she said, suddenly inspired. She led him down a series of cobblestone streets until she stopped at a small panini shop. "We used to come here all the time. All the university kids and those studying abroad come here."

They waited their turn in line, admiring the university pennants hanging above their heads. "I never asked you; did you go to college or acting school? I don't think I ever read about that," she asked, suddenly curious. She kept her voice low, but over the din of the crowd, she felt confident talking.

He smiled. "You read about me?"

She rolled her eyes. "Kind of hard not to."

"That one," he said suddenly, pointing to the NYU banner.

"I might have guessed!" she said with a smile, given that he was raised in New York.

"I was very fortunate to go there. It allowed me to live at home. Zio Angelo helped with the tuition."

"But your father..."

"I didn't have much of a relationship with him then," Lucca said quietly. "And my mom certainly didn't have the money at the time. She refused to take any money from him. She didn't want to be beholden. I worked a couple of jobs, too."

They were at the front of the line now, and they both stopped to survey the menu board on the wall and remark about the meats and cheeses in the case. They chose two different paninis, deciding they could each share a half. Smiling, they went to a table outside near the street, away from people, to wait for their food. She saw Lucca glance around for his security team, spotting them near, but still giving them space. That seemed to relax him, and she decided to resume their conversation.

"So what kind of jobs?"

"What?" He looked at her, confused. "Oh, college jobs. Well, of course I was a waiter."

She nodded. "The obligatory server job every actor must have. What else?"

"I scared people."

She looked confused. "Um, what?"

He laughed. "I was a zombie in a Haunted House."

She shook her head. "I'm sure you pulled that role off."

He looked smug. "I was amazing. It paid well, too."

"Anything else?"

He looked uncomfortable.

"Um, we don't have to talk about it anymore if you don't want to." She suddenly felt tense. Was it something bad or did he do something he was ashamed of?

He looked away and mumbled.

She narrowed her eyes. "Excuse me?"

"I was Prince Charming."

She burst out laughing and Lucca frowned. She clapped her hand over her mouth. "Sorry."

"I knew you'd laugh."

"Sorry! Truly." She bit her cheeks and tried to think of something painful. It wasn't working.

"Go ahead. Laugh all day," he said, clearly annoyed.

"Lucca, I apologize. Okay, now I just have to ask. Was it in a play or something?"

"Not quite."

"Okay. Um, where?"

"Little rich girls' parties."

Ellie snorted to keep from laughing. She had to ask: "So you went to little girl's parties and did what?"

"Well, I brought the glass slipper, of course."

This time Ellie couldn't contain herself. She was laughing so hard, she had to wipe her eyes. "I need a minute."

He shook his head. "Obviously, you have no respect for the range of acting that was required," he said smugly.

"Okay, even you have to admit it's funny."

He smiled grudgingly. "It is. Just not cackling, laughing funny like you've been doing the last few minutes."

"I don't cackle," she protested.

"Uh huh. People down the block heard you."

She rolled her eyes and was about to continue her protest when the owner of the sandwich shop came out with their order. Ellie had not seen him earlier.

"Ellie!"

"Franco!"

"What are you doing here? It's been years! So good to see you, Pepino!"

"Pepino?" Lucca asked dryly.

Ellie shot him a look. "Franco, it's wonderful to see you, too. Our paninis look amazing as always."

Franco, balding and much shorter than Lucca, glanced at him now, sizing him up. "Who's your friend?"

Ellie looked uneasy. Lucca stuck out his hand. "Lucca," he said simply.

"Franco," he said, pointing to himself. "You look familiar. You been in here before?"

"No, I haven't. I'm looking forward to it, though," Lucca said, giving him a ready smile. His sunglasses were still on, but Ellie guessed there was probably clear amusement in his eyes.

Franco switched to Italian then, telling her about his wife and children. Lucca stayed silent as they caught up. Franco finally asked Ellie about her art. She explained she was working in Tuscany on a project.

"You should come to *Firenze* and paint on my rooftop again," Franco smiled.

"I'd love that! I'll take you up on it." She smiled at him.

He gave Lucca another thoughtful look before returning his gaze to Ellie. "You come back again, Pepino. We'll talk."

Franco shook Lucca's hand again, still thoughtful.

They sat down again, and Ellie carefully switched a half of their paninis to each other's plate. "I'm so hungry. I can't wait to eat this. This was my comfort food when I lived here."

"I have so many questions," Lucca said, ignoring his sandwich.

She took a big bite of her four cheese panino and chewed. Maybe if she kept eating, he couldn't ask them.

"Let's start with the obvious top choice. Pepino?"

Ellie swallowed and stalled before answering. "Okay fine, yes, Pepino. I ate so much cheese when I was here, he told me I was like a mouse. And there's an old Italian song called 'Pepino, the Italian Mouse.' He played it for me once. It was hilarious. I used to babysit for him and his wife, too. They have two adorable kids. And in exchange, I would go up to his rooftop and paint. He has an amazing view."

"I'd love to see those paintings," he said softly.

She felt herself turning pink. She looked down at her plate before shrugging. "I sold them all. I don't have them. I probably have photos somewhere."

"You really are exceptional, Ellie. I know you're still feeling challenged artistically, but it's coming back. You have to realize that."

She shrugged, looking away. "I think it is. And I'm happy with the recent work, but I still have nothing at all that I'd even think about finishing for Madeleine."

"She didn't give you any guidelines?"

"No, she just said she wanted it to feel like home."

"Tall order," he remarked.

She nodded, lost in thought.

He took a bite of his choice, the turkey with brie, pesto, and sundried tomatoes. "Wow, that's good. I forgot how great paninis are here."

She agreed, and they continued eating.

He finally pushed his plate away. "I don't think I can eat another bite."

She smiled. "Two more bites, and I'm done."

He laughed and took another bite of his, too, before sitting back and sighing.

They sat there for a long time talking about their memories of the city. Lucca's were from when he was very young. She couldn't help asking: "Did you come back here as an adult?"

He took off his sunglasses and rubbed his eyes. He looked a little weary. "It hasn't been my favorite city. I suppose I have some good memories from here, but the one I have that over-shadows everything is the last trip I had before my parents split up. We came up to spend the night and do some shopping. I don't know what happened, but they were yelling so loudly at each other. They told me to stay in the bedroom at the hotel, but I could hear them perfectly. I was probably nine or so. I turned up the TV really loud. I could still hear them."

She put her hand over his. "Lucca, I'm so sorry. How awful for a little kid."

"I wished I had different parents. I went to school with kids whose parents were so happy and mine—well, they were just so miserable."

She looked at him now, feeling self-centered. "Lucca, I feel horrible. Here I've been complaining about my life and..."

"Stop, don't do that," he said quietly. "You don't need to compare your challenges with someone else's. Mine were mine, and yours were yours. It made us who we are today, I guess." He gave her a small smile.

She looked at him with narrowed eyes. "And who are you, Lucca? I mean, I know the person you are with me. You're kind and considerate. Even humble. You make me laugh. But sometimes I'm wondering if I'm getting to see only a piece of you."

He looked away, a guilty look crossing his face. "I don't know. You've seen the arrogant, like to get my own way side, too. What's left?"

"A lot," she said softly. "You don't have to act around me."

She held his gaze for a minute. His blue eyes were almost mesmerizing. She finally physically shook herself, glancing around at the tourists and college kids around them. Somehow, things had closed in on them, and she felt their future hanging over them. She stood and cleared their plates and trash before he could make a move. She grabbed his hand. "Come on. The world's best gelato is up the street."

THE REST OF THE DAY, Lucca found relaxing as well as frustrating. After digging into Ellie's favorite gelateria, he did agree it was superior. He teased her about having an extra stomach, though. He was stuffed, and she was busy licking her second scoop of gelato, savoring it. He had to finally look away— her pleasure in eating a simple cone was getting to him. In fact, everything about her was making him a little crazy. He knew most of his frustration was because he was anxious to sit down and hash out their relationship. They had to decide what was going to happen next. He had to film this movie, but he had some ideas after that, and he wanted to talk to her about them. He assumed she would want to stay in Italy. Meanwhile, he'd be moving around a lot. It was not conducive to sharing a life with her for the short term. But when he was done, perhaps then they could move ahead with a relationship. He had been serious about never marrying, but he certainly could see himself living his days with Ellie. He never tired of her and she certainly never bored him. He found her fascinating and even though she had pressed him at lunch about showing her his real self, he felt like he had let her see more of him than most people, except his family.

He couldn't believe he'd told her about his parents' fight that day. What he didn't tell her was how normal that was for them. There were countless fights prior to that. He had found movies his salvation and turned up the volume of old westerns he had found on TV. At least the gunfire and horse hooves drowned them out. He had wanted to grow up to be a cowboy, he thought wryly. He suddenly realized Ellie was talking to him. "What?"

She was standing on the corner of an intersection, staring at him. "You were miles away."

"Sorry, I was just thinking. What were you saying?"

"I was asking if you wanted to go back toward the Duomo. We could shop for a little leather or walk across the Ponte Vecchio," she suggested.

"Let's walk back that way and see what we find," he said, grabbing her hand. They walked past street performers, standing and watching for a minute. One man was painted silver and stood like a statue, only moving every few minutes.

"That's kind of creepy," she whispered. He nodded. "But look at his discipline. I'm not sure I could stay so still for so long." He threw a considerable amount of money in the performer's open box.

They walked on through an outdoor leather market. She bought a wallet and a purse, explaining she wanted to send them to Brigid and her husband.

"Any baby yet?" he asked.

"No, it's too early. Probably another month or so. But I wanted to get her something for the baby, too. Maybe we can go find a baby store here."

"I could take the presents back for you," he offered.

She stopped walking, turning to him. She looked at him seriously. "When are you leaving?"

"It's on the list to talk to you about," he said uneasily, mentally kicking himself. He should have waited. People brushed past him, and he ushered her to a bench by a carousel. He took off his sunglasses to look at her. "I wanted to tell you about it. I have a movie coming up. I'm going to have to leave soon."

She nodded, looking away from him.

"Ellie, it's just going to be a break. I'd ask you to come with me, but I'm going to be moving around. I don't think you want to be a part of that. You can stay here and paint."

She was still not looking at him. He could almost feel her emotionally pulling away from him. He gently touched her face, turning it toward him. He leaned in and kissed her lingeringly, trying to show her how much he cared for her. He pulled back, his eyes searching her face.

"Ellie..."

"OH MY GOD, IT'S LUCCA DELAROSA!" He turned his head to see two American teenage girls. He shifted uncomfortably. He spoke Italian to them, telling them that he didn't understand. They merely laughed and yelled to their friends who had been sitting nearby. "You guys, it's Lucca Delarosa!"

He stood quickly. "Let's get out of here," he said, grabbing her.

He didn't know how it happened so fast. Suddenly he was mobbed, kids clustering around him, clutching on to him, taking a selfie, talking at once—yelling to their friends. He tried to push away, but there were too many. He saw two men in black with impressive cameras come out of nowhere. Great, now they had attracted paparazzi.

He had been forced away from Ellie and he glanced over to see her backing up, her eyes panicked. "Go to the car. I'll meet you at the car," he yelled, desperate not to lose her in the crowd. She melted away. His security was trying to hold people back, but it was impossible, there were virtually too many of them. A black SUV pulled up. "Boss, get in—it's ours," shouted one of his security team. They almost physically picked him up, hauled him away from the crowd and threw him in the back before climbing in. The SUV shot away from the curb.

Lucca put his head back. He was covered in sweat. His heart was pounding. "That hasn't happened in Italy before," he choked out.

His lead security for the day, a young man named Hugo, turned around to look at him. "Probably the city. It's crawling with college-age girls. They're all here for study abroad. Mike told us to have a car on standby, thank goodness."

He nodded. "Let's get to the garage. I yelled at Ellie to meet us there." They sped through Florence's streets before arriving at the garage where they had left their cars. No Ellie.

"Maybe she is still trying to work her way here. I mean, if she had to walk—she'll be behind us," Hugo said, helpfully.

Lucca nodded, but he felt uneasy. "I'll call her…" It immediately went to voicemail. She had declined his call.

"Well, that's not going to work," he muttered. He got out of the SUV and leaned up against his car. He looked down at her hat in the front seat. She had left it, saying she didn't want to lose it. He picked it up, willing her to come. He looked at his watch for the twentieth time. "Maybe we should drive around looking for her," he suggested.

They looked at him skeptically. "These streets are like a maze. The chances of us finding her are slim."

Lucca tried another idea. "You guys go drive around and look. I'll stay with the car."

They looked uncomfortable. "That's not going to happen, sir. Look, Tim will go drive around. I'll stay with you. We're not leaving you alone after that mob."

"I'm in a parking garage!" he almost shouted. "Who's looking for me?"

Hugh looked at him seriously. "My butt is already on the line.

Mike's going to go nuts when he hears how we let you get surrounded. I'm already about to lose my job. Can you imagine my report—telling him that Tim and I just left you alone?"

Lucca felt guilty. He had never thought about how it affected them. "I'm sorry, guys. It wasn't your fault and I'll make sure Mike knows that, but right now I'm just feeling desperate to find Ellie."

"Maybe she'll call you," Tim offered.

"Yeah, maybe," he agreed, but couldn't help feeling a growing sense of dread.

ELLIE WALKED AROUND AIMLESSLY for the next thirty minutes. What the hell was she thinking? Her entire life, she hadn't been able to go out in public with her parents. She had been in countless tabloids, her life made public even though she hadn't signed up for fame. And now here she was again with a world-famous movie star. This time was different. She put herself in this position. Of course, he was going to be recognized. They had been lulled into some fairy tale that he was like Superman or something and no one could tell that Clark Kent and the superhero were the same. A baseball cap, a beard, and sunglasses. She rolled her eyes. Hardly the most creative disguise. She couldn't believe she had put herself in this spot yet again, even after he had warned her.

She sat down on a bench, lost in thought. She watched people go by, mainly tourists in this area, going to their hotels to rest in the heat. She was tired, and she looked at her feet, seeing a blister developing. She had worn sandals today, wanting to look her best. Even that was different for her. The usual Ellie would be in tennis shoes, not caring what the world thought. But she cared about what Lucca thought. As she sat there, she unwound the day. It had been wonderful. He had finally opened up, and she had wanted to learn more. In fact, she wanted to learn everything about him. She suddenly felt incredible sadness and her shoulders drooped. Why couldn't he just be a regular guy?

A bus approached, and she realized she was sitting at a bus stop. She waved the driver away, but he was stopping anyway to let passengers off. She found herself staring into Lucca's crystal blue eyes. She physically jumped. Those eyes. The smirk from his clean-shaven face. She hadn't seen that for a while. He mocked her from a poster on the side of the bus. It was advertising his upcoming movie. Above his gorgeous face were the words *Menace: Coming this Fall.*

She almost laughed out loud. Menace! That was him. A menace to society alright. She suddenly felt a new sense of clarity. It wasn't her fault! It was his. She hadn't wanted any of this. She would have lived her life without him easily. But no, she had to go on that plane to take the cake, and then he wouldn't leave her alone, telling his family she was his girlfriend and putting her into such an awkward spot. Sure, she could have rebuffed him at the wedding, but he had worn her down. And then the whole stalking thing and moving into the villa. Once again, it was out of her hands. I mean, she wasn't made of steel. Of course, she had been attracted to him. Siena had been a dream. He had to go be all sweet to that single mother, winning Ellie's heart. And he had to take her on picnics, to Lucca and buy her a hat.

She stood now. She was angry—almost angrier than she had been in her whole life. How dare he? How dare he push and push when he knew how much she had wanted a life away from Hollywood! And then he had met her parents and learned how much she had been through and yet here he was, charming her, holding her hand, kissing her. He even used those eyes on her own mother! He had no feelings! Anybody with any kind of character would have walked away! They would have left her alone. She was finally getting her love of painting back, and yet he still made sure he was a presence in her life.

Deep down there was a part of her instinctively telling her she was being irrational, but she couldn't stop. The anger felt so good. It felt liberating. She had ignored his call. Now she picked up her phone and texted Lucca that she'd be there in a few minutes. He asked if he could come pick her up, and she ignored it. She started walking toward the garage. It took her a little longer, limping a little with her blister. That made her even angrier. She changed herself for him! She never did that.

Finally, she wound herself through Florence's confusing cobblestone streets, walking farther than she needed to. By the time she approached the car park she was tired, thirsty and in pain. She was also even angrier.

"Oh my God, Ellie, are you okay? You look...well you look tired," Lucca said quickly, as he saw her approach. He immediately came to her and grabbed her shoulders, relief on his face. He bent to kiss her, and she turned her face, his kiss landing awkwardly near her ear.

She saw the security men walk away, giving them privacy.

"Does it really matter how I look?" she asked coolly.

"Well, no, I mean, I just meant that..." He was stammering now. "Listen, Ellie, I'm sorry. I would do anything I could to rewind the clock. We were having such a great day. I'm not sure why I attracted attention today, of all days."

"You always attract attention, Lucca!" she said louder than she intended. She took a calming breath. "You *will* always attract attention. Look at you. It's ridiculous. Besides, you were staring at me from a bus!"

"What?" He looked at her, confused.

"Your face. Your big ol' face is on a bus. Your eyes were looking at me! Every woman in this city is probably looking at it! Of course, you're going to get noticed. You're famous! It's time you just accepted that," she shouted. She bit her lip.

Lucca stared at her, his eyes searching her face. "I know I am, Ellie. I did try to warn you," he reminded her curtly.

He put his hands on her shoulders, and she wiggled, trying to escape his grasp. "Let me go!"

He immediately dropped his hands. "How about we drive home, grab a swim or showers and make some dinner? Relax a little. We can talk about this when we have calmed down."

"You mean when *I've* calmed down? No, thank you. I don't need to say much more. I'm done, Lucca, We're done. This has to end now. Before I lose myself, before I become someone I don't even recognize. It's over."

He backed up sharply, his face impassive. "Just like that? That's it?"

She looked at him directly in the eyes. It was important he see how serious she was even if this was the hardest thing she had ever done. "Just like that. We're done."

"Ciao, Lucca." She turned around and began to limp away.

"Ellie, where are you going? At least let me drive you home!"

She turned to look at him one last time. "That's not my home."

ELLIE WALKED around the corner to a side street to ensure she was hidden by Lucca exiting the garage. She dug out her phone.

I need your help.

Her dad's response was immediate. He would send a car for her as soon as possible. And in fact, it was less than fifteen minutes before a black sedan pulled up. In the meantime, she did feel a twinge of guilt—it wasn't necessary to worry everyone. She started to text Lucca, but instead, switched over to Mike and let him know she was going to her parents for the night. She told him it was all right to let Lucca know.

Mike answered immediately—his usual, *Okay, Ellie. Whatever you need.*

The driver seemed to sense her mood, and after a few perfunctory replies on her part, he kept silent. She was glad, her mind spinning. The day had taken such a turn. She told herself she was free. She had broken ties before it got worse. He was going away anyway. It would be a natural ending.

The car entered the gates to her parents' Tuscan villa, stopping at the guard stand to be cleared. The driver wound the car up the hill toward the villa, its creamy white exterior glowing pink in the evening sun. Its wrought-iron balconies and dark brown shutters made it look almost like a castle. In fact, her dad had dubbed it *Montgomery Castello*. She smiled. It was good to be home.

She opened the door quickly before the driver even had time to come around. Her mother was walking toward her in a long flowing red sundress, her hair loose and wavy around her shoulders. "Eleanor," she said, smiling and hugging her. She pulled back and scrutinized her as usual. This time, Ellie didn't hold back. She burst into tears.

twenty-four

Ellie stared at the ceiling. She had slept well after her crying session in front of her mother. Miranda had led her inside the house and let her finish sniveling. She wisely hadn't asked any questions. Ellie winced, knowing now they'd be coming this morning. Her mother had pushed it all aside, intent on feeding her instead, taking out leftovers and plying her with them. Ellie had picked at the food, but just listening to her mother's chatter relaxed her a little. Only after she was feeling more like herself did her dad appear. Ellie knew he'd probably been hiding—he never could cope with tears. He had given her a big bear hug that almost sent her on another crying jag, but she had fought it back and gave him a watery smile.

She had climbed the stairs to her old room, which gave her comfort. She loved visiting Italy with her parents when she was a teenager. They didn't come to this house as often as they should have, but she had some great memories of small breaks in her parents' schedule when they'd gotten away. Memories of their family being like regular people flooded her. She remembered one Christmas they had decided to come to Tuscany. It had just been them—no chefs, no nannies—only Mike and his team, who had stayed out of their way.

Ellie felt now like she was a teenager again. She dressed finally in the same dress she had worn yesterday. She bandaged her foot, but left her sandals off, padding down the stairs slowly.

"Mom? Dad?"

She got herself some coffee and looked outside. Her parents were sitting outside on the patio, near their infinity pool. They were looking out over the restful hills of Tuscany, sipping their coffee. She opened the door, and her father glanced over at her.

"Ellie, sweetie, come join us. We have all kinds of fruit. Your mom made muffins yesterday. A few more weeks here, and I'm going to have to lose weight."

Ellie laughed and rolled her eyes. "Highly doubtful, Dad. You look great."

"Awww thanks, honey. But you're my biggest fan, next to your mom. You wouldn't tell me the truth even if I was packing on the pounds."

"Dad, I'm more than a fan," Ellie retorted sharply.

"Poor choice of words, honey. I'm sorry."

Ellie took a breath. "No, I'm sorry. I didn't mean to bite your head off." She grabbed a zucchini muffin and sunk her teeth into it. She chewed for a minute. "Good muffins, Mom."

"Thank you, dear," Miranda said with a smile. "You just eat that and drink your coffee. And when you're done, you can tell us why you're here."

Ellie grimaced. Her mom always got to the bottom line quickly.

"Lucca and I are...well I mean to say is that Lucca and I..." She looked at her parents. They were clearly not going to help her. "I guess you can say we are over. Whatever it was. We're done."

Monty stared at her, his gray eyes concerned. "Did he hurt you, Eleanor?"

"No, Dad. No! I mean, he didn't mean to. He can't help who he is, just like you guys can't help who you are."

"What does that mean?" Miranda asked. "Exactly who are we?"

Ellie rolled her eyes. "Mom, you know who you are! You're the most famous woman in the world—probably. I mean, maybe there's royalty that outdoes you, but you are American royalty, that's for sure. And Dad is no better. He's a superhero to most men. You saw how Lucca was even at a loss for words. That's how it always is."

Miranda looked sad. "I wish I could change the past, Ellie. Maybe we should have raised you somewhere else besides L.A. I don't know. Your father and I have spent hours talking about it, regretting that we kept you in the public eye. It's jaded you so badly."

Ellie looked at her mom, her eyes wide at her mother's regretful tone. "You guys did the best you could. I always knew you loved me, and that's more than a lot of kids I grew up with had. I'm sorry—I don't mean to sound like a spoiled brat, and I don't want to complain. It's just not what I want now that I'm an adult."

Miranda looked at her daughter thoughtfully. "I never thought you were complaining. I just knew it was difficult."

"Are you in love with Lucca?" Miranda asked, her beautiful brown eyes looking squarely at Ellie.

Ellie felt the color rising in her cheeks. Ever since she was a little girl, she had a difficult time lying to her mom. She could easily fool her dad, but not her mom. Miranda had some kind of instinct, and every time Ellie had tried to be less than honest, it failed.

She was busy inspecting her hands, and her mother was waiting her out. She was like a seasoned interviewer that way. She just let the words hang out there until Ellie would answer. Ellie finally looked up and decided to answer just as directly.

"Yes."

Miranda smiled at her husband. "I knew it! I said to your father, 'Emerson' I said, 'Our Ellie is in love, or I'm not Miranda Montgomery.'"

Ellie smiled weakly. "Mom, falling in love and then being together are two different things."

"You want to tell us what happened? Why is it over?" Miranda asked softly.

"It just got overwhelming," Ellie said. "I couldn't take it, and so I told him it was over."

"Just like that?" Monty asked, his eyes widening.

"Why does everyone keep saying that?" Ellie exploded.

Monty looked confused. "Say what?"

Ellie shook her head. "Never mind. Yes, I ended it."

"You ran," Miranda stated flatly.

"I didn't run. I told Lucca it wasn't going to work, and I texted Dad for a ride. That's it."

Miranda rolled her eyes. "You ran. You always do."

Ellie stood abruptly. "Stop saying that, Mom. I don't always run!

Miranda frowned at her. "Eleanor, sit down while I'm speaking to you!"

Ellie found herself sitting down meekly. She never could disobey that tone.

"Honey, you're my daughter and I love you, but you're a runner. You started running when you were little. You packed your bag and headed off."

"Mom, I was five!"

"Yes, I know, dear. But it didn't quit. You ran to your friend's house instead of going to your ballet recital. You ran to your grandparents when there were those headlines about us getting a divorce."

"I was scared! I knew it wasn't true, but I was upset."

"You ran to art school here. There were a number of places in the U.S. you could have gone. And you ran from that nice boy you told me about who had the crush on you in art school."

"I always loved Italy—that's why I wanted to come here. And that relationship was not going to go anywhere, Mom. He wasn't serious."

"You ran after your show in New York."

"I told you, Mom. I couldn't be anonymous there anymore."

"And you ran yesterday," Miranda said triumphantly, acting like a prosecutor, trying her best case.

Ellie sighed and put her head down on her folded arms. She finally lifted her head up and rubbed her eyes.

"Okay, okay, I admit it. I sometimes run. But I was right yesterday. Okay, I could have been a little more articulate, definitely a little less angry, but we were heading that direction. Lucca told me he was leaving soon to film a new movie. And then there was his face on a bus! What was I supposed to do?"

"I'm not sure about the bus part, honey, but I know that man was falling for you if he hadn't already. Don't you think maybe you could have let him in on the decision a little?"

"It doesn't matter," Ellie muttered. "He wasn't looking for anything serious. He told me that upfront. His parent's divorce was really ugly. He said he'd never marry, and I'm not sure if he'd ever want to be with someone long term."

Miranda looked helpless, for once at a loss for words. It was Monty who spoke up in his quiet voice, "You'll never know for sure now, will you?"

And Ellie felt like she had just been punched in the gut.

ELLIE ASKED her father to drive her back to the villa after lunch. She might as well face the music. Her parents were right. She had been horribly unfair to Lucca, and she should have at least sat down with him when she was calmer to discuss things instead of ranting at him in a parking garage. It was not one of her finer moments. She had let all her anger of her childhood bubble up in one moment and tossed it with Lucca's fame for good measure. She couldn't even remember half of what she said, but she knew it wasn't something to be proud of.

She glanced at her dad. He was dressed in jeans and a polo, his biceps bulging as he handled his vintage Maserati. He loved the old car and tended to take the curves a little fast. He had his sunglasses on, the wind blowing through his thick gray hair. He was oddly silent during the drive.

"Ellie, I want to repeat what your mom said earlier. If we had to do it over, we would have gotten you out of Hollywood and away from all the cameras, honey. We had lived with it for so long we were naïve about how much you would be hounded and how it would affect you."

She was silent for a minute. "It wasn't the easiest thing, but I meant what I said. I had you guys. You were always there for me. And I don't think I appreciated it as much as I should have. At least you have a good marriage."

"Yeah, sounds like Lucca had a really tough time of it," Monty said. "A bitter divorce like that can really screw up kids—you know that. You saw what happened to some of the kids you went to school with."

"I know, Dad. And before you lecture me, I also know I owe Lucca an apology. I shouldn't have said the things I did when I was so angry. I should have thought about things longer, and you were right—as much as I hate to say it. I should have heard him out."

"You don't often tell me I'm right," he said and then smiled smugly. "Kind of feels good."

They waved to the security guard at the gate and drove up the hill to the villa. "Do you want me to come in with you?"

"Oh, thanks, Daddy. But that would be kind of awkward, I

think. I mean, you're pretty intimidating as it is. Lucca may think you're there to beat him to a pulp."

"Only if he hurts you, sweetheart. And actually, I told him he had to worry more about your mother on that score."

She leaned over and kissed his cheek. "That was honest of you! Thanks for the ride. I love you."

"Love you, too. We'll see you at some point, honey. Let us know what you're doing and where," he added pointedly.

She nodded, getting out. "I will, Dad. And you, too! You guys are making some big changes."

Her parents had told her they were heading back to L.A. to get their house ready to sell and move to New York. She was still stunned they were going to leave Hollywood behind and take on Broadway but was excited for this new chapter for them. They had been so enthusiastic about it that she had almost forgotten her troubles.

She waved, watching her father drive away, confidently twisting the car through the hills. She went to open the front door and saw an envelope with her name on it. Grabbing it, she opened it to see it was a note from Mike, letting her know her things had been moved back to the guesthouse. She frowned at the next paragraph. He let her know they were headed back to California. He told her to stay in touch and be careful. He ended it with "Love you, kiddo."

She stupidly tried the door, but it was locked. She had written the code down in her phone, but she realized she didn't really need to go inside anyway if no one was there. She slowly walked down to the guesthouse. She had been dumped. Or had she done the dumping? Lucca had just left. Not even a note. She pulled out her phone. Not even a text. Her heart sank—he had followed her lead.

She entered the code to the guesthouse, and walked in to see her suitcase in the bedroom. She went into the studio to see all her canvases spread out on the floor and her painting supplies laid out.

Her mind was blank. She was stunned. She had come back to talk, and he had just...left. She walked into the living room and sat on the couch. Should she text him? What was she going to say? "Sorry, I got a little carried away. We're not really done." She groaned out loud and rubbed her eyes. What a mess she had made of the whole thing...again.

She walked into the bedroom and changed into a pair of shorts and a shirt, and realized she was not motivated to do anything. She laid down on the bed, watching the ceiling fan circling, and eventually closed her eyes.

THE DAYS SEEM to drag on from there. Ellie got up at sunrise, lugged her easel and palette box around the countryside and painted for hours. She then usually forced herself to stop, return to the villa and go for a swim. There was still some security officers on the property, but they just waved from a distance.

She had been pleasantly surprised to find her refrigerator loaded with fresh food. Someone had gone shopping for her. Too bad she was seldom hungry. She made herself a sandwich for dinner most nights, completely uninterested in eating. She often went outside and sat on the deck, but when the stars emerged, she went inside. She didn't want to think about the hours spent under them with Lucca.

She looked at her phone often, wondering if Lucca would text her. The ball was clearly in her court, though, but to say what? She heard from her parents regularly, and knew they were worried even though she tried to sound upbeat and positive. Brigid checked in as well—still pregnant and very uncomfortable. She said she wanted to live vicariously through Ellie. Ellie had refrained from telling her too much, because selfishly she couldn't bear to go into it.

Her painting was going surprisingly well. She was happy with the colors and hues she was adding to her Tuscan scenes. She would need to go buy some more paint soon. Sorting through her canvases, she had found the unfinished one of Lucca she had been working on. She carefully put it aside. Instead, she looked at the real photos he had shared with her from *Il Palio*. Their silly selfies were fun to remember. They looked so happy. She had more photos, too. Photos of fun things they had seen in Siena, Lucca and even Florence—the photo of her sandwich at Franco's that she had taken. She even had photos of Sophia. She hadn't even gotten a chance to say goodbye to her.

In addition to Lucca, what was on her mind most was the recent email she had received from Madeleine, who mentioned they would return in about ten days. Though she hadn't asked Ellie how it was going, Ellie read those underlying threads. She knew Madeleine was being sweet not asking, but was probably dying to. She looked at her finished canvases, and though she was pleased with a few of her pieces, nothing rose to the level that she had envisioned giving to Madeleine and Bruno.

She took a walk up to the villa to clear her head. It was a cloudy day, but the view from the top was still amazing. She loved looking over the hills, the sunflowers in the distance, the golds and yellows against the greens. Every view seemed like a work of art, and she realized that's why she enjoyed painting it. It was like a second home to her—almost the place she would call home, she realized. It wasn't like she would ever want a painting of L.A. hanging on her walls. The thought of that almost made her laugh.

Suddenly, Ellie had an idea. She got out her phone and hit the number for Gemma, her former roommate and Madeleine's daughter.

Gemma answered immediately. "Ellie! I've been thinking about you! How are you? It's been so long. I don't think I've heard from you since Christmas," Gemma admonished her.

"I know, I know. I'm terrible that way. Time just flies. I'm so sorry. I meant to pick up the phone so many times."

Gemma laughed. "It's okay. I forgive you. You've just been on my mind. Mom said she commissioned you for a piece. How's it going? I hope better than my sculpting!"

"Well, once again, we are on the same wavelength. We always were connected, weren't we?" Ellie chuckled. "Actually, I was stuck for quite a while. I'm finally starting to really see something that I feel good about. You know how it is. I'm much happier with the way things are flowing now, but nothing I create seems like anything I want to give your mom. She's so special and oh my God, why didn't you tell me she was marrying Bruno?"

"I'm sorry! I'm sorry!" Gemma laughed. "Talk about fast. Those two hit it off and asked me to keep it really quiet. The next thing I knew, I was watching them get married. It was all so surreal. It was a real small ceremony. But she's so happy, and you should see Bruno. He's just beaming. Who knew?"

"That's amazing. I'm so happy for them," Ellie said, smiling. She still couldn't believe the small world.

"Have you met Bruno's hot, famous son?" Gemma asked. "I about fell over when I saw him at the wedding. But he was super nice."

Ellie felt herself blushing, even though Gemma couldn't see her. "Um, yeah, I actually did meet him. He was nice," she stammered.

"Spill it."

"What?" Ellie asked. "Spill what?"

"You're completely lying. I can tell by the tone of your voice. You're holding back. Did you have something with him?"

"Oh my God, Gemma. I swear you're worse than my mother!

It's a long story, and I…er, don't really want to talk about it. We did get to know each other, though, but that was completely separate from his being here at the villa."

"He was at the villa?" Gemma asked, clearly surprised.

Ellie bit her lip. "Oh yeah, for a while. That's a whole other story. Look—I promise I'll come to Amsterdam soon, and I'll be thoroughly interrogated by you. And I did call you to catch up, but I wanted to ask you something. It's a random question, but I wanted to know where's home for your mom?"

"The villa, of course," answered Gemma promptly.

"Yeah, now, but I mean, if someone asked her what place brought her joy and comfort, where would she say? Would she say Tuscany?"

"Hmmm," Gemma was thoughtful. "I mean, now it does. She's lived there for a while. But I think she would say the Cotswolds. You know, that's where she grew up."

Ellie's mind began to race. She knew Madeleine was from England, but never really talked about where she had lived. "The Cotswolds, really? Isn't that a region in England with towns that have unique names? I've heard of it but never been there."

Gemma laughed. "Yes, exactly. She was from Stow-on-the-Wold. She grew up there, her grandparents and family were all around. She took me there several times, but now with everyone gone, she doesn't really visit often. She loves that area, though."

Ellie smiled. "That's it, Gemma. I want to paint something from there. Tell me where she took you."

"I think that's brilliant. She doesn't have any artwork from there," Gemma said. She began to tell Ellie about the town and surrounding countryside. It sounded idyllic and full of rich colors, just like Tuscany.

Gemma went on to talk about her sculpting, her husband's job, how she had been preoccupied trying to get pregnant. Ellie made appropriate comments but was only listening with half an ear. She was already formulating a plan, and it was as if a puzzle piece had been worked out.

Hanging up finally after Gemma's recap, Ellie began searching for places to stay. Soon, she had a small cottage to rent, plane tickets and a rental car. She was on her way to Stow-on-the-Wold. She looked around regretfully. She longed to stay in Italy, but right now it was too much of a reminder of her time with Lucca. She would take this escape and after that, she wasn't sure. Deep in her heart, she knew she would return. Italy was always going to have her heart.

twenty-five

Ellie drove hesitantly down the street. From what she could see out of the small windshield of her rental car, the town of Stow-on-the-Wold was as cute as could be.

She drove slowly through the village, passing people out walking and biking. She turned down a little street where she came upon the cottage she had rented. She had felt fortunate there was one close to walking distance to the town, but clearly, she was in the country. She glanced around, smiling. She definitely was in the country. She had passed green fields with sheep grazing, stone churches with cemeteries and larger estates—the manor house sitting farther away from the roads. Fields were abundant with little ponds glistening in the sun. She had even passed some castles on the way that she would have to go check out. She smiled at the wildflowers and colors dotting the rolling hills.

She pulled up to a small stone cottage, with bright pink wild roses growing up the front and smiled. It was sweet looking on the outside, and she hoped the interior was just as cute. The gabled rooftop and the window boxes on the shuttered windows were alive with blooms. Unlocking the door with the key she had picked up at the rental office, she walked in and smiled. Over-stuffed furniture covered in quiet colors was accented with colorful floral pillows. Exposed beams ran the length of the living room. The small kitchen had been modernized, but was still quaint, with small antiques and an old-fashioned chest acting as the island.

Ellie climbed the cramped staircase to a bedroom and bath-room—the comfortable furniture mingled with antique tables and a dresser. Someone had worked hard to make the place very charming. She brought in her suitcase and then her groceries that she had bought at a local market. Putting everything away, she then went back to retrieve her new new custom canvases, paints and an easel she had bought in London. The city had looked tantalizing; she always loved its rich history and vibrancy. But she was here to do a job, she reminded herself. Visiting London could come later. It wasn't a long drive.

She made herself dinner and eagerly walked to the village, watching the stone buildings become golden and then pink in the evening light. Taking photos and strolling around, she decided to return tomorrow for breakfast and get more of a feel for the town. The building in the center that she had assumed was a church was the town library. She finally located the village church with its rounded door that looked like something from the *Hobbit*. She nodded and smiled to people as she walked. The village seemed to have a lot of tourists.

Returning to the cottage, Ellie frowned. It felt a little lonely. She put on some music to fill the void and sat down, pulling out a book. Distracted, she looked at her phone again. She thought a dozen times a day about texting Lucca just to tell him she was sorry. It weighed on her, but every time she went to do it, she didn't know what to say. She didn't like the idea of him hating her, but maybe it was for the best. In the end, he was one of the nicest men she had ever met. He might just want to forgive her and move on, but that was impossible. There was nowhere for them to go. She had done the right thing in the end—at least for him. This made it easy for him to walk away from her. She frowned. She didn't want to make it easy.

ELLIE HAD SUNK into the deep, comfortable bed with its many pillows, sure she was going to get a great night's sleep. Not much time had passed when she realized she was wide awake. Turning the light on, she rearranged her pillows and picked up her computer. She found herself searching for articles about Lucca—something she had never done. What started as a small search sent her going down rabbit holes. Disgusted with herself, she closed her computer and put it on the nightstand, turning out the light again. Her mind was racing with all the photos and history she had found. Who hadn't he dated? He had been with every glamorous woman in Hollywood and beyond. At first, she regretted searching for him, but then she realized it had sort of cleared her mind. It reaffirmed her conviction that she should never have started anything with him. He was just like every actor, and the sooner she moved on, the better. With that, she shut her eyes and willed herself to sleep. It was then she admitted deep down he wasn't like any actor.

In the morning, Ellie woke feeling far from refreshed, but she got up, took a shower, and dressed. Forcing herself to leave the cottage, she went to the coffee shop she had seen the night before. A giant coffee and a warm scone with lots of fresh butter and some homemade jam went down deliciously easy. She was feeling better about things. People were cheery in the town, saying good day and asking how she was. She already liked it.

Walking around, spending time taking photos and studying the architecture kept her busy. She went into a few antique shops and soaked in the charm. Going home, she decided to get in her car and roam the countryside, taking photos and admiring the rich colors and textures. Returning home, she sketched out some ideas and threw the pad down in disgust. She had expected this to be easier. She picked up the pad again and flipped through the pages and found those initial sketches she had done of Lucca on the plane. They were quite good, given how quickly she had to sketch before he noticed.

She set up her easel where she thought there was the best light. She walked over and picked up the partially done portrait she had painted of Lucca. She didn't want to leave it behind, but had felt silly dragging it to England. She put it on the easel and found herself starting to work on it again.

Hours later, she stopped and evaluated it before going to clean her brushes. It was better than she expected and so the next morning, she vowed to continue and keep her mind clear. She painted using the sketches and her photos as her guide. She was in unfamiliar territory; portraits had never been her strong suit. She loved analyzing the shapes of people's faces, but she had always struggled with eyes—and Lucca's challenged her completely. She stopped briefly to gobble down lunch and then continued working. Finally, at the end of the day, she willed herself to stop. There was finish work to do, but the portrait was for the most part complete. She looked at it now clinically and admitted it was some of her best work.

One reason she didn't like painting portraits was because it was hard to break down the wall—the person's character on canvas. This time, she had to admit she succeeded. Smiling, she quit for the day, turning the easel carefully around so she wouldn't spend the evening analyzing it. Tomorrow she would finish it, and then she wasn't sure what she'd do with it. Selling it would never be an option; it was something just for her. It was something she needed to do and keep for a while. Suddenly, her heart felt lighter. Tomorrow, she would begin Madeleine's piece.

twenty-six

What a difference a change of scenery made. Ellie was painting nonstop, it seemed. What once had almost seemed like a chore was back. Her love of her craft was showing as she painted scenes around the Cotswolds. She had envisioned a landscape of the countryside with the village of Stow-on-the-Wold in the distance. She took her backpack with her easel and pallet box to a nearby field and worked all day. It was coming out better than she could imagine, though getting the green hues just right was challenging. She was obsessed with getting the painting finished and had to stop herself when her muscles ached and she found herself chasing the light.

When her day was done, she took long showers and then walked to the village. She knew some of the shopkeepers by name now, and everyone was very friendly and a little curious of the American girl. It was good for her to be around people—at night, she found the cottage's walls closing in on her. Tonight, was one of those times, but she found herself too exhausted to go for a walk. She had returned to the cottage late and now poked at her dinner. It was hard to cook for one, remembering some of the meals she had cooked for Lucca and the guys at the villa.

Glancing up at the mantel, she smiled. She had finished the portrait of Lucca, and had propped the canvas up there. It was probably not doing herself any favors, but she had grown accustomed to glancing up and seeing him there—she had captured his easy grin and she was proud of the painting. It made her feel a little less alone.

Her phone ringing interrupted her thoughts. Smiling, she saw it was her mother—again. Her parents were taking turns calling her, pretending they had things to tell her. She knew they were still worried and curious about her sudden move to England. Though she had explained about wanting to paint something from Madeleine's hometown, they seemed skeptical.

"Hey, Mom, calling to check on me again?" she teased.

"Of course," Miranda answered promptly, and Ellie imagined her smiling. Miranda continued, her voice uncertain. "How are you?"

"I'm doing okay. Like I told Daddy yesterday, things are going really well. I'm thinking of staying for a while longer and painting, even after I finish Madeleine's piece. It's so stunning here."

"Good, good," her mom said distractedly.

"Mom, you sound funny. Is there something wrong?"

"Wrong. Oh well, it kind of depends on how you look at it," Miranda hedged.

"You're scaring me. What's going on?"

"Well, honey, I just don't want to upset you, but I wanted you to know in case any reporters or paparazzi somehow found you."

"Why would reporters care about me? Did you and Dad do something?"

"Well, of course not, dear," Miranda said with an edge. "But someone caught a photo of you with Lucca in Florence. It must have been right before those kids mobbed you. And well, they figured out who you were."

Ellie laid her head back on the sofa. "How bad is it?"

"Well, it depends which way you look at it," Miranda said again.

"Mom, you're killing me. Just send me the link, okay? I better see it myself."

"Honey, don't get angry with Lucca. It's not his fault, and you know it. And none of it is true."

Ellie felt tears well up in her eyes. She had pushed it all to the back of her mind. Now Lucca's easygoing grin was mocking her from the mantel.

"Fine, Mom. Just send me the link, okay?"

"You got it, honey. Talk tomorrow?"

Ellie smiled weakly. "Yeah, Mom, we can talk tomorrow."

She hung up and waited for the ding of her text. Pressing the link, she saw the headline:

Lucca Delarosa Steps Out with Eleanor Montgomery —Will he star in Emerson Montgomery's New Film?

Ellie groaned. "Cause he couldn't possibly be interested in me—just me without my parents," she said out loud to the silent room. She looked at the photo of them. They were both seriously talking on the bench. They had been so in the moment they hadn't even noticed anyone. It wasn't the best photo since they were both so serious, but as always, Lucca looked devastatingly handsome, reaching out to cup her cheek.

She threw her phone down beside her on the couch and stared at the ceiling. Suddenly, she was back to being that awkward teen who was finding out boys were just using her for so many reasons. She had been so stupid and naïve back then.

Angrily, she wiped her tears away. She knew Lucca wasn't using her. He was just as famous as her parents—and of course, he hadn't even known they were her parents up until a couple of weeks ago. It still hurt that the press would print the lies that he would use her, though. As if she had no other appeal.

Ellie went upstairs and washed her face, giving herself a pep talk in the mirror. She realized she was lonely, and that was part of her problem. Picking up her phone, she called Brigid.

"Finally, you call me," Brigid grumbled.

"Hello to you, too."

"Sorry, I'm sitting here feeling like a balloon that's ready to pop. I can't do anything. I've read every book in the house, and Matthew won't let me near the bakery. They are probably running it into the ground," Brigid said. "Please, Ellie. I'm begging you. Tell me some good stories. I need to get my mind off this kid who is bouncing around and using my ribs like a punching bag."

Ellie winced. "I'm sorry I've been out of touch, Brigid. But things are okay. I'm okay," she clarified.

"Have you seen the headlines?" Brigid asked tentatively.

"Yeah, my mom just called. I saw them."

"He wasn't using you," Brigid insisted.

"Of course not, I know that. You don't have to tell me," Ellie said. "But man, does it bring back all the memories."

"I know, I know. I have them, too. I had boys pretend they liked me just to get to my dad," Brigid said sadly.

"I know, Brig. I always forget it wasn't only me. I'm sorry."

"Don't be. You had it ten times worse than most of us. But I'm glad you're not blaming this on Lucca."

"I'm not, but it's still the last thing I need. I hate any kind of publicity, you know that."

"Well, at least you're holed up in that Godforsaken place, whatever it's called. No one will find you there!" Brigid laughed.

"That's kind of true," Ellie agreed. "I think I bring the average age down by a few years here. You should have seen the busload of tourists who came through yesterday. They were very sweet, but just a few decades older than us."

"Are you going to tell me what happened with Lucca?" Brigid

asked softly, changing the subject. "God knows I've got time on my hands."

Ellie sighed and slowly began to talk. She hadn't realized how much she had bottled it up. Starting at the very beginning, it took a while, but she finally got it all out. She hedged a few places—she didn't need to spill everything. When she got to the end, there was silence.

"So that's it? You just left him there? That's it?"

"Why does everyone keep saying that?" Ellie rolled her eyes, frustrated. "Yes, that was it. We were done, Brigid."

"But what if you aren't?"

"We have to be," Ellie insisted.

"You love him, don't you?"

"Yes," Ellie admitted softly.

"Then go to him. Talk to him! Work it out. There has to be a way or at least end it better. If this was a movie, I'd walk out."

"You always did like a happy ending," Ellie said and then gave a weak laugh. "But I don't see this one having a happy ending at all."

"Well, not with you being so freaking stubborn. At least reach out to him."

"He's filming a movie right now. He's busy. I'm not going to bother him," Ellie said. "Plus, I feel like the window has closed. He might have cared, but now too much time has passed, and too much damage has been done."

"Ellie, if I wasn't so pregnant, I swear to God I'd fly over there just to have the pleasure of slapping you! Call him!" Brigid insisted. Then she let out a groan. "I have to go. My husband is calling me. Who knows what is happening now? Just call Lucca and let me know when you do. Take care, Ellie, bye."

Ellie sat back and realized Brigid was right, but she couldn't bring herself to do anything. After all, it wasn't exactly like Lucca was trying to text her either. Besides, he was probably so immersed in his film, he wasn't giving her a second thought. She willed herself to get up. Maybe she would take a walk to the village.

LUCCA WASN'T IMMERSED in his latest movie. After returning to Los Angeles, he had gotten everything in order and traveled to the location shoot in New York. After a couple of grueling weeks filming, production had halted temporarily. An argument between the lead actress and the director was taking on new heights and there was talk of recasting the film. Lawyers were arguing, and Lucca was frustrated. They had done as much work as they could do without the actress' involvement, but now they waited.

His driver had let him off in front of the elegant brownstone on the Upper East Side. He pushed his baseball cap over his eyes and kept his head down as he strode up the stairs to the front door. He had no feelings at all toward the building. His mom had moved there after he had left to go to L.A. He rang the bell.

His mom came to the door, moving slowly. "Lucca?"

"Hi, Mom." He smiled tentatively.

"Why didn't you call?" she asked abruptly.

"Sorry, I wasn't sure if I'd be able to come by. I'm filming and we halted temporarily. I thought I'd come see how you're doing."

"It's been a long time."

"Uh, Mom, can I come in?" he asked uneasily.

Instead of answering, she nodded and backed up.

He stepped into the entryway and gave her a brief hug before taking a long look at her. She looked tired and frail, and was dressed more casually than he had ever seen her. She was wearing velour pants and matching shirt, and her brown hair looked odd to him—he looked closer and saw she was wearing a wig. "Mom, are you okay?"

She looked nervous. "Let's go sit in the living room. Do you want anything to drink? Tea?"

"No, thank you," Lucca answered politely, feeling the hair on his neck stand up. It was like they were strangers. He sat down on the couch, looking around at the modern furniture. The place looked cold and uninviting. He tried to keep the edge out of his voice. "Do you want to tell me what's going on?"

She looked down at her clasped hands in her lap. "I didn't want to bother you, but I've been dealing with some health issues."

"How bad?"

"Breast cancer," she said. "But they think they caught it in time. I had surgery and went through chemo and radiation, and now they have agreed that I can get back to work. I'll have to go in to be scanned every few months, but I should be okay."

Lucca sighed in frustration. "Mom, why didn't you call me? You've been going through this all alone? I could have helped."

She stared at him, her eyes without expression. "What would you have done?"

"Well, I would have made sure you had good doctors and had help here at home and whatever you needed."

"I was fine by myself. I didn't need your help," she said firmly. "I don't need anyone's help."

"I know that, Mom," he said quietly. "But I would have liked to be here for you."

"Lucca, we haven't lived together since you were in college. It isn't like we're a traditional mother and son."

"I'd like to be," he said simply.

Her blue eyes—the same hue as his—stared at him before finally looking away. "That was a long time ago."

He got up and roamed the living room, looking out the front window. He turned to stare at her.

"It doesn't have to be. Mom, I'd like us to be closer, but I think we both have to want it. Do you want it? Or do you just want to stay angry at me because I became an actor?"

"I'm not angry at you because of that," she said abruptly. At his raised eyebrow, she frowned. "I'm angry at myself. I should have encouraged you instead of trying to make you into something that you weren't. I made the same mistake with your father, and look where it got me."

Lucca stared at her, confused. "You hate my father."

She shook her head sadly. "I don't hate him. I hated what we became. Sit down, Lucca. It's time we talked about this. I thought about it a lot when I was in treatment."

"I thought you were upset because I reconnected with him."

She avoided his gaze again, her lips twisted. "No, I was just jealous."

"Why?"

"Because I don't understand either of you, and you're just like him!" She took a deep breath, finally looking at him. "When I met your father, he was studying art history. He wanted to go into academics. I encouraged him. I thought he'd be a professor or something respectable like that. But then, after we married, and I agreed to uproot my life and live in Italy, he told me he wanted to be an artist. I was never around any kind of art in my life—you know that. I grew up on a farm in Indiana with a strict routine: chores, school, homework, church and that was it. I couldn't wait to leave and go to college. Then I met your father and the thought of living in Italy was so enticing." She sighed.

"Go on," Lucca said quietly.

"I was like a fish out of water there. At first, Tuscany reminded me of home with the amazing views and farmland. But then I realized it *did* remind me of home. I wanted city life. And then your dad came up with the idea of being an artist. And between you and me, I don't know about art, but I didn't think he was very good. We argued constantly—mostly about money. I went to work in the bank and loved it, but then I got pregnant with you. We were happy for a time. You were such a sweet child." She smiled weakly.

"I kept working at the bank, and he kept painting, only he wasn't having any success at all. I wanted him to get a real job or go back to school and teach. He wouldn't hear of it. Finally, he got a low-level job at an art gallery. That didn't bring home much. If it wasn't for your grandparents, we would have been living on the streets. We fought a lot."

"I know," Lucca said bitterly.

She looked at him, her eyes filling with tears. "I'm so sorry, Lucca. Things just got out of control. And then I told him I was leaving with you, with the understanding that you'd spend summers in Italy. I was just so bitter and angry we failed. It was hard. I had to go back to school at night and work during the day. I had to work hard to get to where I am."

"I saw you. I know you did, Mom."

"You showed an artistic side early. You wanted to play the piano, remember? I nixed that. Then you wanted to join the theatre club at school. It scared me. You were just like him. I wanted you to be able to go to college and make something of yourself."

"Mom, Dad made something of himself, too. He's one of the premier art dealers in the world."

Her eyes widened. "Do you think I don't know that? I admit it still stings in a way. Then you told me how close you were getting with him. You and I—well, we've had trouble connecting, haven't we? We're two different people. The guilt has been enormous, Lucca. When I was going through chemo, I often wondered if I would have an opportunity to apologize to you."

She looked at him now, sincerity in her eyes. "I am very sorry, Lucca. I lied to you, and I shouldn't have. I just didn't want you to have a relationship with him since you and I didn't seem to be able to have one. That was unfair. Whatever our troubles were, he would have been a good father to you. He probably *is* a good father now."

Lucca gave her a small smile. "Thank you for saying that. I think over the years I've come to accept that you and dad are just very different. You do know there's room in my life for both of you. There always was."

"Aren't you playing a psychologist in this new movie?" she asked suspiciously, amusement in her eyes.

He nodded.

"So you're using your newfound knowledge on me?"

"Whatever works, Mom. Whatever works."

twenty-seven

Lucca looked out the window of his penthouse hotel room, gazing out over the New York skyline. He took a sip of red wine, his thoughts whirling. His heart felt lighter than it had for some time. The talk with his mom had gone well into the night. They had ordered Chinese and had some good laughs, talking about some of the fond memories he did have growing up. Their time together was long overdue.

In the end, he realized how much his upbringing had shaped him. While his mother taught him hard work and a strong ethical background, his father had influenced his artistic side. He also knew their problems had soured him more than he had realized. He had been thinking about that a lot since he had left Italy. He had wanted to talk to his mom about Ellie, but even putting it into words right now was difficult for him.

After Ellie's harsh words in the parking garage, he had told Mike to get ready to leave immediately. He didn't want to see her or have anything to do with her. It angered him that she could simply walk away. Rationally, when he woke up in the middle of the night, he understood the chaos of her childhood and how she didn't want to repeat that as an adult. Still, it hurt him deeply that she could so easily move on. He knew it was unfair to blame her entirely when he had told her that he was never making a commitment to anyone. Now, after his talk with his mother, his eyes had really been opened.

Lucca hadn't wanted to admit to himself that it was Ellie's words that day that haunted him. When he told her about his parents' last argument in Florence, he had deliberately down-played it. The truth was, it was a whopper, and he had heard it all. He remembered his mom's words as if it was yesterday: "I'm done. It's over." It had been devastating for him. When Ellie had directed those same words at him, he completely shut down. All his life, he avoided confrontation. When things got heated in any relationship—work or private, he simply left or gave in. He didn't want to ever induce arguments of any kind. It had been so challenging for him to confront his mother and now he was so happy he had.

He rubbed his eyes. He missed Ellie so much. He hadn't real-ized how much until now. He had immersed himself into this part, and now that he had the time to focus on how they ended, it weighed on him. He knew when she had left him in Florence that he was in love with her. He had thought about what it would take to stay and tell her that, but he couldn't face the rejection. He was also angry. He had repeatedly tried to have a talk about their relationship, and she had continued to put him off. Perhaps if they had decided what the next step was, they could have handled the situation in Florence. How could she just walk away? And not even a text...again.

This movie was so ill-timed on top of everything else. Now, iron-ically, he had time on his hands. Even without the production delays, his agent had negotiated the filming schedule so Lucca could be free for a couple weeks to promote his new movie. He was flying to the premiere in London, doing back-to-back interviews for the day, and then flying back to the U.S. for several talk shows later in the week. He had filmed the movie last year, and there had been some kinks in postproduction, but it was finally finished. He had played a Scotland Yard detective and had spent a few months filming in and around London. It would be nice to go back—though he wished he could stay there longer. He needed time to think.

He turned at the knock on the door. Mike poked his head in. He looked apprehensive. "Hey, boss, there's something I need to show you."

Lucca strolled over and sat down, indicating a chair. "Go ahead, Mike."

Mike handed him his tablet. "Miranda Montgomery texted me this link a little while ago."

Lucca's heart did a backflip as he gazed at the headlines. He scrolled through with disgust. "These are all lies. Of course, I wasn't using Ellie." He glanced at Mike. "Do you think she's seen it?"

Mike nodded. "Miranda told me she let her know. She was concerned reporters might find her."

Lucca grimaced. "I hope not. Maybe we should increase security at the villa."

"She's not there."

"Where the hell is she?" Lucca asked angrily. He had figured once he left, she would stay there, safe and happy.

Mike shrugged. "Not sure. Miranda was pretty cryptic. She probably didn't want to jam me up with you, so she didn't say."

Lucca put his head in his hands and then rubbed his neck. "Thanks for showing me."

Mike nodded soberly and stood. He looked nervous for a second. "Lucca, whatever Ellie told you about her childhood, well, times it by ten. The kid had it really rough. I was there. I wish things had been different for her. She hates the limelight. I'm sure now that she's calmed down, she might feel differently. I just wanted you to know that. I've never seen her as happy as when she was with you."

Lucca looked up at him. "I've been thinking about her nonstop, Mike. I'm going to get her back," he said quietly. He picked up the phone. He needed backup. He called Emerson and Miranda Montgomery.

∽

ELLIE STARED AT HER PHONE. She had woken up to a text:

I'm more sorry that I can say about the headlines. If there is anything I can do to make it better, I will. I'm hoping we can see each other soon. I don't like the way we left it, Ellie. I'm booked up for the next couple of weeks, but if you agree, I'll make it happen. I really need to talk with you.

Ellie had read it a hundred times this morning. It wasn't the text that got her so much, it was the single heart emoji he had added. That heart emoji meant everything to her. She was being beyond ridiculous staring at it.

She sipped her coffee, sitting outside her usual coffee shop. She had no idea what to do. She missed Lucca so much. But what kind of future could they have? And where? She was making great progress on Madeleine's painting. Soon she would be done with it. She had found out that it worked with the rental agency if she stayed on through the fall. She would keep painting the scenes around her. She had been thinking about talking with Bruno about possibly even putting a show together at some point. She needed him to see her work and decide if it was worth it. She would need his feedback. The thought of resurfacing again and showing her art gave her chills and excitement.

She picked up her phone again. Lucca deserved an answer.

Thank you, Lucca. I've wanted to text you…

Her finger hit the delete button. She tried again.

Hi, Lucca. I saw them. I have wanted to text you so many times. To be honest, I didn't know what to say to you except I'm so sorry for the way I acted in Florence. It wasn't fair to you. Maybe we can talk when you're done with your movie.

Her finger hovered over, and she finally added a pink heart.

She re-read it a few times and finally hit send. It was the careful balance she had wanted. Friendly, but also contrite.

He immediately answered.

Ellie, I won't be done for months. On top of that, there's been a few delays. We need to talk before then.

She frowned. *I don't think I'll be in the states soon.*

Where are you?

She bit her lip. *England.*

London? I'm going to be there in about ten days. Can we meet?

She put her phone down as if it was on fire. That soon? She wasn't ready. She gathered herself together and forced herself to answer.

Sorry, no I'm outside of London right now. I don't think so. But maybe in a few weeks. I'm trying to finish this piece.

There isn't anything I can say that will change your mind, is there?

Her heart was pounding. She needed more time to be strong. She decided just to answer: *No.*

Always the chatterbox.

She smiled. *You know me. Can't stop.*

I guess I will have to wait then if I can't change your mind. I WILL wait, Ellie.

Ellie stared at her phone, not knowing how to answer, when another text popped up.

I'll even let you knock me down if it makes you feel better.

Her eyes filled with tears. *I'd like that.*

The knocking me down or the seeing me?

She bit her lip. Time to be honest: *Both.*

She stuck her phone in her pocket and walked through the

town square to home. She felt unsettled now. She pushed it aside. Time to go paint.

ELLIE PURPOSELY KEPT HERSELF BUSY. She drove all around the Cotswolds, weaving in and out of the little villages. She dragged her easel and palette box all over the countryside, even buying a pair of boots so she could stand in the muddy fields. She knew a lot of people in the village now, and they all greeted her. She purposely smiled and waved but didn't engage in conversation. Conversations led to questions, and she wanted to remain private.

She took long walks on the country roads. Exhausted, she was sitting on the couch, sipping tea. She had turned on the television in the cottage for company, which she often did, listening with half an ear. She closed her eyes, wondering what she should do about dinner. She was starting to get weird—being alone all the time. Maybe she should get a cat.

It was Lucca's voice that woke her thirty minutes later. She sat straight up, glancing around disoriented. Had she dreamed of him? Then she looked over and saw him on TV. He was talking to a reporter, laughingly discussing what it had been like to film in London. The interview over, Lucca faded into the background, and the reporter mentioned tomorrow night's premiere and the theatre in the West End.

Those brief moments of him talking and laughing rushed over her. She had gotten so used to staring at his face on the portrait, she had forgotten all the dimensions of his personality. Her heart ached, and she missed him so much. Without thinking, she ran up the cottage's small staircase and grabbed a suitcase from under the bed. She started randomly grabbing clothes. She was going to London, and she would see Lucca, no matter what!

ELLIE HUNCHED down a little in the crowd in front of the theatre. She had thought about texting Lucca that she was coming to London but wasn't sure what to say and put it off. She promised herself she would contact him once she arrived and settled into a hotel. The trip had taken much longer than anticipated, though. She had gotten lost around Oxford, cursing whoever invented roundabouts, which automatically disoriented her. Arriving in London in the evening, she had checked into a hotel where she had stayed before. Realizing the time, she had darted out to grab a taxi to the theatre. She knew Lucca's premiere would be starting soon, and she admitted she wanted to see him, glimpse him—anything. Then when it was over, she would text him she was in London.

A sizeable crowd had formed, and police were guarding the rope lines that had been set up around the red carpet to the theatre. A black car pulled up, and Ellie's heart raced. The crowd cheered, and Ellie found herself being pushed forward. She was closer to the front of the rope now, and she ducked behind a tall man.

She didn't need to bother. She watched as the female lead of the movie got out of the car, followed by her husband. They posed for photographers, waving to the cheering crowd. Ellie came out of hiding then, watching her intently. She knew the woman played Lucca's love interest in the movie. It was then she realized with a heavy heart she probably could never watch one of Lucca's movies again. It would be torturous to see him hold or kiss another woman. Had he just been acting with her? Killing time? She was having doubts right now. She watched the gorgeous woman strolling into the theatre in her short, sequined dress. Ellie could never be that. She didn't want to be that. Even now, she was in jeans and a short raincoat, her hair in a ponytail. She grimaced. This had been a spectacularly bad idea.

Ellie hadn't noticed another car pull up, but the crowd's cheers had begun again. She glanced over this time to see Lucca bound out of the car. He was so handsome in his tuxedo, his smile and wave to the crowd genuine. She could see his deep dimples from here, the beard now gone. Her heart was beating so fast. Now she wanted him to see her. She wanted him to know how proud she was of him and how much she loved him.

"Lucca!" she yelled along with the crowd, realizing with a heavy heart her voice was being drowned out. She tried again. "Lucca!"

He had turned back toward the car, and she watched him hold his hand out. It was then she saw one long, attractive leg emerging from the car.

She blinked hard, her heart sinking in her chest. She watched as Lucca helped a young woman out of the car. She was breath-takingly lovely, and Ellie recognized her as an up-and-coming actress. The crowd roared, and the woman giggled, hanging on to Lucca. He gently smiled down at her—Ellie had seen that look. In fact, he had looked at her that way. She wanted to tear her eyes away but found herself transfixed. It was like watching a train wreck. Time ceased and the noise around her muffled. She stared, as if watching them in slow motion, smiling and waving. She didn't realize she had been thrust so far forward. It was then that Lucca turned his head, and those startling blue eyes were looking straight at her. Time froze for a minute before Ellie turned abruptly and pushed her way through the crowd.

LUCCA OPENED HIS MOUTH. He was about to shout for Ellie. He realized quickly that if he did, it would raise attention toward her. She was so far gone she wouldn't even hear him anyway. He had stepped away from Bethenny, the actress he had grudgingly agreed to bring to the premiere. She looked at him now, masking her confusion. He had to use all his acting skills to bring a smile to his face and grab her hand as they entered the theatre. His mind was a whirling mess. Ellie was the last person he had expected to see. Why had she come? The realization of what she had just witnessed hit him hard. Knowing Ellie, she was already twenty steps down the wrong path.

He cursed inwardly. He needed to contact her. He reached into his pocket and remembered his phone sitting on the charger in his penthouse suite. He had walked out without thinking. He let go of Bethenny's hand now that they were inside and waved Mike over frantically. Mike was busy, talking into his phone, but he quickly responded, ending the call.

"Mike, Ellie is here! I saw her in the crowd. I need your phone. I have to call her."

"No time. We're getting you out of here."

"What? The premiere..."

"There's a gas leak in the next block. This whole place could blow..."

Mike grabbed him and Bethenny, ushering them outside to what had become a chaotic scene. Police were everywhere, directing people away from the area. Sirens were blasting. A member of Mike's security team grabbed Bethenny, and Lucca and Mike began sprinting with the others. Mike yelled back at him: "A car will never get through this mess. Just stick with me."

They were running with the crowd, but Lucca stopped when an elderly woman in front of him fell. He yelled for people to stop as he helped her to her feet. People swarmed around him, and he tried to protect the frail woman, tucking her under his arm. He'd carry her through the chaos if he had to. That's when he looked up to see Ellie running straight at him, the fear on her face evident. He saw her fighting through the crowd to get to him.

"Ellie," he yelled. "Turn around! Run!" What was she doing? He saw the fear in her eyes. "Please, Ellie, run the other way!"

Suddenly, an explosion shook everything around them. People were frantically pushing. Debris began raining down on them. He felt someone grab him and the elderly woman and thrust them toward a building. Mike. Another explosion shook again. By the time he caught his breath and looked around. Ellie was gone.

twenty-eight

Ellie walked through the crowded streets of London. She was grubby, and she smelled like smoke. People were everywhere, and she heard snatches of conversations—speculation that it was a bomb.

She was still shaken. After seeing Lucca get out of the car with Bethenny, she had pushed her way through the crowd. It was only at the corner on the next block that she had slowed down to a walk and witnessed fire trucks pulling up. She had overheard them talking about an imminent disaster that could level the whole area. Not knowing if it was a fire or a bomb or what, Ellie just knew she had to get back to Lucca. She had found herself running full speed toward the theatre. Dang, those walks weren't exactly cutting it for her cardio. Her lungs were dying when she finally had to stop because she was going against the crowd. The relief had been so great when she saw him helping a woman to her feet. All she wanted to do was hug him for hours, but instead, the explosions rang out, and she had been forced along by the throngs of panicked people. She was worried if she stopped, she'd get jostled to the ground. Finally, after several blocks, Ellie had reached into her jacket pocket for her phone, only to discover it was gone...again. It must have fallen out of her pocket in the chaos.

There was no way she was going to get a hired car or taxi, so she kept walking. It was starting to drizzle. Great. That's all she needed. Finally, she entered the hotel lobby, and the desk clerk ran toward her. "Miss James, are you okay? Were you in the blast?"

She smiled weakly. "Yes, unfortunately, I was near it. But I'm okay. I'm just going to go up to my room to shower."

"Would you like some dinner? We can send some food up!" Ellie smiled weakly. She knew the concierge from years ago, and he was eager to please. Agreeing, she told him to send up whatever he wanted. Food didn't sound good, but she knew she'd feel better if she ate. Turning on the TV, she went to take a hot shower. She was just towel drying her hair when the food arrived. The news coverage on the TV was all about the blast and Ellie sat down, and sipped the brandy the concierge had sent up. It burned her throat but was strangely comforting.

Police were confirming to reporters what they knew. They were still combing through the rubble, but they were hopeful there we no fatalities. Still, several people had gone to the hospital with injuries. Ellie didn't realize she was holding her breath until she saw a photo of Lucca flash on the screen. They mentioned the crowded streets and Lucca's movie premiere, even flashing video of him and Bethenny getting out of the car. She winced. In all the chaos, she had almost forgotten about that. The reporter continued talking about the premiere, which was cancelled for now and said the famous actor had left London.

Ellie reached for the room's phone. She didn't know Lucca's number. Who memorized a number these days? The only number she knew by heart was Mike's. It went to straight to voicemail.

She felt a lump in her throat. "Mike, um, this is Ellie." Swallowing a sob, she continued. "I lost my phone. I wanted to talk to Lucca. He's okay, right? And you're okay? I mean, they said so on the news, but I was just hoping they were right. I guess you guys are up in the air by now." She took a shuddering breath. "I...well I wanted to tell him that...oh, Mike. I don't know. I made such a mess of everything. I know he was with that actress tonight, but I'm hoping there's still a chance for us. I've been so wrong and so stupid. You know me—stubborn Ellie, right? And now I've probably lost him. I think he saw me but will you at least tell him I came here because I wanted to see him..badly. That I would have given anything to talk with him and tell him I'm sorry. There's so much more. Like a lot more, but um, that's it, I guess. Bye."

Ellie hung up the phone and burst into tears. She knew it was delayed shock, but she couldn't stop crying. Letting it out was something she wasn't good at, but she cried for several minutes, before sitting up and sipping the brandy some more. Remembering Lucca's tight valve analogy about crying, she realized it did feel good. She didn't cry often and now she was making it a habit.

She laid down on the couch, her stomach in knots. She wasn't really sure what she even said in her rambling message to Mike, and had just blurted out whatever came into her head. Tomorrow may bring regrets. For right now, she needed to just close her eyes.

LUCCA HUNG up his phone and paced his hotel room. He had been on the phone for the last hour with studio executives, his agent and others, assuring them he was fine. Police were still investigating, but it appeared to be a gas leak and nothing intentional. He was relieved. He had been worried that it might be terrorism or something sinister.

He was furious at Ellie, and wanted to know if she was okay.

The least she could do was answer her damn phone. He had called it dozens of times and texted. Nothing. It went straight to voicemail. His ears were still ringing and he was exhausted; it had been so disorienting. Debris had fallen everywhere, and he had lost her in the chaos.

Mike entered the suite, his face unreadable.

"Any word from Ellie?" Lucca asked. He was hopeful if she didn't want to speak to him, she would at least contact Mike.

"Actually, yes. I was in the briefing with Scotland Yard. She left a voicemail, but I think it was more for you, then me." He handed Lucca his phone, a gleam in his eye.

Lucca lifted the phone to his ear. As he listened, slowly a smile spread across his face. When he was done, he looked at Mike, smiling for the first time in hours. "I need to find her."

"Already working on it. The number just goes to a hotel chain. There's four in the city. We're calling them all—we may have to go in person, though, to persuade them that it would behoove them financially to confirm if she's there. But I suggest you get some sleep now and let me worry about it. The whole city is locked down. Police are out everywhere just making sure it stays peaceful, and that it doesn't erupt into looting or anything. You both need rest. You can talk with her in the morning."

"I'm going to call her parents," Lucca said firmly, already picking up his phone.

"Do you think that's wise? You may get them all stirred up. They probably don't even know she was in London."

"I guess you're right," Lucca said, clearly frustrated.

"Look, just get some sleep. By the sound of it, she is pretty spent. The two of you need some rest before you're going to be able to sort this out. Take my advice."

Lucca thanked him quietly and went to pour himself a drink and sit down on the couch. He knew Mike was right. He focused on breathing. What a disaster. He wanted to talk to Ellie so badly. Just hold her. Forever. He needed to tell her that.

ELLIE WOKE UP DISORIENTED. Darn brandy. Blinking in the blinding light that entered her hotel room, she realized she hadn't bothered to shut the curtains. It was still early, and she had slept on the couch for several hours. She sat up, trying to loosen her neck and stretched her sore body. What an awful night. It had gone from euphoria of seeing Lucca to devastation at seeing him with the young, gorgeous woman. Then they'd almost been blown to bits.

Her phone call to Mike came back to her. She was mortified. When she was running back to find Lucca, all she wanted was to be with him. It had all come to her with such startling clarity. In the chaos, she had forgotten about him being with the young actress. Had he moved on? And even after see her and knowing she was in London, he had simply taken off. Lucca was probably back on a movie set today, clearly forgetting about her. Hope sprung lightly in her mind—maybe Mike wouldn't play the message for him. With a sinking heart, she knew he would. Mike was a straight-up guy and wouldn't keep anything from Lucca.

Ellie stood and stretched some more. Originally, she had planned to stay in London for a few days. That had lost its appeal. She would return to the cottage—her refuge for now. First, she needed to get a phone—her parents would kill her if she disappeared again.

She quickly dressed and threw the rest of her things back into her suitcase. Soon she had checked out and was driving out of the parking garage. She chose a phone store on her way and headed in that direction. Time to get out of Dodge.

twenty-nine

"What do you mean, she's gone? Lucca yelled at Mike. "I thought you figured out what hotel. Why didn't you get somebody over there to make sure she didn't leave?" Lucca knew he was being irrational, but he was at the end of his rope.

Mike stared at him hard, with narrowed eyes. "I did confirm it in the early hours this morning. As it was, I got up first thing and went over there because I thought she would only listen to me. I didn't think she would get up so early to leave. I should have known."

Lucca felt like a heel. He saw the fatigue in his security officer's face. "I'm sorry, Mike. I didn't mean to snap. I'm on edge."

"I get it. I get it. Ellie can frustrate the hell out of a person. Sure you want to be with her?" Mike was now looking slightly amused.

"Without a doubt," Lucca answered. He looked at his watch. "Now I'm going to call her parents. They were traveling back to California to tie up some loose ends, so it's not even midnight there."

He wasn't surprised when Miranda picked up right away. "Lucca, are you okay? We saw the news about the explosion!"

"Yes, thank you. We weren't harmed. But Miranda, listen, Ellie was there."

"Ellie was there? Did she go with you? Is she okay?" Miranda was clearly confused, and her voice rose frantically.

"She is fine. Fine. Please don't worry. She left Mike a voicemail that she was okay. She called from a hotel phone—she lost her cell phone again."

Miranda sighed. "No wonder! I texted her a couple of times last night. I'm glad you told me."

"Yes, well, there's more. You should know I took Bethenny Sanchez to the premiere." He paused only for a second, anxious to explain. "It meant nothing. It was a favor to my agent who represents her, too, and I also hoped it would get reporters off the whole story with Ellie."

"Did Ellie see you?" Miranda asked softly.

"Unfortunately, yes."

Before she could speak, he continued persuasively. "I know you didn't want to tell me before. But now I need to know. Where is she staying? She's checked out of her hotel already in London. I need to get to her, Miranda. I need to be with her. I have a lot to say to her."

There was a long silence. "I told you when you called the last time, Lucca, she's a runner. When things get bad, Ellie runs."

Lucca smiled, remembering Ellie's voicemail and the love he had heard in her voice.

"I know, Miranda. But this time, she ran *toward* me."

THE PHONE STORE wasn't open yet when Ellie arrived. Frustrated, she sat at a coffee shop next door and ate two donuts, suddenly starved. Once the store opened, she was first in line and soon got a phone. She started driving back, as it was still uploading. Hearing dings and sounds, indicating texts and voice-mails were coming in, she didn't stop—she'd look at them when she got home.

Ellie drove back the way she came and was feeling confident this time in her navigation skills. Everything was fine until she got to the bridge she had taken with ease yesterday. Today, there was roadwork and a detour. She had to wait in a long line of cars before finally being able to take the detour and go around. The detour threw her off, and she finally pulled to the side of the road to activate her phone's navigation system. For some reason, she had no service. She drove a little and found a bar. She threw her phone back on the seat and continued. She thought she was on the right road. Finally, pulling alongside two bicyclists, she asked them directions. She wasn't that far off, but she turned around and took a different exit at the last roundabout. Now things were looking familiar. She drove easily to the village and toward the cottage, driving toward the little alleyway where she parked the car.

She picked up her phone. There were dozens of texts and missed calls. She scrolled through Lucca's. He obviously had been frantic, trying to see if she was okay. She smiled. He even explained why he was with Bethenny in case she was angry and purposely not answering his texts. There was no text about her voicemail to Mike. Mike might not have told him, after all.

Hey Lucca, I'm sorry. I just got my new phone. I lost it in the crowd. Can we talk soon?

She hit send before she could analyze her feelings, grabbed her bag, and started walking toward the front of the cottage, staring at her phone.

"How about we talk right now?"

She looked up to see Lucca standing a few feet away. He was wearing jeans, a T-shirt and a leather jacket. For once, his hair was disheveled as if he had been running his hands through it.

Her heart was beating out of her chest. He was looking at her, exhausted, his heart in his eyes.

She didn't care anymore. She dropped her bag and ran to him, launching herself into his arms. It was what she had wanted to do so badly the night before. He held her tightly for a long time before finally loosening his grip and pulling away, his incredible eyes searching her face.

"Are you okay?"

She nodded, unable to speak.

"Ellie James Montgomery. You're crying."

She gave a watery smile. "I *can* cry, you know."

"I've never seen you cry before."

She shrugged. "Now I can't seem to stop."

He grabbed her, hugging her tightly. He pulled away, looking at her for a minute, his hands on either side of her face. Slowly, his mouth descended and kissed her. She melted into his kiss, feeling his firm, strong lips. It was like coming home, and she sank into the kiss. It went on and on until she felt her knees almost giving out.

He pulled away then and gave her a brilliant smile. "I don't want to stop doing that."

She smiled weakly. "They said on the news you left."

"I'm right here. Let's go inside," he said quietly. He went to pick up her bag from the ground. "I think we have some talking to do."

She nodded, suddenly embarrassed, remembering her voicemail. She felt uncertain. Opening the door, she waved him in. "Come on in. Do you want something to drink?" She leaned against the now shut door.

He shook his head, staring at her.

She felt her nerves bubbling over. "Um, how did you know where I was?"

His gaze met hers. "Your parents."

"Oh geez, you called my parents?"

He nodded. "I have a few times, actually. I visited them when I was in New York, too." He looked around and then meaningfully at the couch. "Can we sit down?"

She gave a nervous laugh. "Oh yeah, sorry." She walked over to the couch and sat down. He followed, lowering himself slowly down. Glancing around, his eyes went to the mantel.

His eyes widened. "What exactly is that?"

Oh my God, she had forgotten about the portrait! "Uh, so I was just playing around."

He stood and walked over to it, picking up the canvas. "Ellie, this is really eerie."

She looked down at her hands. "I know, I'm sorry. I was just kind of experimenting. I've never done a portrait I liked before."

He looked up at her, clearly amused. "I didn't mean eerie in a bad way. It's just a little crazy how you captured me. I mean, it looks almost like a photo. It's just kind of startling."

She looked at him, biting her lip.

He smiled at her, his dimples showing. "Do my eyes follow you around the house?"

She laughed then. "No, I purposely made sure they didn't."

He laughed, too. "Leave it to you to figure out restrictions." He put the painting down carefully and came back to the couch. He grabbed her hands, looking at her steadily. "I've missed you so much."

She glanced away. "I've missed you, too. But I just have to know. Are you here because of the ridiculous voicemail I left Mike?"

He turned her chin so she had to look at him. "That wasn't ridiculous, Ellie. I felt your love. I heard your love. I would have been here with you, though, even without that voicemail."

She gave him a small smile but felt her face flushing. "Okay, fine. I'm so in love with you, Lucca. Happy now? Why am I always the one to go first?"

He grinned.

"Stop grinning. It's not funny." She gave him a small push on his chest.

"You can't knock me down when I'm already sitting," he said and then laughed. "Yes, I'm *very* happy. And I'm hoping to get even happier after we clear the air." He suddenly turned serious. "Ellie, I love you more than I've loved anyone in my whole life. My whole career, I've had to act like I was in love and yet, I didn't have a clue what it felt like. Now I do."

"What does it feel like for you?" she whispered, hoping he felt the same as her.

He smiled gently. "Terrifying and fantastic all at the same time."

She grimaced. "For me, too."

She grew serious, her eyes searching his face. "Lucca, I need to tell you something. I'm so sorry about what happened in Florence. It wasn't all about you, but it was all directed at you. I've done a lot of thinking about my childhood, and I've realized how I let it get in my way as an adult. I shouldn't have left like that."

He stared at her. "I think we both had our issues that day. It definitely brought back bad memories for you, but it did for me, too," he said softly.

She looked at him, confused, and he sat back, keeping one arm around her. He told her about how it resurfaced all the hurt from his parents' last fight in Florence. "So when I heard those same words, I just became that nine-year-old boy again. I just wanted to put a pillow over my head and make it go away. I left instead. I realized how much I've avoided confrontations over the years. I didn't wait for you to figure out how you were feeling and come back to the villa. This time I was the runner."

Ellie turned toward him, stroking his arm now. "I shouldn't have used those words. I should have waited and calmed down."

He smiled at her. "Ellie, when have you ever waited and

calmed down? You can work on that, and I can work on confronting the bad stuff when it happens."

He leaned over and kissed her deeply. They finally broke away, both breathing heavily.

She looked at him, uncertainty on her face. "I want you to know that it doesn't matter anymore. You being famous is part of who you are. I can do it. I *will* do it if it means being with you."

He smiled, tucking a strand of hair behind her ear. "You're sure? Because you understand it will be forever, right?"

"What do you mean? You said you're never getting married."

"Let's just say I've had a change of heart about that."

He sat back, taking her with him, her head on his shoulder. He told her about his talk with his mother. "They made a lot of mistakes—both of them. But that doesn't mean you and I will. My mother couldn't compromise, and I think my father gave up trying as well. We *can* compromise—I will, and you have already told me you will."

She sat up, looking at him with raised eyebrows. "And just how are *you* going to compromise?"

He laughed. "Ellie, I love how you cut to the bottom line!" He grew serious. "I've been thinking about this for a long time. I want to form my own production company and produce content out of Italy. I even talked with your father about it, and he's been very encouraging. I want us to live in Tuscany if you're up for it. I can move about more freely there. We can raise our children there."

"Children?" she squeaked. "Lucca, if this was a movie, you would have really rushed the final scene."

He smiled. "Okay, so I'm not a screenwriter. But I think I could be successful at producing the content I want to."

"Are you sure you wouldn't miss being an actor?"

He shook his head. "I don't think so. I've done it, Ellie. And the last few years, I've grown so restless. When we were in Italy, I could breathe."

She stared at him. "If you're sure, Lucca. I don't want you to make this move for me. If it's only for me, it will be disastrous in the end."

"It's not. It's for me. Come to Italy with me, Ellie," he breathed, his lips descending on hers.

"Yes," she whispered.

thirty

Ellie took a small sip of prosecco. She smoothed her hands down her simple black dress. Nervously, she patted her hair, which was twisted up for the occasion. She glanced around the crowd, milling about the Florence art gallery that Bruno had chosen for her show.

She had stayed another month in the Cotswolds after Lucca had left to continue working on his last film. She missed him terribly but looked forward to their constant video calls. He had slipped over twice, flying all night just to spend two days with her. She didn't know if it was because she was in love or what, but she painted like she couldn't stop. She had traveled all around, taking in the rustic scenery, and she captured those images on canvas. At Lucca's encouragement, she had her artwork from England crated and sent to Tuscany.

It had been time to decide it if was worthy to show anyone. They had agreed that Lucca would first call his dad and tell them about their relationship. While Lucca had assured her Bruno and Madeleine were ecstatic for them, Ellie felt a little awkward. She finally left England and arrived at the villa, eager to show them her work, but also apprehensive about how her former mentor would feel about her being with his son.

She shouldn't have worried. Bruno, taller and larger than Lucca, had wrapped her in a bear hug upon her arrival and squeezed the breath out of her. Madeleine had greeted her warmly as well, and they had sat down to an exquisite dinner to catch up. Bruno had teased her about Lucca, but Madeleine had shushed him, changing the subject when she saw Ellie squirm. She had been grateful—it felt weird to be there without Lucca. She had eventually got up her nerve and shown Bruno some of the photos of her artwork. He looked at them one by one, a thoughtful expression. It was only when he reached the end that he had looked up with a big smile, and she knew she had his approval. He started immediately to put together the show in Florence. Now it was her big night, and her heart wouldn't stop racing.

"Ellie, you captured my home perfectly," Madeleine whispered to her. Without realizing it, Ellie had gravitated toward the painting she had finished with Madeleine in mind. Bruno had insisted on showing it, with a small sold sign below.

Ellie hugged her. "I wanted you to have a piece of your own home to bring to the villa. I have to say the place brought me so much inspiration."

Madeleine smiled, an eyebrow going up. "Was it the Cotswolds, or was it that extremely loveable man—who also happens to be my son-in-law—who is coming through the door right now looking like he can't wait to see you?"

Ellie's eyes widened. She thrust her glass at Madeleine without thinking and ran over to throw herself in Lucca's arms. He kissed her passionately before hugging her tightly. "I'm so proud of you," he whispered in her ear.

She drew back, her heart melting at the love in his eyes. Now she no longer cared that they were in public or who saw them. She just wanted to hang on to him. He looked so devilishly handsome in his dark suit, his tie the same color as his eyes. She smiled. "You haven't even seen everything yet."

"I've seen most of it. It's going to be a breath of fresh air. Mixing Tuscany's scenery with the Cotswolds—there's so much depth and so much texture to your work."

Ellie laughed. "I thought you said you don't know art."

He hugged her. "But I know the artist. Very well, I might add."

He drew away again and looked at her, his eyes searching her face. "Is it okay if I'm here? I almost didn't come. I don't want to take away from your big night. I probably will be recognized," he said, glancing around. The room was full of people browsing.

Ellie smiled. "It's time to make great memories in Florence. And I think it will be fine. Art goers aren't really the type to mob you, though you may get the occasional request for a selfie."

"I don't want to take anything away from your big night, Ellie."

She laughed. "I don't care about that, Lucca. I'm just so surprised you're here. I thought you were still filming."

He smiled. "No, we wrapped. It was all I could do to get out of there. I'll have to go back for postproduction work, but then I'm all yours."

Her heart gave a somersault. She had a lump in her throat and gave him a hug, unable to speak. Finally, she grabbed his hand, "Come on, my parents are here, too. I just wanted the people I loved to be here. Let's go talk to them."

Suddenly, her night was perfect.

ELLIE TUGGED on Lucca's hand. "Slow down, Lucca. I can barely keep up with you. Where are we headed? And are we stopping for coffee?"

He looked back and smiled, continuing to lead her through

the streets. He stopped then as they entered the Piazza del Campo. Ellie smiled, remembering *Il Palio*.

"It looks so different now," she said, glancing around. There weren't very many people around at this time in the morning, other than the ones crossing the piazza on their way to work or errands. Ellie and Lucca walked to the very center of the piazza, holding hands still.

"But why are we here?"

Lucca stopped walking. He was wearing khakis and a light blue button-down shirt that reflected his eyes more than ever. She noticed how relaxed he seemed these days now that he had decided the future. He smiled at her, his eyes glancing down over her floral blue dress and sandals. "You dressed up today."

"Well, you said we were going to be doing important stuff. I wasn't sure what that was."

"This," he said quietly, getting down on one knee, and holding a ring box open.

"Lucca! Get up, everyone is going to notice you! We'll get mobbed." She glanced around frantically and realized how ridiculous the statement was. Two older Italian gentlemen were sitting at a table, intent on a chess game.

"Hardly a mob, here, Ellie. I'm not getting up until you say yes."

She laughed. "You haven't asked me anything!"

Lucca rolled his eyes. "Do you want me to get up, or do you want me to ask you what I came here to ask you?"

Her eyes were huge. "I want you to ask me," she whispered.

"Ellie James Montgomery, Injured Cake Deliverer, World-Famous and Talented Artist and most of all, my soulmate, will you marry me?"

"Lucca Leonardo Benedetto Delarosa, Formerly of Holly-wood, California, now Tuscany, I will definitely marry you."

Lucca quickly jumped to his feet and gave out a whoop, grabbing her and twirling her around. They glanced around as the men stopped their game to watch. "Brava," they heard one say. Lucca smiled, kissing her several times before pulling back. He slid a glittering emerald, surrounded by diamonds, on her finger, and Ellie admired it. He knew how much she loved color.

"How did you know my real name?"

"What?" She came out of her trance and laughed. "Your father, of course. He told me he wanted to name you Leonardo, but your mom and he compromised."

Lucca smiled gently, pushing some strands of hair away from her face. "Well, at least they compromised on something."

"You're sure about this, Lucca?" Ellie looked at him tentatively.

"Ellie, I dragged you out at sunrise to put an engagement ring on your finger. I'm pretty sure I'm sure."

He kissed her slowly. "I love you more than I could possibly tell you, but I promise to spend the rest of my life showing you."

She threw her arms around him. "I love you so much, Lucca. So much that I promise never to knock you down."

He threw his head back and laughed. "We can negotiate those terms later."

They walked hand-in-hand through the piazza. As they strolled by the two men, one nodded: " *L'amor move il sole e l'altre stelle.*" Love moves the sun and the other stars.

Ellie gave Lucca a brilliant smile.

epilogue

Ellie couldn't believe it was her wedding day. It had been such a whirlwind. She and Lucca had made all the decisions at their breakfast picnic. He had arranged it at a nearby vineyard after his proposal. They had laid down on the blanket, talking quietly about what they wanted. They were both firm in a quiet wedding, surrounded by the people who meant the most to them.

Her mother wasn't too happy that the wedding was happening so fast, but Miranda knew better than to argue with her stubborn daughter or now her equally stubborn future son-in-law. Lucca and Ellie wanted a small, intimate wedding at the lemon grove as soon as possible. Mike had agreed, knowing it was the most secure location.

"That might mean a dress off the rack," Miranda had wailed.

Ellie smiled, shaking her head. Miranda got on the phone right away, calling her favorite designer, who volunteered to fly in immediately to discuss the details. Ellie had stayed firm in her resolve to look like herself. She had described to the designer a very simple slip dress of white satin, which dipped dangerously low in the back. She smiled at the heated look she undoubtedly would get from Lucca. Her hair she chose to wear up because Lucca had once told her he liked it that way because he could kiss her neck. When her mother suggested a tiara, Ellie burst out laughing, shaking her head firmly. She decided against any type of headpiece or veil.

"Oh good, you're up," whispered Brigid, coming into Ellie's room, holding her baby at her shoulder.

"Did my goddaughter get you up early?" Ellie asked, reaching for the baby. "Come here, Norah, sweet girl."

Norah stared up at her, stretching her little arms. Ellie reached down, gently kissing her. "She's so precious, Brigid."

Brigid smiled. "Yes, she is. Not so much at two in the morning. But we are very blessed. I'm just glad she's entered the world. I thought she was going to stay inside me forever."

Ellie laughed. "I would have postponed the wedding until she was out. I had to have you here. I hope it wasn't too soon to travel."

"Oh no, it's fine. Especially on Lucca's private jet," she said with a laugh. "Vanity makes me wish you would have waited a few more months so I could lose some of this baby weight, but thanks for letting me choose a dress that hides it."

"You look beautiful," Ellie said, still looking down at Norah.

"You do, too, Ellie. You really look happy."

"I am happy," Ellie agreed softly. "I'll be even happier in a few hours.

Later that afternoon, the wedding went off without a hitch. Ellie and Lucca had chosen to get married at the entrance to the gazebo in the lemon grove. The love on Lucca's face when she and her father walked down the field on the makeshift runway was all she needed to see. Her heart tugged when she saw him wiping tears steadily from his eyes. She was his family now, too.

The ceremony had been brief, with Brigid and Marco standing on either side of them. Sophia, who had been staying with Margherita while Lucca filmed, now sat up front, a white bow around her neck. Once officially married, they had turned to see all the people they loved, laughing and clapping them down the aisle. She had been so touched that all of Lucca's family had wanted to be a part of it. Well, most of them, anyway. Lucca's mom had chosen not to attend, telling him it would be too hard on her after her cancer treatments. She had invited them to dinner the next time they were in New York. Lucca had been at peace with it, telling Ellie he was meeting his mother where she was, and it finally felt good.

Margherita had done her magic yet again. The tables outside under the lemon pergolas were perfectly set, and everything was draped in white fairy lights, with greenery and bright flowers bursting from pots. They had dined on several courses leisurely. Ellie had glanced over, smiling, watching her parents holding court. They blended in so well with Lucca's family. People were now standing, eager to stretch their legs and have another glass of prosecco.

"Margherita, we can never thank you enough. This is the most beautiful wedding we could ever ask for," Ellie said as she hugged her.

"I had a feeling about you two," Margherita said, her eyes lighting up. "I knew you would figure it out."

Lucca laughed, giving her a big hug. "I'm glad we didn't let you down."

Margherita beamed at them before turning to go, catching her high heels on the stone. She would have fallen if two strong arms didn't reach out.

"Oh, thank you, Mr. Donnelly," Margherita said, flushing, glancing up at Mike.

Mike smiled gently at her. "It's Mike, and you're welcome."

He turned to Ellie. "You look breathtaking, sweetheart."

"Grazie," said Lucca before Ellie could speak. Ellie shoved at him and hugged Mike. "Thank you," she whispered.

"I knew you and Lucca would be here getting married when I

saw you at the last wedding," Meara said, breaking up the moment, reaching over to hug Ellie.

"Meara's always right—or she'll tell you she is, anyway," said Kate with a laugh. Ellie laughed at the two of them. She had gotten to know them much better in the last few weeks. She and Lucca had traveled down a few times, and the women had gone shopping together. Just the other night they had thrown her a little bachelorette dinner party with Brigid attending, as well as Kate's friend, Teresa, who had flown in rather mysteriously.

"Look at Teresa over there," Kate commented, amusement in her eyes. "It's like she's mesmerized. I don't think you have to worry about her, Ellie. She can't seem to utter a word to Lucca." They all laughed, but Kate still teased her. "Not that you would need to anyway. That guy is so in love with you."

Ellie smiled. "I know. Thank God, because when he looks at me, I feel like Teresa looks!"

Lucca was heading over now, his face filled with tender amusement. "Katie, I left Teresa sitting down over there."

Kate laughed, shaking out the folds of her pink gown. "I better go throw some water on her or something." Two strong arms came around her from behind. "Not before you dance with me," Marco said, kissing her neck.

Kate smiled at Lucca and Ellie. "I feel like this is déjà vu. Could you guys go dance already?"

Ellie laughed. "We are just waiting on one thing."

Lucca looked at her inquisitively. He turned when he heard a commotion. The cake was being wheeled out, sparklers shooting out colorful flames. She grabbed his hand, and they walked over to it.

"Ellie, did you decorate the cake?" Lucca asked, astonished. "When did you have time?"

"When you were having all those secret meetings with Stefano and Marco!" Ellie said, giving him a teasing smile. "By the way, you still haven't told me what those were all about."

"I promise I will on our honeymoon."

Ellie sighed, leaning into him, thinking of the two weeks they would be sailing on Marco's yacht.

He smiled. "I thought Brigid was going to do it all."

"She did, but I wanted to help. It seemed like going full circle. Besides, I had to write the inscription."

He bent his handsome head to read it: *Amore sotto le stelle.* Love under the stars.

He bent to kiss her. "Our first night together was under these stars. How did you know that was the night I fell in love with you?" he whispered.

"Because it was the same night I did, only it took me a little longer to realize it," Ellie said, her hand tracing his jaw. "You're my Tuscan star."

also by tess rini

Looking for your next sweet romance from Italy?

Check out the next in the series—
Teresa and Stefano's story: ***My Christmas in Capri***

E-Book Available Now!
Paperbacks available at Amazon or your favorite bookstore
Continue on to read the first chapter!

My Christmas in Capri: Chapter One

Stefano Rinaldi glanced impatiently at his watch for the tenth time. Since he was planning to be in Naples for the day, he had agreed to pick up his sister-in-law's closest friend, Teresa Rossi, at the airport. He checked the app on his phone and then the airport's information board. Her flight had arrived. Where was she?

Taking out his phone, Stefano texted again. Frowning, he waited. Nothing. And no replies to his last two texts. Did she miss the flight? Possibly customs could be backed up—the airport was very crowded this time of day. He agreed to meet Teresa where travelers exited customs, so as to not miss each other. Maybe she misunderstood—but there was no other way for her to exit.

It had been a long day, and he was in meetings for most of it. As Executive Vice President of his family's dynasty, Oro Industries, Stefano had worked hard to ascend the corporate ladder. His role now was to ensure their products' distribution lines in wholesale and retail were on target and thriving. Ranging from limoncello to lemon soap, olive oil, and lemon candy, Oro's products were continuing to grow in markets all over the world. And then there were the many local businesses Oro had acquired over the years. He loved his family, but every day, he hated his job a little more. With his brother, Marco, at the helm, he felt guilty for not being more enthusiastic. Marco, who had recently taken over as CEO, needed Stefano to keep a tight hold on things while they navigated through some tough times. Marco inherited his title from their uncle—*Zio* Angelo. But with the role, came managing the corporation's Chief Financial Officer—Angelo's closet friend. Stefano grimaced, thinking back to the fraud they uncovered at the hands of the detestable man. It had caused a lot of pain. The corporation was hopefully through the worst and Marco was finding his feet, but Stefano didn't know what the future held for him personally.

He had taken off his tie and left his suit jacket in the car. Now he longed to get home and change out of his white dress shirt and dark gray slacks. He needed time to unwind, but that probably wouldn't happen. The house was packed with family. At least he could cook dinner and possibly have some solitude while doing it.

If it was anyone but Kate, he would have said no. He was fond of his new sister-in-law, and it wasn't that out of his way. Except, well, he was picking up Teresa. There was just something about her. He met her when she arrived for Marco and Kate's wedding, and she had unnerved him. At first, he was highly physically attracted to her, but then he watched her practically drooling over their cousin, Lucca, a famous movie star. Next came her nonstop chattering with their brother, Nico. Whatever it was about her got under his skin in a way most people didn't.

"There you are!" Teresa came hurrying toward him as if he were the one who was late.

Quickly remembering his manners, he tried to wipe the impatient look off his face. "*Benvenuta*, Teresa," he said to welcome her, kissing her on each cheek.

She accepted his greeting, juggling her purse, backpack, and rolling suitcase. She smiled up at him, her wide mouth showing perfect white teeth—he forgot how petite she was—he was almost two heads taller than her. Her dark head of curls, stopping a few inches below her ears, was perfectly styled, as if she hadn't been on a long plane ride. Her big brown eyes, under their distinct brown brows, were crinkled at the corners, and he noticed a smattering of freckles across her small nose. She was wearing white jeans and a multi-colored top, with big gold hoops in her ears. He blinked a little at all the color before him.

"Sorry if I kept you waiting. Uh, I left my phone on the plane. So stupid—and the crew was nice enough to go get it for me.

Then I made a couple of quick stops to buy a few things. Then customs took forever—man, they were thorough. You'd think I was a criminal. But I'm ready!"

"Let me have your bags, and we will go to my car," Stefano said politely, as he grabbed them and headed toward the exit. Teresa was almost running in her sandals, trying to keep up with him, and he slowed down courteously. She was chattering already. *Dio*, it was starting. He realized she asked him a question. *"Mi dispiace?"*

"Have I made you late or something? You seem to be in a hurry. I'm sorry about this. I told Kate I could get a ride. She was already upset with me for not taking Marco's plane, but that seemed silly—just me on a private jet. I mean climate change and all..." Her voice trailed off.

They entered the parking garage, and Stefano made a few small noises to appear as if he was listening. He indicated his large black Mercedes that he used around the city. Opening the door for her, he went to put her bags in the trunk. Getting in the car, he started it and the hard rock music from his deluxe stereo system blasted. He quickly turned it down without comment, but he saw her raise his eyebrows in surprise.

Driving out of the airport's exit, he began to deftly navigate the evening traffic. He realized she finally was silent, and guilt nudged him again. If Marco or Kate found out he was rude, he would get an earful. "Did you have a pleasant flight?" he asked politely.

"Yes, thank you. Though long. It was sweet of Marco to upgrade me. I've never in my life flown First Class. Have you?"

Stefano's lips twitched at the thought of flying anything but First Class or private. He knew he would sound like a snob, but it was his reality. "Well, yes, it is very comfortable."

"They were soooo nice. I slept a lot, though. I worked yesterday, and I was exhausted."

"How is your work at the hospital?" asked Stefano, remembering that she was an obstetric nurse.

Teresa was looking at the window and seemed to be contemplating the question. "Okay," she mumbled.

Sensing she didn't want to talk about it, he decided not to ask any more questions. Instead, he concentrated on his driving, winding through Naples' crowded streets. *Dio*, this was awkward. He shouldn't have offered to pick her up. The silence now was deafening, and he searched his brain for what to say next.

Suddenly, his nose twitched. What was that horrible smell? He glanced over at the rustling to see Teresa shaking a wrapped burger out of a bag onto her lap. She then reached in the bag and grabbed a French fry. He was so distracted, he about drove the car off the road. "What the hell?"

She looked at him with wide eyes, glancing around at his spotless vehicle. "I'm sorry! Do you not allow eating in your car?"

It took him a minute to find his voice. "I do not have rules about eating in my car. I just do not allow that kind of horrendous food in it—or anywhere in my life, for that matter."

Teresa took a big bite of her burger. "What's wrong with it?" she asked after swallowing. She took another bite quickly, grabbing a napkin to wipe a little ketchup off her face.

"Well, it is disgusting, number one. Number two, it is going to kill you."

"What a way to go," Teresa said, smiling at him. "Want a fry?"

"No!" he almost shouted. Taking a calming breath, he asked, "Where did you get that stuff?"

"Oh, it was conveniently right after customs. I was so happy to see it. I was starving. I mean, they kept offering me food on the flight, but it was all plane food, if you know what I mean. And I ran out of the goldfish that were in my backpack and my animal cookies only lasted until we were over Greenland, I think."

He shook his head. "Goldfish?"

"You know, the little cheddar crackers? They are required on any trip—plane, car, train. But I shouldn't have left the other goldfish bag in my checked luggage. And the animal cookies were delicious—I like the pink-and-white ones with the sprinkles. They are mandatory as well."

There were absolutely no words to add, and he decided to stay silent. Finished eating, she put the wrapper back in the bag and crumpled it. She glanced around, looking smug. "Not a crumb in your car. I was careful."

"Except the smell is going to linger forever."

Teresa rolled her eyes, stuffing the bag in her purse. "You'd be so lucky. If they made a car freshener with this scent, I'd buy it for sure!" She settled down now in her seat, almost looking sleepy.

"You can fall asleep if you want," he said quietly. If she slept the rest of the way, it would solve his problem of keeping this conversation alive.

She nodded, not looking at him. But she didn't close her eyes.

They drove for a few more miles, now beginning to leave Naples behind, heading toward Sorrento. They would be at his family's lemon grove in about an hour. The entire family was home, getting ready for his cousin Lucca's wedding. Lucca and his fiancé, Ellie, a renowned artist, were marrying in just a couple of days. Their meeting had been unique, and he almost smiled, remembering their turbulent relationship in the beginning. He realized Teresa was talking again and apologized for the second time. "*Mi dispiace?*"

"No, I'm sorry, Stefano. You didn't need to pick me up. But since you did, let's just take this opportunity to discuss something."

He raised his eyebrows. What could they have to discuss?
"Why do you dislike me so much?"

306

Get your Kindle copy of My Christmas in Capri!
Paperbacks available at Amazon or your favorite bookstore

Dear Reader:

Thank you so much for traveling to Tuscany with Ellie and Lucca. I loved telling their story—especially Lucca's sense of humor and Ellie's feisty nature.

A lot of work went into research—including even consulting with an artist friend of mine on how and where Ellie would paint. Note the important details such as that green is the most difficult color to paint! Thank you, Susan, for all your tips! Siena is one of my favorite Tuscan towns and it *had* to play an important role in this book!

If you want more…there is! Tour through more regions of Italy in this series: From Italy With Love. We'll travel all over, but we'll always swing by the Amalfi Coast to say hi to the family.

Grab some delicious Italian cuisine or a pint of creamy gelato and enjoy more from Italia! Remember to sign up for my newsletter at Tessrini.com/newsletter to read a bonus chapter from *My Secret Positano.*

Cin Cin!
XO, Tess

about the author

Tess Rini has spent her professional life focused on non-fiction writing, from her journalism degree to her editing and writing magazine articles and content for local government. She has published one non-fiction book under a different name.

Tess was raised on a self-induced steady diet of Harlequin romances and so it was inevitable that she should try her hand at romance writing. The idea took off when she combined her love of Italy with her love for romance novels.

When not writing, she can be found relaxing in her Oregon home, traveling or cooking Italian cuisine (her specialty!) for her husband, four daughters and son-in-law. Keeping her company while writing or watching Hallmark movies is her adorable, but anxious, golden retriever.

Sign up for her newsletter at Tessrini.com/newsletter to read a bonus chapter from *My Secret Positano* and stay up on all the latest Italy news.

Website: tessrini.com
Or follow her on social:
Facebook @tessriniauthor
Instagram @tessrininauthor

www.ingramcontent.com/pod-product-compliance
Lightning Source LLC
Chambersburg PA
CBHW021236060726
47590CB00005B/1773